THE ABANDONED

by

Jonas Saul

PUBLISHED BY:
Imagine Press Inc.
Ebook ISBN: 978-1-927404-41-6
Paperback ISBN: 978-1-998047-08-6
Hardcover ISBN: 978-1-998047-37-6

The Abandoned
Copyright © 2015 by Jonas Saul

All rights reserved. No part of this publication may be reproduced, stored in a retrieval system, or transmitted in any form or by any means (electronic, mechanical, photocopying, recording, or otherwise) without the publisher's prior written permission.

This is a work of fiction. The characters, organizations, and events portrayed in this novel are either products of the author's imagination or are used fictitiously. References to real people, events, establishments, organizations, or locations are intended only to provide a sense of authenticity and are used fictitiously. Any resemblance to actual events, places, organizations, or persons, living or dead, is entirely coincidental.

Imagine Press Inc. does not have control over, or any responsibility for, any author or third-party websites referred to in or on this book.

The Sarah Roberts Series

Dark Visions (One)
The Warning (Two)
The Crypt (Three)
The Hostage (Four)
The Victim (Five)
The Enigma (Six)
The Vigilante (Seven)
The Rogue (Eight)
Killing Sarah (Nine)
The Antagonist (Ten)
The Redeemed (Eleven)
The Haunted (Twelve)
The Unlucky (Thirteen)
The Abandoned (Fourteen)
The Cartel (Fifteen)
Losing Sarah (Sixteen)
The Pact (Seventeen)
The Terror (Eighteen)
The Chase (Nineteen)
The Betrayal (Twenty)
Sarah's Return (Twenty-One)
The Hunt (Twenty-Two)
The Delivery (Twenty-Three)
The Trap (Twenty-Four)
The Ultimatum (Twenty-Five)
The Depraved (Twenty-Six)
The Condemned (Twenty-Seven)
Payback (Twenty-Eight)
The Unknown (Twenty-Nine)
Wrath (Thirty)
The Damned (Thirty-One)
The Game (Thirty-Two)

The Decoy (Thirty-Three)
The Disappearance (Thirty-Four)
The Whole Truth (Thirty-Five)
Alex (Thirty-Six)
Parkman (Thirty-Seven)
Darwin (Thirty-Eight)
Aaron (Thirty-Nine)
Remains To Be Seen (Forty)

The Jake Wood Novels

The Immortal Gene (Book One)
The Immortal Target (Book Two)

Standalone Novels

'Til Death Do Us Part
The Drowning
The Woman in the Woods
The Threat
The Specter
The Mafia Trilogy
A Murder in Time
Frequency of the Dead

Co-Authored Novels

Collision Course (Written with Gary Ponzo)
There Will Be Blood (Written with Rania Stone)
The Soulless (Written with Rania Stone)

Short Story Collections

Twisted Fate (Tales of Horror)

Twists of Fate (Tales of Hope)

Chapter 1

SARAH ROBERTS MADE IT through security at Toronto International Airport without incident. She collected her passport and boarding pass from the guard, placed her billfold with her only credit/debit card in her front pocket, and started across the corridor, where she entered a small magazine kiosk. Near the back, she lifted a thick Vanity Fair off the rack and looked over the top of the pages at the man who had been following her.

He was gone. He hadn't followed her inside the store. Maybe he was simply staring at her figure, her hair. Not everybody had devious intent. A limited number of people knew why she was at the airport, so it couldn't be that.

Aaron and Parkman had dropped her off. A long few days in Toronto—harrowing days—had just ended. The nightmare of the Torture Club was over. A black book containing a list of names that could implicate dozens, if not hundreds, of people involved with the Torture Club, had gone missing. Once Sarah retrieved that book and delivered it to the authorities, she could take a much-needed break. She had killed people and come close to being killed herself. The risk of being sent to prison for decades hung over her head the entire time. This experience had mentally cost her in ways she hadn't discovered yet, but she would forge on regardless because that's what she did. Sarah Roberts forged on. And her dead sister Vivian knew this about Sarah, hence the directive to fly to Amsterdam today in search of the missing black book.

With the magazine placed back on the shelf, Sarah meandered slowly through the store, stopping at the paperback shelf. The new Stephen King novel sat beside the new Clive Barker. She browsed for a few moments, lost in the world of fiction.

Clutching her boarding pass, Sarah left the store and started for her gate. She bought a black coffee at a Tim Horton's kiosk and scanned the patrons and travelers for the blond man who had been watching her, but she couldn't locate him.

Maybe she'd imagined it.

She continued toward her gate. Her flight to Amsterdam would start boarding in twenty minutes. This trip was an exercise in blind faith. She had no description of the man who possessed the black book. There was no location he'd be at or his final destination. All she knew was that he was heading to Amsterdam.

After all she had gone through in Toronto, it felt good to leave Canada. Even though she had felt unlucky, she now felt like she was abandoning Aaron. He was her purpose for coming to Toronto in the first place. They talked at his apartment the other night and then again last night at the hotel, but there was still a lot left unsaid.

She promised him that as soon as she located the black book, she would return with it and turn Vivian off for a spell. She needed downtime. She needed *Aaron* time. That's what she felt Aaron had been missing all along, and Parkman had agreed. Pick a spot on the map, and they would vacation somewhere tropical. Just the two of them, even if that meant Sarah had to be drunk on whiskey the whole time to keep Vivian out of her head.

Black book first, then Aaron. Then vacation.

She hopped onto a people-mover, stood to the right, and sipped her coffee. It was going down good, smoothly.

Up ahead, a man with the same color hair as the guy she thought had been following her sat at gate B14.

She scanned her boarding pass for her gate number.

B14.

When she looked up, the blond man was reading a newspaper, his legs crossed.

She reached the end of the people-mover and stepped off, now slightly in front of him. Across the walkway and into the gate's waiting area, she took a chair that faced him, leaving two rows of people between them.

Elbows on her knees, coffee supported with both hands, she leaned forward and studied his lean face. He appeared to be educated, either in business for himself or the government. Mid-forties, clean-shaven, attractive in a George Clooney kind of way, but with a pale complexion.

She set her coffee between her feet and rechecked her boarding pass.

Then her hand numbed.

Vivian?

It started up her arm.

Right now? Seriously?

Four seats to Sarah's left, an overweight couple in their sixties chatted while doing a crossword, their carry-on bags at their feet.

She lunged off her chair just as the numbing reached her chest, and she blacked out.

***

Voices came from a distance like she was underwater. Her hands ached. Something tugged at her, drawing her sideways.

Was she floating? Falling? Pain in one of her shoulders.

In a quest for answers, never one to dawdle, Sarah surged forward and upward.

Her eyes popped open.

The shoulder pain was from a circular saw injury she'd received recently. Injuries plagued her, but she had learned how to handle them. Purpose minimized the pain.

The concerned faces around her moved back. The man who had been doing a crossword attempted to wrest his pen from her grip. The ache in her hands intensified as she clung to the Bic pen.

Airport security stepped into view.

"Excuse us. Make some room."

Sarah released the pen, and the man stood up and moved aside.

"Are you okay, ma'am?" a female security guard asked.

Sarah nodded. Everything felt back to normal, except she was lying on the floor three chairs from her coffee that was getting cold while Vivian had her fun.

It had been a long while since Vivian had made her perform automatic writing. So long that Sarah felt mild embarrassment as everyone waiting at the gate watched her, trying to glimpse what the commotion was all about.

"Just afraid to fly," Sarah mumbled. "I pass out sometimes."

They helped her to her feet. She felt the eyes of a hundred people on her back.

"I'll just retake my seat." She offered the guard a half smile. "Coffee's getting cold."

"I'm sorry, ma'am, but maybe you're not fit for travel. Do you have someone traveling with you?"

"I'm alone."

"Maybe you should come with us."

Sarah gently pulled her arm out of the guard's grip and stepped back.

"I'm fine. Just lightheaded. Coffee'll do me just right."

The guard motioned for her colleagues to move closer.

"I'm sorry, but I insist. We'd like you to see the nurse on duty. Then we'll bring you right back out."

She couldn't miss the plane. Nothing could be allowed to let her miss the plane. Sarah nudged past two onlookers, slipped behind them, and dropped to retake her seat. She picked up her coffee, surprised it hadn't been knocked over in the commotion and took a sip.

"As I said, I'm fine," She glanced up as the guard moved closer. "But thanks for your concern."

"Embarrassing?" the guard asked. "Or polite?"

Sarah squinted her eyes and tilted her head. "Excuse me?"

"Pick one." Two male guards were joined now by three more. Onlookers and bystanders were cleared away. Now a semi-circle of airport security surrounded her. "You're coming with us willingly, the polite way, or unwillingly, the embarrassing way. Pick one. We prefer willing."

What is this, Vivian?

Sarah studied the guard's face as she drank from her cup one more time. They weren't about to go away. The longer she dragged this on, the higher chance she would miss her plane.

"Okay, fine. I'll go with you." She stood, adjusted her shirt, and faced the female guard. "Which way?"

"Follow them," she said, pointing at two heavyset men in uniform.

They nodded and started down the corridor past the other gates.

Vivian? Anything? Why are we back to automatic writing?

The guards opened a door that led to another corridor.

"How long is this going to take?" Sarah asked. "I have a plane to catch."

No one responded.

The guards in front stopped and motioned for her to enter a room. Inside, a single table and two chairs were set up under bright fluorescent lights, just like an interview room at a police station.

"Where's the nurse?" Sarah asked. She turned to address the female guard, but she was gone. "What's going on here?" The male guard gestured for her to enter the interview room.

"I have a plane to catch. There's no time for this."

Something wasn't right here. There was an agenda at play she wasn't privy to, and Vivian was strangely silent.

"Please, Miss Roberts, enter the room and take a seat. You won't be catching any planes today."

Her stomach dropped. She ruled out violence. Attacking airport security and running for the plane would never work. This wasn't a back alley or an attempted kidnapping. This was forcible confinement. All the power was in their hands.

"And why is that? I have a plane ticket. My American passport is in good standing. I know I have no travel bans, and I have done nothing wrong. I demand to know why I'm being detained."

"You will be apprised of your situation shortly. Please step inside. The sooner you do that, the sooner we can expedite your release."

"My release?"

"Inside, ma'am. I don't want to have to tell you again."

Sarah waited a few seconds before she entered the room. The door closed silently behind her.

Then it locked.

"Fuck!"

What's going on, Vivian? Talk to me.

She paced the floor and checked for cameras. As far as she could tell, there was no two-way glass in the room or listening devices.

"Hello!" she shouted. "I have a plane to catch."

She yanked out her boarding pass to check if there was a final boarding time and stopped pacing when she saw what was written on it in her own handwriting.

Aaron must hospitalize his new student, then leave

Toronto for one week. This must happen, or Aaron will suffer.

"What the hell is this?" Sarah asked. She looked up at the wall of the room. "Vivian, should I be heading to Europe for a black book? Or should I be staying here? What kind of trouble is Aaron in?"

The lock clicked on the door.

Sarah folded the boarding pass and slipped it into her back pocket.

The door opened. Before anyone stepped inside, Sarah started forward.

"I demand to speak to my lawyer."

The female guard from earlier appeared. The door closed again. It locked from the outside.

"Sarah Roberts?" the woman asked.

Sarah leaned against the wall as if this was boring her. "Of course, you know that because I'm flying under my own name. International Travel Airlines has my ticket in their system, and I've already checked in." She pushed off the wall. "I hate to have to pull this card, but I'm an American citizen. I have rights. This is an illegal detainment. I was sitting quietly at my gate when I passed out. I'm fine." She patted herself down, ignoring the protest of her fresh shoulder wound from yesterday. "See, all fit to travel."

"I admit it," the guard said. "We made a mistake."

Surprised but not willing to show it, Sarah said, "Great. I'd like to get to my plane now."

"Not yet."

"Excuse me?"

"We know who you are."

"What's your name?" Sarah asked. "Then we can be even."

"We know what you did in Toronto. Only twenty-four hours ago, this airport was almost in full lockdown in case an American fugitive named Sarah Roberts attempted to fly out of Toronto. But somehow, after all that was released to the media, you're here, ready to fly to Europe, and the Toronto police have acknowledged that you are no longer a suspect. According to them, you're free to go." She finished with a toss of her arm as if exasperation got the better of her.

"I already know all this," Sarah said. "I'm the girl you're talking about. Moving along now to the present, unlock that door. Let's get this show on the road."

"Someone upstairs is looking out for you," the guard said, almost under her breath.

"Again, I would agree. We done here?"

"Someone powerful just made a phone call. You're to be left alone."

This intrigued Sarah. "Who?" Sarah asked. "How powerful?"

"All the way to the top."

"The top? Like the president?"

"All I know is the phone call came in, and they know everything as if they are here, in the airport. Your blackout. My involvement. Our detainment of you. Everything. All within three minutes of you being in this room."

How the hell?

"And that has pissed you off," Sarah said, her voice low, non-threatening, "because you had other plans for me, didn't you?"

"You're free to go, Miss Roberts."

Sarah's patience was at an all-time low. A dull throb emitted from the split skin on her shoulder blade, elevating her temper a degree. She probably needed to change the bandage, but she didn't have any extras on her.

If this detainment were a personal score, it would anger her. If they were just checking to see if Sarah was free and able to leave the country, if they were just doing their jobs, then so be it. It was time to go. Boarding had probably already commenced.

"Maybe you should rethink returning to Toronto," the guard said.

Sarah edged closer until they were inches apart. "Are you threatening me? What are you, a security guard at the airport? Who are you to tell me I'm not welcome in this city?" Sarah waited for a response, but none came. "Are you interested in a lawsuit? Are you interested in repaying the cost of my flight? Or should I go to the police and lay criminal charges of forcible confinement? I can add to that how you threatened me as well."

The guard stepped back and knocked twice on the door. It unlocked. She clutched the handle but didn't turn it.

"You're free to go," the guard repeated.

Sarah waited. Something else was on the guard's mind. Then the door was opened from the outside.

Cautiously, Sarah moved past her into the corridor. One guard stood on the outside of the door. They exchanged a glance before Sarah started down the deserted hall.

"Don't worry, I'll find my way back," she shouted over her shoulder.

Both guards followed her to the exit at a distance. With the push bar in her hand, Sarah stopped and turned around in time to see the female guard wipe a tear from her cheek.

"What's on your mind?" Sarah asked in a softer voice.

"What were you trying to say back in the room? What was this all about?"

The woman gestured for Sarah to go as she turned away and started down the corridor in the opposite direction. Sarah moved her gaze to the male guard.

"Samantha Mason, that cop's wife who was murdered, was like a mother to her."

It all came together in a second. Samantha Mason, Niles Mason's wife, had been tortured and killed yesterday. Originally the police thought it was Sarah's fault. But now they knew differently. The people affected by loss, the collateral damage that came with the life Sarah lived, was something she rarely saw.

"Tell her I'm sorry. It had nothing to do with me. In fact, I tried to stop it. I was too late when I got to where they were holding Samantha."

"Doesn't matter now," the guard said. "Just go. Catch your flight. The sooner you're out of our airport, the better it'll be for everyone."

Without another word, Sarah slipped out and let the door close behind her. Unexpected, raw emotions swept over her. She *had* tried to save Samantha Mason. But she couldn't save everybody. Maybe people expected too much from her. Maybe it was time for a break after all.

But first, she had to track down the black book. She had to locate the man who had it in Amsterdam and return it to Toronto. Then she would stop being a vigilante for a while.

She looked outside at the airplanes on the tarmac.

Or she could leave through an exit door and walk off into the distance. She could keep walking until she hit a beach, bought a little hut with the rest of the savings her father had supplied her, and settle in for long days of sun and margaritas. Let the world figure itself out. Let them all kill each other.

But the faces of the dozens of girls she had saved from the Torture Club in Toronto passed before her mind's eye. The frail, broken bodies from the horror house in Orillia. All the people before them, too.

And just like that, it all came clear to her. The purpose wasn't them, exactly. The purpose wasn't solving crime like some superhero or gifted vigilante. The purpose was Sarah. Everything Vivian did was through Sarah. She was the vessel. Sarah Roberts *was* the purpose, Vivian's purpose. She had accepted that years ago and never doubted it. She had lived against impossible odds. She had survived where others wouldn't have because she had Vivian. And until Vivian didn't need her anymore, Sarah had to fulfill that purpose. She was duty-bound.

That meant getting on the plane for Amsterdam.

It also meant understanding that as sad as Samantha's death was, countless others were saved. Had the torture club continued its reign, dozens, if not hundreds, of women would have fallen prey to its will. Sarah didn't author this death and destruction of the societal fabric. All she ever did was attempt to mend it. And if people died along the way, all she could do was her damnedest to minimize the damage.

In the end, everything had to be weighed on a scale. To remain idle meant dozens of deaths, if not hundreds. Responding to the call to action meant the possibility of collateral deaths. Without hesitation, she had picked the call to action. Not only was that the right answer, but it was also the better answer. It was also the most fun. Punishing those responsible for the shit they thought they could get away with offered Sarah pleasure like nothing else. Shutting assholes down had become too enjoyable to quit.

She pulled her gaze from the tarmac in the distance, broke her reverie, and headed back to her gate. A new excitement was in her step, a feeling of elation as she knew she was the purpose. By acquiring the black book and returning it to Toronto, she could almost guarantee a whole list of powerful people would have to answer for their actions.

All that with one book.

How hard could this be?

She was ready, energized, and excited to nail this task. Then she would hide in Aaron's apartment until she was ready to listen to Vivian again.

That and a lot of Johnnie Walker Black.

Yes, Johnnie Walker Black.

She ran for gate B14. The remaining people by her gate formed a line as an announcement stated that it was the final boarding call for flight K338 with service from Toronto to Amsterdam. She fell in line at the back and pulled out her passport and boarding pass.

What could that female airport guard mean when she said that someone high up had called in? And how could that caller know what was happening in the airport in real-time? Perhaps they received a play-by-play from the blond man.

That creeped her out. Someone had to be watching her.

The waiting area was mostly empty.

And she was still confused by automatic writing. Why didn't Vivian whisper the message in her head as she'd done before? It was the dramatic automatic writing that brought airport security running. Ultimately Vivian had been the one who caused her delay. But why? What was going on?

There were four people left to board in front of her.

Should I be getting on this plane, Vivian?

Earlier, in Vivian's message regarding the flight to Amsterdam, she had warned Sarah that the plane would crash. But she hadn't warned her *off* the plane.

What do you want, Vivian? Do you want me to willingly catch a plane that is doomed or not?

One person in front of her left.

Then the attendant took Sarah's boarding pass, ran it over a square window in a console that beeped, examined her passport, and handed them both back.

"Enjoy your flight, Miss Roberts."

The other attendant was preparing to close the tunnel doors leading to the plane. Sarah's stomach did another flop and settled low in her abdomen.

Vivian, give up the ghost here. What's your angle? On or off the plane? Running out of time, sis.

When no answer was forthcoming, Sarah stopped halfway down the tunnel.

Is our man with the black book on the plane? If it's going to crash, I don't need to be here, do I?

Nothing.

"Excuse me, ma'am," the attendant said behind her. "You're going to have to keep moving. The plane is preparing to leave."

Sarah started walking again.

Vivian? I need direction here.

At the entrance to the plane, Sarah stopped and showed her boarding pass to another attendant.

"Row fourteen, seat C." She motioned with her hand. "Down this aisle."

Sarah couldn't control the nerves that made her body shake.

How many people willingly walk onto a plane that will crash, Vivian? Help me out here. There's still time. Should I warn the attendants, so we don't take off? Shouldn't I be saving everyone on board?

She located her aisle seat and plunked down beside a tall woman and what appeared at first glance to be the woman's young son. They nodded at each other.

Do you need me on this plane for another reason? Is that it?

One of the flight attendants was closing the plane's door. The tunnel was cut off a moment later. Unless Sarah made a ruckus, she was committed now.

Fuck, Vivian. Sometimes you really piss me off.

She clicked her seatbelt, whispered a silent prayer, and rested her head back.

Moments later, as the plane jerked backward and began to pull away from its docked position, she remembered she hadn't called Aaron to warn him to hospitalize his new student. She had no idea what that meant or if Aaron would even do it anyway.

"Excuse me, but before we take off, do you have a cell phone I could borrow?" she asked the woman to her left.

The response was a shake of the head.

Someone tapped her shoulder from behind.

"Here, you can use mine."

Sarah turned in her seat to look into the face of the blond man from earlier. The one she thought had been watching her. She took his phone, said thanks, and turned back to face forward in her seat. What was his deal? Is he connected to anything happening right now? Or is he a coincidence?

She pushed buttons on his cell phone, scanning through messages and recent numbers dialed as fast as possible to glean anything that would reveal who he was.

The woman beside grunted. Sarah glanced her way. The look on her face was one of disgust. Sarah had asked to borrow a phone and was rifling through the man's privacy. It obviously bothered the woman.

"These new phones," Sarah said. "Can never figure them out." She shrugged.

The woman leaned over and pushed a button. The keypad lit up; the cell phone function shined bright on the screen.

She dialed Aaron's apartment as one of the flight attendants was moving down the aisle checking seat belts and ensuring carry-on baggage was safely stowed under the seat ahead. The cell phone had to be turned off when she got to Sarah's row.

It started ringing.

"Come on, Aaron. Pick up."

On the fourth ring, the flight attendant still six seats away, Aaron's machine picked up. Four seats away, the attendant stopped to help someone put a bag in the overhead bin compartment.

The machine beeped in her ear.

"Listen, Aaron, you will have a new student at the dojo. Don't trust him. Vivian says there's something wrong with him. I need you to hospitalize that new student and then disappear for a week or more. Can you do that for me? Listen closely." The attendant stopped at Sarah's chair. Sarah raised a finger to inform the attendant she would only be a second more. "Hospitalize the student," Sarah whispered. "Then disappear. Do it in that order. But make sure you do it."

Sarah ended the call.

The woman beside her was exchanging odd glances with the attendant. Then the attendant met Sarah's gaze.

"I'm sorry, but you'll have to turn your cell to airplane mode."

"I have one more quick call to make." She needed to try Parkman's cell. They might still be together. She needed to hear Aaron agree to do it.

"I'm sorry, but those are the rules. Airplane mode. We're about to taxi out for takeoff."

They had heard what she said into the machine. The attendant seemed wary of her. To push it would be to raise the alarm. She had done what Vivian wanted of her. She had left a message for Aaron. He would get it today when he got home. He would listen to it and know how important it was to take the advice. He would never *not* listen to what Vivian asked, would he?

"Okay," Sarah said. "Sorry about that."

She turned in her seat, returned the phone to the mysterious blond man behind her, and righted herself.

It was going to be a long flight.

And during the flight, she wanted to take inventory of every face on the plane. She had no idea what her enemy looked like, and Vivian wasn't talking to her. So she would walk the aisles watching the passenger's faces, waiting until she saw a response from one of them.

Could it be that easy? Or could it be the man behind her?

Was that why he was watching her earlier? What was his

role in her purpose? Or was he responsible for the call from higher up?

She would wait until the meals were rolled out and cleaned up. She would wait until the lights dimmed on the nine-hour flight. She would wait until the blond man got up to use the lavatory.

Then she would learn who he was, what he was up to, and whether he was willing to tell her.

Answers were always there for the taking.

You just had to know how to take them.

You just had to know how to ask.

Chapter 2

THE PLANE WILL CRASH.

Even with that knowledge, Sarah got on the plane anyway. She had to surmise that the crash would be a minor one. Otherwise, Vivian would've tasked her to keep the plane grounded.

Her stomach still stirred. With so many unknowns—where was the black book, how many casualties would be due to the plane crash, who was the blond guy in the seat behind her—Sarah could barely think about food.

Yet within an hour of taking off, the meal was being rolled out. The passengers were offered a choice between pasta or chicken. She had picked the chicken but regretted it when she saw the pasta in the woman's dish beside her. Leaving half her meal untouched, Sarah sipped from the small bottle of wine the flight attendant had given her and waited until the trays were collected.

Her seat companion's approximately six-year-old son fussed in the window seat, but his mother did a reasonably good job of calming him down. Sarah figured the woman wasn't interested in small talk after she overheard what Sarah had said on the cell phone prior to takeoff.

That was okay, though. Sarah wasn't here to make friends. She was here to locate and return the black book to Toronto, so Detective Marina Diner could finish her investigation into Toronto's Torture Club.

This would be a simple in and out. Land, use Vivian to find the book, and fly back to Toronto. Nothing to it other than the fact that the plane was going to crash. There's that, though.

She laid her head back and closed her eyes, trying to envision what it was about the blond man behind her that had her worked up. As far as she could remember, without turning around and looking at him, he was dressed in a sports jacket, a collared shirt, and dress pants with shiny black shoes. His hair was almost white blond, but it gave him an older man sexy look, like a James Bond kind of man. But something about him made her believe he wasn't just a businessman on his way to Europe.

He had an agenda, and she was certain it had something to do with her. Otherwise, why did he spend so much time watching her back at the airport? At the same time, she was also certain he wasn't the man with the black book.

Out of repulsion, she tried to avoid the thought that the blond man invoked images of Rod Howley, the dead government agent from the Sophia Project.

But it couldn't be. The Sophia Project had stopped chasing her years ago. Rod had died a horrible death in

Toronto as well as his replacement. During that year, she recalled sadly, she'd lost Dolan and Esmerelda as well. Two people, the world was a darker place without.

Why did it have to be this way? Why were so many people bent on hurting others and destroying lives?

She closed her eyes and thought about all the people she had lost. How her parents had been targeted for death by that Rapturites group. And then how they were tormented and almost killed by Violeta Payne the year Sarah had been shot in the head by Violeta's daughter.

Maybe it would be better if she was a loner. Maybe she should change her name, go underground, and make it harder for fundamentalists to locate people like her parents or even Aaron. Going forward, doing what she does, Sarah always knew there was an element of danger for her loved ones.

They had accepted that, though. Her father loved what she did and supported it. Parkman had never said an unsupportive word. It'd only been Aaron who had tried to school her on her activities. And Aaron had gotten into the most trouble for it.

She wondered about Vivian's message and what it meant for Aaron. Or who was coming for Aaron? Why hospitalize a student and then lie low for a week? What was Vivian not telling her?

It was irritating to have Vivian reveal everything after Sarah finished her tasks. Why not explain everything at the beginning? Get it all out there. Then Sarah could be better armed to deal with what she had to endure.

But Sarah suspected that it had something to do with fate or having to live our lives on earth without foreknowledge of the future. Vivian probably had rules she needed to follow.

Take this airplane. It will crash. And that is all you need to know for now. Sarah was on the plane. She was doing as she was told. And when it was all over, and everything was ironed out, Vivian would explain why she could only tell Sarah this or that and how it led Sarah on the right path.

Sarah reclined her seat farther. The steady drone of the plane's engines propelled them at over five hundred miles an hour. The engines had a relaxing quality about them.

Her eyes shut as Sarah drifted off on the plane that would eventually crash, her dinner tray still not taken, the plane's interior lights still on, and the blond man in the suit still sitting behind her.

***

Sarah woke with a start. Beside her, the mother and her son slept soundlessly.

She rubbed her eyes and looked around the darkened cabin. The window shades were down, and the lights dimmed. The seats to her right were filled with people in various states of sleep. Some watched the TV screens in the headrests of the seat in front of them. One man stood in the aisle, stretching his legs.

Sarah undid her belt and got up to stretch in the aisle.

The seat behind hers was empty. The blond man was gone.

She started toward the lavatory, the narrow aisle difficult to manage as a foot stuck out here and an elbow there.

Three men stood waiting at the toilets. Each door had a little sign saying they were in use. None of the men were her blond man. She sidestepped through the galley and exited the other aisle, where one woman waited for the toilet.

Up one aisle and down the other, there was no movement. Maybe Blond Man was in one of the lavatories. Maybe when he got up from his seat, it woke her.

She started toward the back of the plane. Blond Man was nowhere to be found, so she entered one of the lavatories at the back and used it. When she stepped out, a man crowded her.

"Oh, sorry," she said, looking up. "Here, all yours …"

The blond man smiled down at her. A familiar rush of adrenaline filled her stomach. He had been watching her, following her through the plane. But from where? And why? Neither of them could leave the large metal tube in the sky. Everyone was stuck on the plane until it landed or crashed.

"Long way from your seat," he said.

"I could say the same about you."

She closed the lavatory door and rested her back against it. They were alone, the closest passengers a few feet away, sleeping in their chairs. About four seats up, two people with headphones watched the tiny screen in front of them.

They had time. At least four or five hours before they were due to land. Nothing insane could happen in that time, could it?

"What's the nature of your trip to Amsterdam?" she asked. "Business or pleasure?"

"Both." His reply was short and clipped, but his face remained friendly.

Sarah moved to lean on the metal counter with small doors that housed what the flight attendants used to prepare meals and drinks.

"What kind of business are you in?" she asked.

"Home repair."

She frowned. "Home repair? Like Home Depot?"

"Not exactly. I work for the U.S. Government."

I knew it!

He continued. "When I said home repair, I meant that I travel to various countries worldwide and aid in repairing our image." He chuckled softly and leaned against the lavatory door. "As you probably know, we don't have a very good image abroad. There are a lot of countries that have issues with our foreign policy."

"I wouldn't know much about that. I mean, I read the papers and have a basic understanding of what's going on in the world, but I usually keep to myself."

He changed his position, crossed his arms, and rested his shoulder on the door.

"Tell me," he said. "What happened back at the airport?"

It wasn't an accident that she felt his eyes on her at the airport, and then his seat was behind hers, and now he had followed her to the rear of the plane. A thought slid home: he was here because of her. She was his agenda.

"I'm Sarah," she said, extending her hand. "Pleased to meet you."

"I'm Buck Schaffer, but you can call me Casper."

She mentally logged the name for a Google search when they landed—if they landed.

"Casper? Why's that?"

The plane encountered mild turbulence, which seemed worse at the rear of the plane. Sarah had to balance herself by placing a hand on the counter behind her.

Casper pointed at his blond hair. "Always had this hair. Nearly white when I was a kid. I didn't like my first nickname, which was the first letters of Buck Schaffer, BS. But Casper stuck in high school, and to this day, everyone calls me Casper."

More turbulence shook them. Sarah's stomach did a flip. Vivian said this plane had accident written all over it, and they were at least 38,000 feet above the ocean at the moment.

Hey, sis, at least let me know if the people on this plane survive.

"You okay?" Casper asked.

"Yeah. Fine."

Then Vivian's voice reached her in its dark, echoing quality.

Their survival is up to you, Vivian whispered.

"Oh, shit," Sarah whispered aloud before she could take it back.

"You're not going to pass out again, are you?"

She studied his face. Why wouldn't Vivian help with who he was or what he was up to?

"No, I'm sure I won't pass out again."

"Is that a condition or something?"

He sounded genuinely interested.

"No condition. People faint all the time." She looked at the carpet and shuffled her feet in an attempt to express embarrassment.

"I'm sorry," he said. "I'm not trying to pry."

She looked up and met his eyes. "It's okay."

"It's just, I was surprised by airport security's response. Wouldn't they bring a paramedic over to check on you? Instead, you were surrounded by guards and literally led away. I didn't think you were coming back."

"Me either. But it wasn't important. I made the flight,

right?" She smiled wide, then dropped the smile.

"That you did."

"Tell me something else," Sarah said. "What's your interest in me?"

He smiled, which seemed to light up his face, but he didn't say anything at first.

"No answer?" Sarah asked.

"Let's just say you put on a show back at the airport that caught my eye."

"And that's it? Nothing more?"

"That, and I thought I recognized you."

"Do you?" Sarah asked.

"You're the girl everyone was looking for over the past few days."

The events that took place during her recent time in Toronto had been held back from the media by a gag order. Sarah's name never made the news. The detectives handling the case had been diligent about that. So how did Casper know? Which led her to the next question. How high in the government was he? High enough that prompted airport security to say Sarah had friends in high places? Did Casper get her out of the airport security's clutches? If so, why? What did he want?

"Tell me something," Sarah said as turbulence shook the plane again. This time it continued until the seatbelt light flicked on. They were going to have to take their seats. "My picture and my name weren't in the news. You didn't recognize me because of Toronto. Which means we need to start at the beginning. Who are you, and what do you want with me?"

A flight attendant stepped in behind Casper.

"Excuse me, could you both please return to your seats?" she asked.

"In a minute," Sarah said. "We're almost done here."

Casper raised an arm above his head and rested against the lavatory wall. It gave ample access for the flight attendant to step by him.

"I'm sorry," the flight attendant said, "but I'm afraid I have to insist. The captain has turned on the seatbelt light. You need to retake your seats."

Reluctantly, Sarah nodded. The woman was right. They had to follow the rules or risk escalating the situation. Being charged with air rage was something she didn't want on her record.

The flight attendant moved aside to allow Sarah room. As she eased by Casper, something glinted inside his jacket. She slowed and did a double take just as he dropped his arm. The first image in her mind was enough, but she had wanted the double take to solidify the image.

Then he was gone through the walkway behind the seats and up along the opposite aisle.

"Ma'am," the attendant said behind her as she watched Casper disappear toward the front of the plane. "Your seat. You need to retake your seat now."

"Right," Sarah mumbled and started forward.

On the way back to her seat, she couldn't get the image out of her mind. What puzzled her the most was how Casper got it onto the plane.

How could he smuggle a knife without airport security picking it up?

And the gun stuffed in a holster? How could he have done that?

Unless he was an air marshal of some kind, but wasn't that only on domestic American flights? She hadn't heard of international air marshals before.

Her seat came up on the left. She would sit, think about it, and then when the seatbelt light flicked off, she would turn around in her seat and ask him about the knife and the gun holstered in his jacket. If his answer worked, she'd let it go. If it didn't, Casper could be why this plane crashed, which meant she had to do something about it. She would have to do something about Casper.

Four seats from hers, she slowed.

Casper had left the back of the plane half a minute before her. He would have beat her back to their seats.

But his was still empty.

Casper, the ghost, was gone.

Chapter 3

Sarah retook her seat, adjusted her seatbelt, and waited. Casper would resurface unless he bought two plane tickets, giving him a seat elsewhere on the plane. Maybe he worked for the airlines.

She rested her head back as turbulence shook the aircraft. A man to her right woke with a start, adjusted himself, and tried to go back to sleep. The boy by the window to her left slept undisturbed. His mother wasn't doing so well.

"You okay?" Sarah asked.

The woman nodded. "I don't like the shaking."

"Me neither. But these planes are made to handle it."

She wasn't sure if she was consoling her fellow passenger or trying to convince herself, as she already knew this plane was doomed. But what bothered her more was the immediate danger of Casper roaming the plane with weapons.

She undid her seatbelt and got to her feet.

Casper's seat was still empty. She started up the aisle and stopped at a divider. After a moment's pause, she pulled the curtain aside and stepped into first class. Small televisions displayed several different shows intermittently throughout the seats. Some were watching while others had fallen asleep in front of their TVs.

Sarah continued forward, intent on locating a senior crew member before returning to her seat. She pulled it back cautiously at the next curtain in case Casper was there. He wasn't, but two crew members were talking, each having a coffee.

"Can we help you?" the tall, dark-haired one asked. "You should be in your seat during this turbulence."

"I need to speak to your senior crew member."

"That's me. My name is Jasmijn Luna."

"I'm Sarah. I was speaking with a man who was sitting in the fifteenth row, seat C." She stopped talking to grab a handle protruding from the bulkhead to balance herself as turbulence continued to assault the plane.

"Is he still in his seat?" Jasmijn asked.

"No. I haven't seen him."

The flight attendants exchanged a glance. "Well, I'm sure he's still on the flight somewhere."

"Are there any air marshals on this flight?"

"Why do you ask?"

"Because the man I was speaking with is armed."

Another exchange between the women. They didn't appear to be taking her seriously.

"When you had your meal, did you choose an alcoholic beverage?" Jasmijn asked.

Sarah narrowed her eyes. "Don't take this lightly. You have an armed man roaming this aircraft. I saw the gun under his jacket. What is the protocol for dealing with situations like this?"

Jasmijn undid her seatbelt and stood to her full height. She was over six feet tall with heels.

"Look, Sarah, you were chatting with a man at the back of the plane, quite far from your own seat. When asked to go sit down, at first, you refused. We still have the seatbelt light on, and you're walking around the plane telling stories about men with guns. Our security is good enough these days that no guns are on board."

"One man. One gun."

"You're becoming a problem."

"And the gunman isn't a problem?"

"There is no man on the plane with a gun," Jasmijn said sternly. "Security-wise, it's a near impossibility."

"He has a knife as well."

"Look, Sarah, I'm going to need you to walk back to your seat and stay there for the duration of the flight. Speak of this to no one. Can you do that?"

If it meant avoiding the inevitable plane crash, she would have to locate Casper on her own. Jasmijn was making it abundantly clear she wasn't willing to listen.

To avoid looking desperate or worse, Sarah nodded. "I'll go back to my seat. But this man is armed, and he's dangerous."

"How would you know he's dangerous? Are you in law enforcement?"

"You could say that."

"What are your credentials?"

Sarah shook her head and stepped back to the curtain. "I'll head back to my seat now."

"If we see this man, what was his name? Did you get a name?"

"Yes," she said without thinking.

"Well, what was his name?"

"He goes by the name Casper." She avoided using his real name, Buck Schaffer. That reduced her credibility instantly. There was no use continuing this conversation.

The attendants looked at each other, then back to Sarah. "Casper, as in Casper the friendly ghost? And now you're saying you can't find him. You said he disappeared."

Sarah pulled the curtain aside and stepped past it, letting it fall back in place behind her. On the way to her seat, she realized how easy it was to lose credibility with just one word.

Where could he be? Hiding in a lavatory? Or two plane tickets, two seats? But why?

She scanned all the faces until she reached her seat in the fourteenth row. Casper's seat remained empty. No crew members were close by. Only pausing for a brief moment by her seat, she continued toward the back of the plane, scanning faces in search of the friendly ghost. Near the back, she crossed to the other side and started up the aisle.

The attendant from earlier approached her.

"Ma'am, you need to retake your seat. The seatbelt light is still on."

"Where is the man I was talking to?" Sarah asked. "You saw us talking back there by the lavatory. Where is he now?"

"I have no idea. He's probably in his seat, as you should be."

"He's not in his seat." She leaned in close so none of the other passengers could overhear her. "That man was armed with a gun and a knife."

The flight attendant gasped and pulled back to look into Sarah's eyes. The surprise on her face was evident.

"I don't know how he smuggled these items onto the plane, but he's a credible threat to the safety of this aircraft."

"Okay," the attendant patted Sarah's arm. "Come to the back with me."

They headed aft, Sarah in the lead. Once there, the woman yanked a curtain in place, concealing them from the other passengers.

"What makes you feel he's a threat?" the woman asked. "Do you know this man?"

"I don't know him. He's sitting behind me in row fifteen. He's a threat because the weapons he has were most likely smuggled onto the flight."

"You appeared to know each other when I saw you earlier."

"We were talking. When he raised his arm, I saw the weapons."

"Where is he now?" she asked.

Sarah shrugged, frustration building. "I have no idea. I asked you the same question."

"He can't just disappear." She peeked past the edge of the curtain and then let it fall back into place. "I take what you've told me seriously. Please, go back to your seat. I will talk with my superior. I know what this man looks like. We will get to the bottom of this very shortly. But please, go back to your seat. I will come to talk to you when I know more."

"When's the earliest we could land?" Sarah asked.

The attendant glanced at her watch. "We're less than two hours from Amsterdam. That would be our best airport as we're over the ocean right now. We'll be rolling out the breakfast soon. Then we do cleanup and prepare for landing. Just take your seat. We'll look into this."

Sarah nodded and started away. Short of being branded paranoid or accused of causing a disturbance, she decided to remain in her seat for the duration of the flight. Whatever Casper was up to, she was sure he'd planned on her seeing the inside of his jacket. But why? What could he gain by it? Especially if he knew who she was as he had claimed.

When she got to her seat, the chair behind hers was still empty. Casper was hiding out somewhere on the plane, and what ate away at her stomach was that he was probably plotting something that would prove disastrous, and there was nothing she could do to stop him. Her attempts came across as annoying the crew and being disruptive.

So she would sit in her seat and wait, just like all the other passengers. She would wait until he showed up or the plane landed.

Or crashed.

But that was just it. She couldn't wait. It wasn't in her to wait. But what else could she do? She had notified the crew, one of which could identify the man. Short of causing a panic on the flight, she had done all she could do.

The little boy by the window seat was awake. He nudged his mother and whispered something to her. The mother looked at Sarah.

"Toilet," the mother said.

Sarah nodded and got up to let them out. Once they were both gone, she sat down and affixed her seatbelt.

Vivian. Anything?

The seatbelt light went out with an audible ding. The plane had been flying steadily without much turbulence for the previous few minutes. Then the interior lights came on. It was time to serve breakfast. The smell of food floated through the cabin as an attendant wheeled a tray out from behind a curtain about ten rows up from her.

Moments later, her seatmates were back. After they sat down, the mother leaned over to Sarah.

"There's a man back there asking to speak with you."

Sarah spun around in her seat and stared down the aisle. Another crew member was heading her way with a silver cabinet on wheels filled with breakfast items.

"Where?" Sarah asked when she spun back around. "What man?"

"A tall blond man. The one you borrowed the phone from. He's standing by the toilets. Asked me to tell you."

Sarah got up without another word and started for the back. When she approached the cart, she had to wait for the attendant to retreat four seats and turn into an opening so she could pass. She muttered an apology, hopped by him, and continued toward the lavatory.

At the doors, both were occupied. She moved past them, checked behind a curtain, and slipped to the other side, where she looked up and down that aisle.

Nothing. If Casper had been here, he was gone now. Or he was inside one of the lavatories.

She moved back and waited outside both doors to see who would emerge. While she waited, two other men joined her, also waiting for the use of the toilet.

There was a thump as a lock disengaged, and then the

door on her right crumpled inward like an accordion and opened. A woman in her seventies stepped out and walked past Sarah. One of the waiting men gestured at the door for Sarah to enter. She shook her head and gestured for him to take it. He thanked her and stepped inside, closing and locking the door behind him.

One more bathroom occupied. He had to be in there. Where else could he be? She took one more look around her and prepared for the door to open, wondering the entire time what his purpose for the cat-and-mouse game was. What was his end game?

The door's lock clicked, and the little red *occupied* button switched to a green *vacant* sign. She waited.

Then the door slid inward, and a teenage boy stepped out. He nodded at Sarah, then stepped past her and headed to his seat. Sarah spun on her heels and stared at the passengers that filled the seats facing her. Maybe she'd missed him. Maybe he was two rows away. But why send her seatmates back with a message and then disappear again? Whatever game he was playing, she was done with it. Watching her at the airport, following her to the back of the plane, sending messages—for what gain?

All of it reminded her of Rod Howley and his cronies. She would never work with or for the government. They couldn't be trusted. And their power held no limits.

"Excuse me," a voice behind her.

A flight crew member attempted to pass her with his little breakfast trays and drinks trolley. She stepped aside to let him pass. The second he was by her, the curtain brushing against her back moved, and an arm wrapped around her throat. Then she was yanked inside a small alcove where coffee and tea were brewing.

She grabbed at the arm in an attempt to dislodge it, but it was immovable.

"Don't fight me," a voice whispered into her ear. "I'm a friend."

The blond man's voice. Casper.

He let his arm loosen enough for her to breathe.

"Don't yell out," he whispered.

She thought about jamming her heel into the top of his foot. Or a well-placed elbow in his gut.

"I'm going to give you a present. You will need it before or when you land in Amsterdam."

"We're not going to land properly," she grunted.

"What are you talking about?"

"The plane is going to crash."

There was a moment of silence from behind her. His forearm didn't move.

"Bullshit," he whispered.

Was that fear in his voice? If so, he believed her. Which meant he knew who she was.

"Did Vivian tell you that?" he asked.

Confirmation.

She took the slack opportunity to spin around and face him. Their eyes met from inches away.

"How do you know about my sister?" she asked, her jaw clenching. "Who are you?"

He appeared to contemplate his answer, studying her face. Then his eyes relaxed, and he blinked.

"I've been watching you—"

"Why?" she shot back.

"Studying you, really."

"I asked you why."

"Because you're worthy of study."

"That's not an answer. Satisfy me or lose the ability to walk properly for a few months."

"What?" He eased back, frowning.

Sarah lashed out with her foot, brought it in behind Casper's leg, and yanked forward, buckling his knee. He dropped in front of her, where she grabbed his throat with both hands and lowered her face until their noses were touching. The back of his head bumped the counter and couldn't retreat any farther. He remained pinned under her grasp.

"Answer shit faster," she spat, anger fueling her strength. "Why me? Why now? Who are you working for?"

She lessened the pressure on his throat.

"I'm with a black organization in the U.S. Government. Something like the CIA and NSA wrapped together."

"What's the interest in me?"

"You've caused ripples."

"So it's my fault, is it?"

"I'm not assigning blame."

The curtain slid aside behind her. Sarah spun around, not releasing her grip on Casper. "We're not done here."

The flight attendant jerked, made a face, and jammed the curtain back into place.

"Speak faster," Sarah said. "The truth."

"I don't have all the truth."

Sarah eased back off him and stood by the curtain. "Get to your feet and tell me what you can."

"I'm supposed to follow you. Stay close. Make sure nothing happens to you."

"I can stay close to me and protect me all on my own. I'm a big girl now. I don't need you. What else?"

"Eventually, I'm supposed to bring you back to the States."

"No. Not going to happen. The U.S. Government doesn't manage my travel itinerary." Her words were accompanied by spittle.

"There's too much danger," Casper said, shaking his head. "You don't understand."

"No, you don't understand. What I do has never been *controlled*. Even I can't control my sister. You're entertaining an illusion if you think you or your government can control it."

"We aren't willing to control it."

"Then what?" Her frustration grew by degrees. "Why are you here?"

Casper took in a long breath and sighed. "We're trying to save you. You and everyone you know."

The curtain ripped aside. Sarah spun around.

Jasmijn Luna, the senior flight crew member, was flanked by four others. She looked past Sarah to Casper.

"I will only ask once," Jasmijn said. "Retake your seat, Sarah Roberts, and remain there for the duration of the flight or I will be forced to have you restrained until we land, at which point, charges will be brought against you."

Sarah raised her hands in surrender. "I'm going." She offered Jasmijn a half smile. "You won't have any more problems with me."

She pushed past Jasmijn and started up the aisle to her seat. What could Casper have meant when he said he was trying to save her and everyone she knew? What did the government know or think they know?

The breakfast dishes had all been cleared away. Morning sunshine beat through the windows as the plane prepared for its final descent into Schiphol Airport.

People were restless, moving in their seats and around the cabin. They were close to landing, and the tourists wanted to begin touring. It felt like an exciting time for everyone around her, but she was hunting a man with a black book, and the government of the United States felt it necessary to send a man to protect her from danger. All this and a plane crash, too.

Yippie!

She sat in her seat and asked her sister for something, anything, but nothing was forthcoming.

All in good time, eh, sis?

Turbulence shook the plane. People retook their seats. The captain came over the loudspeakers and announced that he was preparing to land.

"Ladies and gentlemen, as we start our descent, please ensure your seat backs and tray tables are fully upright. Ensure your seatbelt is securely fastened and all carry-on luggage is stowed underneath the seat in front of you or in the overhead bins. Please turn off all electronic devices until we are safely parked at the gate. Thank you."

Vivian had said this plane would crash. Now that they were preparing to land, and Vivian remained quiet, Sarah could only assume the crash would happen during the landing.

Something Casper had said came back to her. He had a present for her. Something she would need when she landed. What present? Did he already give it to her?

She felt around in her front pockets, then raised her butt and eased a hand into each back pocket of her jeans. Her right hand slid along something cold, steel-like. She pulled out the tip, saw the knife he'd had inside his suit jacket earlier, and slid it back out of sight.

Why give her a butter knife?

"Flight attendants," the captain said over the speakers. "Prepare for landing, please. Cabin crew, please take your seats for landing."

Sarah snuck a glance out the window beside the boy and saw only water. She felt the descent, the slowing of the aircraft, and only hoped that a crash could be avoided. But Vivian never bluffed or lied.

Then Vivian's voice reverberated through her head. Sarah closed her eyes and listened. When she opened them again, land could be seen outside the window. They were descending toward the tarmac, but now Sarah knew differently. The entire tragedy had been explained to her.

She undid her belt, bolted from her seat, and started for the front of the plane just as the pilot jerked the aircraft to the left and began to swing back out over the ocean.

He knows of the danger now, too. We're so screwed.

Sarah lost her balance and landed in a flight crew member's lap before careening off a wall and landing on the carpet. The plane was in a steep turn, the engines roaring to add power, when Sarah looked up into Jasmijn's eyes.

"You're asking for trouble, Miss Roberts."

Chapter 4

SARAH RIGHTED HERSELF AND leaned against the wall as Jasmijn worked to unbuckle her seatbelt, which seemed stuck.

"You're going to have to listen to me," Sarah said, aware of her precious little time.

Jasmijn glared at Sarah. "There's no listening to you, young lady. When we land, we'll let the authorities deal with you."

Jasmijn's belt disengaged. She got up and started away, probably thinking of returning with help to restrain Sarah. Before she could get two steps, Sarah caught Jasmijn's foot and tripped her. The attendant was able to grab the upper portion of a seat to arrest her fall before she hit the plane's carpeted floor. When she righted herself, Sarah was already on her feet and moving toward Jasmijn. She grabbed Jasmijn's arms and manhandled her back to her chair, shoving her down as the plane righted itself.

"Listen," Sarah ordered, jabbing a finger in Jasmijn's face. "Don't talk. Just listen."

Jasmijn regarded Sarah with a stern look of disgust. Or maybe it was anger. She had probably never been dealt with in such a way on any flight.

"In approximately twenty seconds, the captain will call you."

Jasmijn's eyes widened. "Why?"

Ignoring her question, Sarah continued. "He will inform you that he had to abort the landing. He will circle for as long as he can to burn off the rest of the fuel and to let emergency services prepare and organize themselves on the ground."

"Why?" Jasmijn asked again, more adamant this time.

"Because we're going to have a bumpy landing."

"How would you know this?"

"My sister told me. But that's not important. What is important is that you must find a way to remove all the people from rows six to twenty."

"Six to twenty ..." Jasmijn said, her voice echoing the words as if she was unsure why she was even saying them.

"Yes, six to twenty. Maybe remove rows five and twenty-one, too. Just to be sure."

Her eyes wandered left, then right, then refocused on Sarah.

"What? Why? Why are those rows important?"

"Because the plane will break in half somewhere near row fourteen. The split will affect five or six rows before and after row fourteen."

Jasmijn blanched. Sarah wondered how often someone sat Jasmijn down and told her the plane would crash. Not many from the way she was handling the information.

Sarah peeked out the small window in the door beside Jasmijn. They were back out over the ocean, the land moving away from them.

A curtain blocked them from the view of the passengers, which Sarah was grateful for. She didn't want panic on her hands.

The phone on the wall rang over Jasmijn's head.

Right on time.

She met Sarah's eyes but didn't move.

"Get it." Sarah nodded at the phone. "It's the captain."

On the third ring, Jasmijn pulled the phone to her ear. She identified herself and listened, nodding once, her eyes never leaving Sarah.

"Yes, sir," she said, then replaced the phone. "The captain said the front wheel isn't responding properly."

"I know. It's retracted. It's stuck in a sideways position."

Jasmijn acted like she'd been struck in the head, rearing back from Sarah, her jaw slack, eyes wide.

"Yes," she whispered. "That's what he said."

"Now, I need you to remove those people. Take them to the back of the plane. Fill all empty seats and have men get on the floor and lock arms to ground themselves."

Something like recognition flashed across Jasmijn's face. Using the wall behind her, she pushed herself up to stand. The look of amazement moments before had turned to defiance now.

"You don't give the orders on this plane. We have had trouble with you since you boarded—"

"Oh, come on," Sarah cut in. "What, I've been out of my seat a few times? Yeah, real trouble. That's me."

"I will not take passengers out of their seats and have them lock arms somewhere else on the plane. The captain assures me we can land with the defective front wheel. He'll keep the nose up as long as he can, reverse thrusters in place. We'll have a small amount of travel on the front wheel, and emergency services will be mobilized along the runway. This in no way is a crash landing. We will be fine, and you will go to jail for orchestrating a terrorist act on my plane. You could only know about the wheel if you sabotaged it."

"What's your horse's name?" Sarah asked.

Jasmijn blinked. She moved away from Sarah and stepped into the aisle.

"Excuse me?" Jasmijn asked in a terrible posh accent.

"Your horse. The one you rode in on. That high bugger. What's his name?"

Jasmijn wagged a finger at Sarah. "You're in a load of trouble."

Sarah stepped closer to her. "If you don't do as I say, a lot of people will die on this flight. I'm trying to save lives here."

"No, you're trying to kill people. I can see it in your face."

"You know, sometimes I make people earn a fuck." Sarah looked down at her fingers as she checked a nail, shaking her head as if Jasmijn had disappointed her. "I don't give many fucks away. They're not free, you know. But with you, I think I can make an exception. As I said, I usually don't give a fuck, but with you, I'll let this one go."

"You're insane." Jasmijn had backed away to the wall beside the curtain's opening. "When we're on the ground, you can explain yourself to the Netherlands police."

"I told you the captain would call," Sarah said, holding back a shout. "I told you why. Then I ask you to move passengers for their own safety. But you refuse. So tell me who the police will be more interested in. You or me? Who's trying to save passengers here?"

Jasmijn backed through the curtain and disappeared.

"Shit," Sarah mumbled under her breath. "That didn't go well."

Soft tremors of fear rippled through her at the thought of a crash landing. Overrunning the end of the runway, the plane breaking apart.

Hey, Vivian, did I have to be on this doomed plane? I mean, really?

She started up the aisle toward the front of the plane. It was time to make an announcement. The passengers needed to know who she was and why she knew what she knew.

It was time to save lives whether the flight crew agreed with her or not.

And she had a knife, thanks to Casper.

She only hoped she wouldn't have to use it.

Chapter 5

BUCK SCHAFFER MADE HIS way to the front of the plane. He slipped into the alcove outside the cockpit door where the flight crew made coffee.

After turning his cell phone off airplane mode, he waited to see if the plane was close enough to land for his phone to latch onto a cell tower, but it didn't. He began texting anyway. As soon as the phone picked up a tower, the message would send automatically.

He typed that he was in contact with Sarah Roberts. He was currently with her and would stay with her while she was in Europe. Then he would bring her back to the U.S. whether she wanted to go or not.

He was the one man who would convince her to go as she learned to trust him. He had a few plans for Sarah's Amsterdam trip that would endear her to him. He couldn't fail because Sarah was just one girl, one pliable girl. Even the smartest person could be outwitted if done correctly, and his plan was foolproof. Sarah would be his, like melted butter on popcorn. All he needed was the right temperature and the right atmosphere, and she would do as he said.

Or Sarah Roberts would be taken out.

His mission was simple. Sarah's compliance or termination. If she were willing to work with him, things would go smoothly. If she refused, it would be better for all parties involved that Sarah was dead. Killed in a public display would serve his purposes the best.

A part of him wanted her dead. The workload was minimized in that case. He would have less to do. But alive, she swept fear into the hearts of their common enemy. Even though his mission was to win her over, thereby keeping her alive, murdering her would be just as pleasurable.

Alive or dead, Sarah Roberts *would* serve her purpose. He would see to it. So far, she was already the unwitting actor in his dangerous play.

When the plane landed, she would be arrested for smuggling a concealed weapon onto the plane. How would she explain the knife? Would she say he gave it to her? A man who disappeared like a ghost and wasn't on the plane's itinerary. As far as ITA is concerned, he was never on the plane.

Her story wouldn't hold. The American Embassy was prepared for the inevitable call. Leaving her to her own devices with the Netherland authorities would keep her off Amsterdam's streets long enough to stay out of Buck's way.

Then he would swoop in, break her out, and she would learn to trust him.

Or she would prove too difficult to work with, become

unreliable, and he would kill her and dump her in the canal. The newspapers would run with the finding of a popular American girl bobbing in the dirty canal waters.

Whatever end result came about worked for him.

He hit the send button on the text, slipped his phone away, and checked to see that his gun was ready.

The plane banked sharply. He held onto the counter for balance.

Alive or dead, Sarah Roberts *would* serve her purpose.

Alive or *preferably* dead.

Suddenly, a woman screamed about the plane crashing. Someone struggled, then grunted.

Buck "Casper" Schaffer yanked the curtain out of his way and looked in on the pandemonium.

Chapter 6

SARAH PREPARED TO ADDRESS the passengers at the mouth of the aisle that led back from row one. She had seen the teenage boy from the lavatory earlier. He smiled at her. A good-looking boy with glasses and a nice smile. Instead of addressing everyone at once, she decided to talk to the boy first to make him an ally.

She knelt by his seat. "What's your name?" she asked.

"Conner Quinton."

Sarah nodded at the woman beside him. "Is this your mother?"

Conner nodded. "Her name is Sara."

"Oh, hey, nice name. I'm a Sarah, too." She adjusted her legs as they cramped. "Where's your dad?"

Conner shot his eyes skyward, then looked back at Sarah. "My father is gone. Died serving his country."

Conner's eyes welled up with tears.

Sarah placed a hand on his forearm. "I'm sorry for your loss. But I need you to do something for me that'll make your father—and mother—proud."

"What's that?"

Conner's mother leaned in closer to listen.

"Your birthday is coming up in, wait for it …" Sarah listened for Vivian. She held up a finger, then lowered it. "July. I think it's the seventeenth."

"That's right!" Conner exclaimed. "How did you—" He looked at his mother and then at Sarah.

She addressed Conner's mother. "You have a great network of family and friends. You're doing a wonderful job with Conner. But I need him to man up right now. I need him to be strong not just for you but for me and everyone on this plane."

"How so?" Conner's mother asked. "What do you want him to do?"

"Wait for a few seconds. The captain will explain. I'll cover the rest."

Sarah sat down in the aisle and stretched her legs. Other passengers watched her, but she didn't care. Once the captain announced the situation, people would be more willing to listen to her. At least, she hoped so.

A moment later, the captain came on. He explained there was a problem with one of the wheels and that everything would be fine. They were in the final approach, and emergency crews were on standby. Could everyone please place their heads between their knees and hold them there until the plane came to a full stop. The flight crew will open the doors and deploy the chutes. Leave everything behind.

Sarah got back on her feet. The air in the cabin had

thickened. People wore panicked, pained expressions. Over half of them had already lowered their heads.

"Conner, here's the problem. Rows five to twenty-one are going to split apart during the landing."

He gasped and reared back, clutching his mother's arm.

His mother leaned across him. "We're in row six," she said.

Sarah nodded. "I know. You need to move to the back of the plane to be safe. The plane will be okay, but we will overshoot the runway with the bad wheel. Once on the grass, the body of the plane will crack open under the stress. Rows five to twenty-one will break up. I need all these people"— she swung her arm wide—"to huddle at the back of the plane. I need your help."

Conner locked hands with his mother, looked into her eyes, and nodded. His mother nodded back.

"We'll help," Conner said.

"Good. We have less than five minutes. Let's do this."

Sarah got to her feet.

"Can I have everyone's attention?" she shouted.

Heads rose from between knees to look at her.

"As the captain said, the plane will land with a defective wheel. Overall, it'll be a decent landing. We have a good pilot. But rows five to twenty-one are where the plane will break apart when it overshoots the runway—"

A woman shouted over Sarah's voice, drowning her out. Someone jumped to his feet and tried to climb over someone else, grunting as he did so.

Like a comedian being heckled off stage, at least five voices rose over each other to quiz Sarah on how she knew this.

Conner and his mother got out of their seats beside Sarah.

"We're not going to risk it," Conner said loud enough to be heard by the passengers in his immediate area. "She knows what she's talking about," he said, jerking a thumb her way. "She knew things." His eyes watered, a tear spilling over his cheek. "Like my birth date. She's psychic or something."

Conner's mother was nodding behind him. "Let's go. Please join us at the back of the plane. These seats are doomed."

The Quintons started aft.

"At least I've saved two people," Sarah shouted. "Is there anyone else who wants to live to enjoy Amsterdam?"

At least half the seats from rows five to twenty-one began emptying. But that wasn't enough. The alcove that led to the back of the plane on the right aisle started to jam up. Then Sarah saw why. Jasmijn Luna and her crew, bent on stopping Sarah, were swimming upstream in their attempt to get to her. Jasmijn's voice was loud enough for Sarah to hear her shouting for everyone to retake their seats, but the people she struggled against weren't listening.

Sarah scanned the rest of the faces and tried to count them, feeling optimistic at the low number. At least fifteen people remained in the doomed rows.

Her peripheral vision caught movement behind her. She twisted to see Casper standing by the cockpit door.

What's he doing up here?

Jasmijn and her crew were getting through. Any second, she would be in the open, at which time they would rapidly close the gap and attempt to subdue Sarah. But there were still fifteen people to save.

A quick look out of one of the windows showed the land below was close and getting closer every second.

"Everyone, listen up," Sarah shouted. "This is not a drill. This is serious. Either leave your seats now and make your way to the back of the plane, or you will die."

Six people got up and started toward the back. They used the aisle Jasmijn was in, offering Sarah a few more precious seconds. She didn't want to use the knife but would if needed. People's lives depended on her. She would save them at any cost.

Her stomach did a flip, and nausea rose in her throat. The ground was dangerously close. She, too, needed to get to the back of the plane.

Jasmijn broke through and ran for Sarah. Four members of her crew, male and female, were pushed back in the rush of the last few passengers heading toward the back.

Sarah waited, her hand in her back pocket, fingers wrapped around the knife, silently thanking Casper for offering it to her.

Jasmijn lunged, no doubt assuming her backup was with her.

Sarah was ready. She feinted left, yanked the knife from her back pocket, pivoted around Jasmijn, and came up behind her as Jasmijn tried to right herself. The blade came up against Jasmijn's throat as Sarah pulled back on the flight attendant to keep her off balance.

"Don't make me slice through the carotid artery," Sarah said loud enough for everyone in the remaining seats to hear. "She'll bleed out before we touch the ground." Sarah jerked her arm. Jasmijn yelped. "Now that I've got your attention, I want everyone else in rows five to twenty-one to get up and run for the back of the plane, or this woman's death is on your head."

All but three men got up and started for the back. One of the three remaining stood and turned toward Sarah. He was in his sixties but still trim. A runner, maybe. Clean-cut gray hair, well dressed.

"I'm a retired police officer," he said. "Let's talk about this. Release the woman."

"There's nothing to talk about. Move away from the area, or stay and watch her die."

The other two men stood and started toward Sarah.

What's Casper doing? Why isn't he helping?

Sarah pulled on Jasmijn, keeping her off balance. Jasmijn's hands were on the backs of a seat on either side of the aisle. Sarah couldn't see her face but had to assume that her eyes were wide and her mouth agape.

"Okay, stay then," Sarah said. "But I'm heading to the back. I don't want to die on this plane."

Jasmijn's flight crew broke through and ran up the aisle.

"Stay back," Sarah yelled.

They slowed and stopped a few feet away.

The plane touched down on its rear wheels with a sudden jolt.

Sarah's stomach dropped, and her knees weakened her resolve. She held Jasmijn hostage near the seventh row. The plane would break apart exactly where they were standing when they hit the end of the runway.

The distinctive sound of a gun's slide jolted her from the moment of paralysis. Casper stepped into view beside her, his weapon raised.

"Get back," he yelled. "Everyone, go to the back of the plane, now."

The crew members turned and retreated through the door they had come through. The retired police officer and his two cohorts, who were willing to stay behind earlier, listened without further protest.

The nose of the plane touched down.

Sarah released Jasmijn and shoved her away. Jasmijn clamped a hand to her throat and ran after her coworkers.

The seats were all empty.

Through the windows on the right, sparks flew up past the wing. They weren't slowing down fast enough.

"Come on," Sarah shouted, but Casper was already running up aisle two, headed toward the cockpit.

Sarah started after him, dropping the knife as she ran.

Something slammed into the plane like a huge fist, shaking its frame. Sarah lost her balance, fell into the seat on her right, and careened off the seat on her left before smacking down onto the thin carpet of the aisle.

Another jolt and the plane creaked like a giant can opener was opening it.

She was lying beside row five. In a heightened state of panic, she got onto all fours and crawled. The plane bounced and bumped as it left the runway. She lifted off the carpet, smacked back down, and bounced again as she tried to crawl past row three.

The plane would stop and break apart at any moment now.

Worried she might be sucked outside when the plane broke apart and then run over, Sarah grabbed the armrests on either side of the aisle and, with great effort, got to her feet.

With one big push, she lurched forward as the plane cracked open behind her. The nose tilted sideways and away. It felt like she made a leap that would take her four or five feet, but she was still falling ten feet later as the cockpit part of the plane rolled away from row five.

Sunlight streamed through the large opening in the fuselage and blinded her before she landed.

The sound dimmed until all she heard was the wailing of sirens.

Chapter 7

EMERGENCY VEHICLES, PERSONNEL, AND hundreds of passengers roamed the area. A small fire that had ignited under the defective front wheel of the ITA flight had been extinguished. As far as Sarah could tell, not a single passenger died in the crash. There were a few broken arms and bruises, and one older woman was taken away on a stretcher, gauze wrapped around her head, but that was it.

The plane was another matter. There was virtually no damage from row twenty-one to the rear of the plane. The cockpit and the first few rows behind it were intact and lying on an angle completely separated from the rest of the plane.

Just as predicted, rows five to twenty had fallen apart and lay in shambles across the grassy area at the end of the runway. The casualty rate would have been fifty or more if those seats hadn't been evacuated.

Sarah hadn't seen anyone from the flight yet. When she

leaped toward the cockpit as the plane broke apart, she followed it down until she body-checked the bulkhead beside the cockpit door. Emergency personnel were rigging a ladder to bring her down. The pilots had already climbed out the cockpit window and were on the ground.

Casper was nowhere in sight.

The ladder touched the broken edge of the fuselage. An emergency worker stuck his head above the rim as Sarah crawled toward the edge.

"English?" he asked.

Sarah nodded. "Yes."

"Are you hurt? Can you manage the ladder on your own?"

"I'm fine. Nothing more than bruises."

"Okay, I'll start down and will remain a few rungs below you at all times. It's only about six meters to the ground. You'll do fine."

She offered him a smile for his kindness and pivoted on her knees to get into position. Once her legs were over the edge, she descended the ladder, emergency personnel surrounding the base. Some of them were police officers.

Is this trouble, Vivian?

At the last rung, she hopped off and turned to address the assembled crowd.

The man who met her at the top flashed a penlight into her eyes and did a quick but thorough check for injuries.

"I'm fine," Sarah said.

The man stepped back and nodded at one of the men in suits.

"Sarah Roberts?"

"And who are you?"

"I'm Inspector Lars Dekker. Please come with us."

"Where are we going?"

"For a little talk."

"We can talk here."

The inspector walked away. "Bring her."

Two officers on either side clamped rough hands above her elbows and half lifted, half dragged her after the inspector.

"Am I under arrest?" Sarah shouted.

"We will discuss that at the police station."

"I'm an American citizen. I demand to speak with my embassy."

"All in good time, Miss Roberts. All in good time."

As they rushed her to a waiting Mercedes, Sarah caught a glimpse of Jasmijn Luna, the senior flight crew member, mumbling something to another flight crew, watching her the entire way.

At the car, before they shoved her inside, Conner Quinton, the fourteen-year-old young man who was the first to stand and head to the back of the plane with his mother, rushed up to the car, his mother in tow.

Inside the vehicle, the doors closed, and a uniformed officer was sitting on either side of her. Sarah watched as Conner leaned down and mouthed two words.

Thank you.

The car sped off, but not before she smiled and nodded at him.

All would be okay. Whatever they planned for her, she saved those people. The plane crashed, and no one died. Sure, she had to resort to drastic measures to get people to listen, but isn't that the way it always was?

She was sure she would have to resort to drastic measures to get the Netherlands authorities to listen before she flew back to Toronto.

All she wanted was a black book, and then she'd leave their country.

As the car raced into the heart of Amsterdam, she knew something else was cooking. She couldn't smell it yet, but something was definitely stirring. Intuition told her Casper had something to do with this.

Hear them out, call the embassy, and be out looking for the black book by the end of the day.

It would be easy. At least a lot easier than being on a doomed airliner.

Anything beats plane crashes.

Anything.

Chapter 8

Inside the police station on Prinsengracht Street, Sarah sat behind a table in a clean interview room. The walls were painted white but so bright and clean that it was as if a luminance oozed from behind the paint. She recalled her time in Europe a few years ago with Parkman. The modern, newer European buildings were always clean and smelled new. It was different from the new buildings back home. She could *feel* the difference but had trouble describing it.

The room was wired for sound, and cameras were fitted into multiple places. This interview was routine, especially for someone who attacked one of the flight crew. But once they saw reason, and Jasmijn told them how Sarah prevented those passengers from dying, they would have to let her go.

The only trouble was it would take time to gather everyone up and interview them. Time to collect the information and deduce her role before the crash. They would investigate her personally. Inspector Dekker would learn who she was and most likely see what she could do— her special ability. That would go a long way in getting her out of here. At best, she would be detained until later in the day. At worst, later in the week. Losing a week could mean the difference between attaining the black book or having it disappear forever.

She needed out of here as soon as possible, and she needed a phone to call Aaron to get confirmation he understood the message she'd left him. Without knowing why yet, it was vital he attacked one of his students and then went into hiding. Something was going on in Toronto, and Aaron's life depended on him doing his part.

Aaron will suffer ...

After flying to Amsterdam and now cooling her heels in a decked-out interview room in a Netherlands police station, Sarah had no way of knowing if Aaron had gotten her message. It made her feel like she'd abandoned Aaron in his time of need. Something she would never do.

And where was Casper? He had run for the front of the plane as it landed, but when the dust settled, he was gone. He still had to answer for how he'd gotten weapons on board that flight.

How long are they going to keep me in here, Vivian?

Why did everything have to be so frustrating? All she wanted to do was help people. Save them from an early visit to the morgue. But everyone worked against her, thwarted her every move. It would be enough to make her quit if she weren't as motivated as she was. If people *wanted* to die and be used and abused, then who was she to stand in their way? Bitterness led to anger. She clenched her fists under the table.

She could still fight, but after all she had endured over the past few years, she had lost something on the inside. An innocence that led to being forever jaded.

She studied the room and thought about the building, the city. Amsterdam. She was already here. She would get the book, head back to Toronto and tell her sister to leave her alone for a while. It was time for a break before she did something that would see her in prison for a very long time.

The interview room door clicked open, startling her. The inspector from the crash site stepped inside, followed by two other uniformed officers, a woman and a man. The inspector waited until the officers were inside before he closed the door and addressed her.

He held a file folder and several sheets of white paper. His expression was void of emotion. He'd done this many times and wasn't giving anything away. The only one who appeared uncomfortable was the woman. Dark hair, and dark eyebrows, she kept her eyes averted from Sarah's. The other officer's beard was cut thin and fashionable. His eyes gave his age away. He had to be in his forties and still wearing a uniform. The loss of promotions for him were probably due to the drink. His nose had broken blood vessels on each side, and he already had a nervous tick about him, like his last drink was more than a few hours ago, and he needed another.

"We met at the airport." Inspector Lars Dekker stepped away from the door and circled behind her, which she thought was dangerous as they hadn't restrained her in any way. "I'm with the Royal Constabulary, one of the four services of the armed forces. A military organization, actually. Familiar with it?" He moved farther around to stand behind the female officer.

Sarah shook her head.

"Audible," he said. "I need audible answers."

"No."

"No to my request for audible answers or no to my first question?"

Sarah stared at the woman and remained silent.

Dekker pushed on. "My rank falls under the Ministry of Defense even though we operate as a regular police force in the Netherlands."

"Why do I need to know all this as a tourist?" Sarah asked. "I'm here to tour Amsterdam, see the sights, photograph the canals, and then head home."

Dekker rested his clenched fists on the table, studying her face. "I fear it's you who has other plans, Miss Roberts."

His aggression toward her was clear. Dekker thought her guilty of something. Someone had fed him lies, and he wouldn't show his cards easily.

"Tell me, what kind of Mercedes did we ride here in?"

"It's a Mercedes-Benz E-Class. We have BMW X5s as unmarked vehicles as well."

"Bit classy for unmarked cars, isn't it?" She tapped the table with her fingers, one after the other. "I have to say I'm impressed. Your English is impeccable."

"Approximately ninety percent of the people here in the Netherlands speak English. Many of them have better grammar than English-speaking natives."

"Bold statement."

"Truth. But we're getting off-topic. Let's talk about the diamonds."

What diamonds?

She leaned back in her chair at the mention of diamonds

before realizing her mistake. Her surprise might be perceived incorrectly.

"Diamonds?" she asked. "I know nothing about diamonds."

"Yes, diamonds," Dekker said. His voice rose with the words.

Inspector Dekker opened the file folder and slid two pictures across the table to Sarah.

"On February 25, 2005, over seventy-five million euros worth of diamonds were stolen from Schiphol's cargo terminal. They used a stolen ITA van to gain airside access."

Sarah studied the photos. One showed the ITA van from security footage, and the other displayed the empty cargo area where the diamonds had been stowed.

"What has this got to do with me?"

"This decade-old robbery was and still is considered one of the largest diamond thefts ever."

The room fell silent. Sarah waited. She was done talking but interested to see where the inspector was headed.

"Diamonds are in the cargo terminal again today," he said. "As we move them to their new home in Amsterdam, security is heightened. So why do you suppose we have you here with us?"

Sarah shrugged and raised her hands. This was ridiculous, illegal, and preposterous. "No idea. You tell me." She tried to check her anger but couldn't. "Maybe you like my hair. Or it could be you wanted to buy me dinner." She slapped the table, making the female cop jolt. "That's it, isn't it? You want to buy me dinner. Fine. With our meal, I'll be wanting an Amstel beer, the original Amsterdam taste. Will there be a dress code?" She looked down at her jeans, then back up to the inspector whose face had colored. "Oh shit, I'm not dressed appropriately for the restaurant you had in mind, am I?"

Inspector Dekker nodded at his colleagues, who both rose from their chairs and headed for the door.

"What?" Sarah nearly shouted. "Was it something I said?"

The inspector opened the door and let his officers out. The door still open, he turned back to face Sarah.

"You're here because we have intelligence that suggests you flew into Schiphol Airport today to steal that diamond shipment. The organization involved in the 2005 theft acknowledged they were working with a pretty blonde woman."

"Why would they *acknowledge* something like that to the authorities? That was ten years ago. I was a young teenager. Come on. You know it's bullshit. I know nothing about diamonds, and I'm not a thief."

"We have an insider. What do you call it in America? A mole? Deep cover? Our sources say we are to watch for a pretty blonde, tough-talking American female who might be armed. When the plane landed, and we heard the stories from the other passengers that you were all those things and that you attacked the flight crew with a knife and a gun, we knew you were the one we were looking for."

"I didn't have the gun!" She slammed the table with both hands this time.

"The courts will figure it all out. According to witnesses, you had the gun. How you got those weapons on the flight is another investigation entirely."

He moved backward out the door. Before closing it, he

said, "Make yourself comfortable, Miss Roberts. I suppose you'll be with us for the duration of your trip and a lot longer. You have broken too many laws and are a suspect in an attempted robbery at the fourth busiest airport in Europe. Your government can't help you. Your situation is hopeless. The sooner you see that, the better. Before processing, I'll send officers down to transfer you to your holding cell."

He closed the door with finality. Her eyes glazed over in anger as she looked down at the two photos the inspector left behind. She crumpled them into a ball, cussed twice, and threw the photos at the closed door in frustration.

In her hopelessness, it was moments like these that she wondered again why she did what she did.

Then she remembered all the women pouring out of the panic room at the heart of the Torture Club in Toronto. All those women had been saved because of her actions.

The people on the plane were saved because she took that flight.

That was her purpose. She had to stay on point. Whatever was going on, it would get resolved soon. She would make it out. She always did.

She had to.

She slammed her fists on the table to feel better.

It worked.

Chapter 9

AARON STEVENS TIGHTENED THE black belt that clung to his waist. It was his dojo, students, and class, but the new student, Juan Lopez, was doing everything he could to disrupt the class.

Juan was trained in commercialized Tae Kwon Do. The kind that sells on street corners all over Canada for a few twenties a month. They don't teach discipline, style, or technique; most of all, they don't teach humility. Shotokan Karate has a code of honor. It is a discipline in itself. But now, Aaron was trying hard to stay disciplined and not lash out at Juan.

The answer was simple. He had to explain to Juan that this wasn't a class he was welcomed at anymore. Removing students was rare, but it had to be done in this case.

Aaron left the bathroom and entered the main area, where his students practiced a new kata. *All* the students but

Juan stood off to the side. Juan was whispering into his cell phone.

Juan had only been to two classes, but it was enough for Aaron to know that he didn't fit in. With Juan's back to him, Aaron approached and tapped his arm. When Juan glanced over, Aaron nodded toward his office.

"I have to go," Juan said into the phone.

Aaron went ahead and left his office door open. He sat behind his desk and pulled Juan's initial fee from petty cash. A moment later, Juan entered the office, closing the door behind him.

"You can leave that open," Aaron said.

"Better not." Juan shook his head. "We wouldn't want anyone hearing our conversation. Might be bad for business."

Aaron leaned back in his chair and raised a finger to his lips. "How's that?"

"You first. Why did you call me in here?" Juan asked.

Aaron studied the Mexican's face. He couldn't read Juan, couldn't understand him. Why join a karate class only to disrupt it? This was a dojo where students came to learn. Juan didn't have to be here but stayed and participated less than half the time.

"I called you to my office," Aaron tossed the money on the desk, "to give you back your month's fee and tell you you're no longer welcome at my dojo."

Juan let out a soft chuckle. "You're firing me?"

"Not firing. You don't work here. Just cancel your membership."

"No, you're firing me. I do work here. I work hard here."

"Call it what you want, but you're leaving now. We don't want you back here. You've been to two classes and disrupted them both. If you know so much about karate, open your own dojo and teach your own style. But you can't do it here."

Juan was shaking his head, his lower lip curled inside his mouth as he bit on it. Slowly, he moved forward until he rested his hands on the end of Aaron's desk. For a moment, Aaron wondered if Juan desired a fight. This wouldn't be a problem, but he wanted to avoid it as it would send a wrong message. The last time Aaron fought a student, he almost killed him, but that was because the student had done a terrible, unspeakable thing to a young girl.

"Tell me one thing, and I will leave peacefully."

Aaron pushed his chair back and got to his feet. In his heightened state of alertness, he was ready. Juan was unpredictable, even a little crazy. With the door shut, it would be Juan's word against Aaron's, and since Aaron had a track record for hospitalizing a student, he needed to quell this fast.

"Where is Sarah Roberts?" Juan asked.

That took Aaron by surprise. He actually took a step back as if he had been slapped unexpectedly. Then anger at such an invasive question consumed him, and he put his hands on the desk to lean forward.

"Why are you asking about her?" Aaron asked.

"People's lives depend on me locating Sarah Roberts."

"Whose lives?"

"Just tell me where I can find her."

"Is that why you're here? Is that why you joined my club? To speak with Sarah Roberts?"

Juan's jaw clenched. Somehow this conversation angered him.

"Will you give me the information I need?" Juan asked.

"Absolutely not. Get out."

Aaron walked around his desk, opened the office door, and motioned for Juan to leave.

"What will it take for you to tell me where she is? Or at least commit to getting her in touch with me?"

Aaron stepped out to the main class area, ignoring Juan's last question.

"Everyone, stop what you're doing. At ease."

The class of twenty-three students and three teachers stopped and turned to face Aaron. His teachers, Daniel, Benjamin, and Alex, all stood rigid, at attention. Alex moved along the side wall toward the front door. Aaron didn't stop him. Someone had to open the front door when Juan was tossed through it.

Aaron gestured at Juan, who remained just inside the office door. "We have a student leaving us today. Normally I would regret his departure, but we've had two classes with Juan, and not only does he refuse to take direction, but he's also determined to disrupt the class. I have politely asked him to leave, but he refuses. So please, class, don't be frightened when I physically remove him." Aaron turned to Alex. "The door." Alex nodded and moved faster.

Aaron turned back to Juan. "On your own or on your head?"

Juan emerged from Aaron's office, his face rigid in anger.

"You will pay for this. And I will still find Sarah."

The last straw and all that, Aaron had had enough. He lunged in, wrapped Juan's arms together as if they were in a straitjacket, hugged him close to lock the arms down, and nose to nose, Aaron said, "You will stay away from her. Don't even speak her name."

"Why? Because you don't want me to follow her to Europe? Or should I wait until she returns? Or maybe I'll ask Parkman to set up a meeting. He'd be none the wiser."

Aaron squeezed harder until Juan's last words were almost cut off. Then abruptly, he let go, forcing Juan away from him.

"Get out. I'll be calling Sarah *and* Parkman. I'll explain who you are and what you just said. Don't ever let me see you again."

Juan started for the door. The class behind Aaron remained pin-drop quiet.

Juan turned back at the door. "You can't explain who I am because you know nothing about me. You can't call Sarah because she's in trouble with the Netherlands authorities. And you will see me again. Very soon." He wagged a finger in the air and squinted his eyes. "Actually, you won't see me coming."

Aaron took a step forward, but Alex waved him off. Alex's foot swept out in a shuffle movement while his right hand nudged Juan's shoulder. It was enough of a push that Juan was clear of the door, but the foot sweep caused Juan to lose his balance. He fell on his butt square on the welcome mat just as Alex closed and locked the door.

"Oops," Alex whispered.

The class behind him roared and clapped with enthusiasm.

But Aaron felt none of their joy. All he felt was danger. There was something about Juan that scared him. Something that went deep. Like he was part of a street gang or worse. Somehow Sarah had crossed this man's path, and now Juan and whoever he represented wanted retribution. It was something like that. It had to be. Otherwise, how did Juan know so much about Sarah?

And what was that about trouble with the Netherlands authorities?

He had to call Amsterdam. But where to start? And now he had to watch his back. Juan threatened that Aaron wouldn't see him coming. What could that mean? He had to call and warn Parkman.

What the hell was going on?

Aaron nodded at his teachers, a clear signal to take the class, as he locked himself in his office and picked up the phone.

After all he had been through in life, he was surprised his hands were shaking.

Chapter 10

IT HAD TO BE at least two hours before the female officer returned and offered Sarah a toilet break. Once she was done, the woman took her back to the interview room. Not a word was exchanged between them.

Reseated, coffee was brought in for her without asking, for which she was grateful. She sipped it and tried to remain calm even though her nerves had other plans. By the time she had taken her last drink from the coffee, the door opened. Inspector Dekker entered the room, followed by two men in suits. One had a lazy eye, a pot belly, and a thick white mustache. Some disease pockmarked the other's face in his past. Either that or a bad case of youthful acne. He was the opposite shape of his partner, slim, trim, and barrel-chested.

"Sarah, these men are with the NTSB, your American agency investigating plane crashes."

"That's fast."

"Fast? How so?"

"The plane just crashed."

"We were already here. Vacation. Got called in to review the preliminary results before the rest of the team arrive tomorrow."

"Yeah, I'll believe that. Sounds like a good story to me."

The men exchanged glances.

Lazy Eye turned to face her. "It's not a *story*. It's a fact."

"Whatever. Your agenda doesn't matter to me. What matters to me is when I can go tour the lovely city of Amsterdam. How about it, Dekker? When are you letting me go?"

"Sarah, the tough girl act won't work here. You are already aware that charges against you are being processed as we speak."

"What kind of charges? What did I allegedly do?"

The three men took seats opposite her. None of them held folders or pulled anything out to write on.

"Let's start with the hijacking of a commercial airliner."

"Hijacking? That's funny." Sarah offered a fake laugh. "How could anyone misconstrue what I did as a hijacking?"

"Every passenger we talked to feels that's the case."

What is their game? They know that's not true.

Dekker continued. "Sarah, you brought a gun and a knife on board. Could you explain how you got those items through security?"

"I did not bring those weapons on board. And if you ask the right passengers, you will learn that the gun was held by a man named Casper."

"Casper?" Dekker asked, eyebrows raised.

The younger, fitter NTSB agent began flipping through

something on his cell phone.

"What are you doing?" Sarah asked.

"Passenger list names are alphabetized on my phone." He flipped two more times, then shook his head. "No one by the name of Casper on the plane."

The trio of men stared at her, waiting for more.

"Try Buck Schaffer. Casper's a nickname."

The NTSB agent flipped through his phone again, shaking his head.

"Nothing. No Buck. No Schaffer."

"Tell us your story. Why don't you start at the beginning?" Dekker asked her. "The more you tell us, the better for you. Like why you have no luggage. Not even a carry-on bag. What woman travels without at least a carry-on? How do you expect to change clothes? Or do you?"

"I wasn't planning on staying more than a day. I'd buy replacements and fly back tomorrow or the day after."

"Why's that? Seems like a short vacation. Or are you not here on vacation? Tell us, what's your purpose in Amsterdam?"

She considered what they had on her. The angry passengers. Jasmijn Luna attacked and forced to listen to Sarah. A story of a man named after a ghost who then disappeared. Diamonds in a cargo warehouse. Whether it was a story concocted for her benefit or all coincidentally true, it didn't look good.

"I want a lawyer," she said.

Dekker shook his head. "It doesn't work like that here. I work for the Ministry of Defense. Your actions against one of our airlines and your potential theft of the diamonds at the cargo warehouse have labeled you a potential terrorist. You have no rights as of this moment. The only way for you to resolve this is by answering our questions in the best manner possible. It will go a long way during sentencing when this gets to court in a year or two."

Shock settled in over her system. "You've got to be kidding me. There is no way what you're doing is legal."

"Test me. Test us. Clam up. Do nothing. Say nothing. Go ahead. Nothing will change the fact that you blurted out, before the captain announced what was wrong, that the plane would have an accident. The senior flight crew member told us you knew everything before it happened. Unless you're psychic, that is simply impossible. The only other possibility is you planned it. So tell us, why did you want to crash your own ITA flight?"

Sarah imagined her face whitening. It took sheer will to find her voice, and when she did, she wondered why she even spoke the words.

"I am psychic," she said.

All three men laughed. When they collected themselves, Dekker turned toward her, a stern expression on his face.

"I wonder what the judge will think of that?" He slapped his knee. "No, the *psychic* defense won't hold up. Please explain how you sabotaged our plane and why. It will go a long way toward receiving better treatment while you're with us."

"I have nothing further to say to you. Look me up. Research my name. You'll learn who I am and what I can do."

"Okay, I will do that. What is your name?"

She frowned. "I'm Sarah Roberts."

"That's the name you gave us, but we know it as a fake

moniker, a pseudonym. The real American named Sarah Roberts was wanted yesterday in Toronto, Canada, on suspicion of multiple murders. Our information is current, and we understand she's still in custody. It's highly unlikely that you cleared your name and got on a flight out of Toronto headed to Europe that fast. Even Amanda Knox took longer to flee the Italian courts. We know that it takes planning to sabotage such a large commercial plane. If you were the real Sarah Roberts and not working with the jewel thieves, then I'll eat my words. But we all know that is not true. So just tell us your name, and we'll get on with it."

"Okay, write this down." She waited until Dekker was ready. "My last name is Fobrains." Sarah spelled it for him. "My first name is Url."

"Url Fobrains?" he asked.

Sarah nodded. "My middle name is Shit."

"Url Shit Fobrains."

"You got it. It sounds like this: *You're all shit for brains.*"

Without laughing, all three men got up and started for the door.

"Fingerprint asshole. That's how you learn my identity. Send it back to the States. Call Toronto. Ask to speak to Detective Marina Diner. She'll verify that I was on that plane and with her until I boarded the flight. Look into things. Investigate me. You'll see a pattern form." The door was almost closed. "A pattern of truth, *asshole.*"

The door closed.

"Shit!" She slammed her hands on the table, making her empty coffee cup bounce once and fall over.

What the fuck is going on, sis?

Chapter 11

Aaron couldn't get through to Parkman, so he left messages at his office in Santa Rosa and on his cell phone. Caleb and Amelia, Sarah's parents, were unavailable, too.

He called his apartment to listen remotely to his messages, but none were on his phone.

Wouldn't Sarah call? Did he miss her call? If so, why wouldn't she leave a message? She had to have landed in Amsterdam by now.

If he wanted to call Amsterdam, where would he start?

It was late. The class had already gone home. His teachers had left half an hour ago. Alone, the lights dimmed, and the doors locked. Aaron sat in his office chair and felt something loosen in the fabric of his life with Sarah.

When strange men came to his class to meet Sarah, it bothered him. He should have subdued Juan and made him talk. But the entire class had been watching. He had a gut feeling someone like Juan didn't go to the police. But that meant someone like Juan would be back. And he wouldn't be alone.

How could Juan know about Sarah? How did he know where she was and what was happening to her?

"What the hell's going on?" Aaron asked the empty office.

After ten more minutes of quiet reflection, he collected his things and locked the office. At the front door, he set the alarm, stepped outside, and secured the front door.

Half an hour later, he entered the side door of his apartment building. The elevator was empty when he stepped on. At his apartment door, he took one last look up and down the hallway outside his door, opened it, closed it, and locked it, then slid the chain on.

He tossed his duffel bag on the floor, kicked off his shoes, and headed to the kitchen for a glass of wine. An Australian Shiraz was left over from the other night. Once his glass was poured, he moved into the living room, grabbed the cordless phone, and sat in the plush armchair.

He hit the *talk* button and listened for the dial tone.

It wasn't there.

He shook the phone, hit the button again, then listened.

Nothing.

"It's dead," someone said.

Aaron jerked at the voice coming from his dining room, the wine spilling over the top of the glass. He set the dripping glass on the coffee table and made to stand, but rough hands landed on his shoulders, shoving him back into the chair.

A large gun entered his peripheral vision.

"Stay seated," a Mexican-accented voice whispered

beside him.

Aaron settled into his chair, the red wine soaking through his pants, his hands slightly raised above the armrests. This had Juan Lopez written all over it. Aaron had been careless. Sarah would be upset with him. He'd let her down.

Listen to them. Hear them out. Find out what they wanted and try to mediate their demands, the whole time looking for an opening. When he saw one, he would break bones. He would fight like someone possessed. And these men would regret coming to his apartment.

"We want Sarah Roberts," the man at the dining room table said.

He sat in the shadows, his features obscured. Aaron hadn't turned to look at the man behind him, so he had no idea who he was dealing with.

"She's in Europe."

"We know this."

"Then why come here?" Aaron asked.

"When she returns, she will need the motivation to come to see us. You're our motivation."

"Leave me your name and number—as most people on this planet do—and I'll be sure to give it to her."

"Listen to something for me," the man at the table said.

"I'm listening."

A recording started. Sarah's voice. Like she was leaving a message.

"Listen, Aaron, you will have a new student at the dojo. Don't trust him. Vivian says there's something wrong with him. I need you to hospitalize that new student and disappear for a week or more. Can you do that for me? Listen closely— hospitalize the customer. Then disappear. Do it in that order.

But make sure you do it."

The recording ended.

"What does that mean?" the man asked. "Who is Vivian?"

Sarah left him that message. How did he not get it? Whatever was supposed to happen will happen because he didn't put Juan in the hospital. He clenched his fists and unclenched them. Sarah was going to be pissed with him.

"I only had one new student recently, and I would've loved to hospitalize his ass."

The man at the dining room table rose and stepped around the table. His suit shone like it was lit from the inside as he came into the light. A bright silver jacket, a white shirt. A professional. Dark hair and brown skin.

"You will come with us now. You will be our guest until Sarah returns."

"I don't think so."

Something jabbed his neck. He reached up, wrapped his fingers around the offending wrist, yanked and twisted, intent on snapping the offending wrist. But whatever hit his neck seemed to work fast. He lost his strength, his will to fight. It was like the anger ebbed out of him as if it were a liquid.

"You will join us, and then you will die when she returns, as I will have no further use for you."

Die? Use ... what?

"Where are we going?" Aaron asked, but he wasn't sure if the words left his mouth or remained a thought.

"Tijuana."

But I can't go ... Aaron tried to say before everything went black, and he slumped in the chair, slid off it, and bumped his head on the floor.

He was out before his head bounced once.

Chapter 12

Amber Dijkstra rolled another cigarette with precision and care. Each piece of tobacco mattered. The amount of saliva to close the paper mattered. Too wet, and the taste was off. Not enough guts; the smoke was too weak.

Her hands shook because she had decided today would be the day she would tell her boyfriend everything. Her boyfriend was also her pimp. And when he heard what she had to say, Amber wasn't sure she wanted to know the outcome. That was why she had asked two friends to join her as backup.

Ten years working the red light district windows for Sven Spaans, and all she ever got was just enough to eat. She had chances in the past to leave this place with several rich clients. One recent client—known as platinum clients—who she had been with half a dozen times over the last year offered her a one-way ticket to London. She could stay hidden in his manor until Sven forgot about her.

But Amber didn't leave. She loved Sven. Even when he beat her, she loved him. Even when he slept with other girls. How was that different from all the men she bedded down daily? Of course, he needed variety. A man needs variety. Every girl knew that.

She lit the cigarette's tip, inhaled long and deep, held it, then blew the smoke out into the stale air of the cobblestoned street. In a few hours, she was supposed to be in her bikini, dancing in the window half a block up, the red and pink lights making her look ten years younger.

When she spilled her guts to Sven, there would be little chance she'd be dancing tonight. When Sven heard what she had to say, Amber was sure she would end up in the hospital. Unless he didn't want to touch her. Although he could still beat her with pipes, baseball bats, and stones.

Just save the face. All the girls got beaten at one time or another, and all the girls knew to save their faces. Without the face, you don't work. Bruises can be covered up. Facial wounds, not so much.

The sun beat through patches of clouds roaming across the Amsterdam sky, warming her, then leaving her in the shade. A soft breeze rose off the canal, moving the cigarette's smoke away and replacing it with a stench of urine and feces. At times, when the wind was just right, the canal reeked worse than an unwashed commode. Or maybe that was her impression of the city that had slowly eroded her, worked her will to live through a meat grinder, and spat out an Amber hamburger of an existence. She wasn't worth much anymore. There was nothing left. Used and abused. The new girls coming up were pert, young, with tits that hadn't been affected by age or gravity. Soon Amber would only be catering to the creeps, the weirdos, and the fetish crowd.

But she used to be a somebody. A painter, an artist. At seventeen, with stars in her youthful eyes, she thought she'd be famous one day like Van Gogh. Sven assured her of her success when they met. A little party here, a little party there, and suddenly, she was doing too many drugs and having too much sex.

She forgets how, but by eighteen, she was in the red-lit window, dancing in a tiny bikini, watching the tourists gawk at her every fifteen minutes, a customer entering the door, negotiating a price to use her body.

Sven explained that to be an artist on a world stage, they had to save money. She could make so much more doing what she did. More than he could ever make working a canal tour boat.

For the love, for the art, for Sven, she had agreed. It was supposed to be temporary. Six months maximum. That was a decade ago.

And now she had to quit. She just turned twenty-eight years old. She was washed up, dangerously thin, the elasticity of her skin gone, and a few teeth missing from a heroin addiction that she never fully kicked.

Sven didn't love her anymore. She knew that. But after a few years in the trade, what else was there for a used-up prostitute?

She dropped the end of the cigarette onto the cobblestone, set her flip-flop on it, and twisted.

Sven wouldn't care if she was quitting. The business was slow for someone her age. What he would be mad at was why she was quitting.

Especially since he never used a condom with her. He swore he used one with all the other girls, but with her, his one true girlfriend, he never did.

Her HIV test came back positive over a month ago. Afraid to say anything, she had tried to believe it was a false positive.

Yesterday's test confirmed she had the deadly disease that led to AIDS.

She didn't feel too guilty about the hundred-plus customers visiting from around the world who slept with her at that time. She had been careful and made them wear condoms.

It was Sven she was worried about. He came to her almost daily, had sex with her in every way possible, and even made her ass bleed a few times.

The likelihood of Sven getting a positive test was so high she worried that he'd kill her with his huge hands.

She looked over the canal and wondered why living mattered anyway if this was all there was to life. Without hooking, what did she have? What could she do?

She pulled out her cell phone and dialed Sven's number.

"Yeah?" he answered on the second ring. He sounded out of breath.

"It's Amber."

"What do you want? I'm fucking busy right now."

"We need to talk."

"I've got a runner. The stupid bitch took off. They caught her at the airport. I haven't got time for this."

"But Sven, we *have* to talk."

A car door slammed on the end of the phone. "I'm heading to a meet. My contact is bringing the runner to a warehouse. I have to do this first. Then we can talk."

"No."

There was silence on the other end of the line. When he spoke, his tone was tight, firm. "What did you say?"

"I said, no." Her hand shook so much that the cell phone jerked against her ear. "Where are you now?"

"Where I always park my car. At my apartment."

"That's only a few blocks from the window I dance in. Come pick me up. We'll talk on the way."

He was quiet for a moment. She thought he had hung up on her. Then he cleared his throat and coughed into the phone.

"Okay. But be ready. And be ready to handle some blood. The girl we're picking up is a runner. She won't walk away from this. Can you handle that?"

"I can stay in the car."

"I'll be there in two minutes. Be outside. Be ready, or I'm leaving you behind."

She clicked off her phone and began rolling another cigarette. After two failed attempts because her hands weren't steady enough, she shoved the tobacco and paper onto the road in front of her, got to her feet, swung her purse with the gun in it over her shoulder, and waited for her boyfriend to arrive.

She would let him have his meeting. Locate his runaway girl. When they were done, and he was calmer, she would tell him she had contracted HIV. She could do this without her two friends because this was where it ended. She had made her decision.

One bullet to his forehead and one to hers. For all the beatings. Payback for the years Sven tortured and sexually abused her.

It was payback because he took away her dreams.

Sven was a dream stealer and a rapist. And rapists deserved to die. Sometimes faster as opposed to slower.

Chapter 13

IT WAS THREE HOURS before they returned. The coffee made her bladder scream, but she didn't say anything at first. She was too interested in what they had to say as Dekker entered with uniformed police officers again. This time he toted a box overloaded with file folders.

Everyone took a seat opposite her as Dekker pulled files from the box.

"What's all this?" Sarah asked.

"You," Dekker said. "We did our research. We looked into who you really are. But something mystifies us."

"I'm sure you're going to tell me."

"How is it you're still alive?"

Sarah shrugged. "Luck."

"Hmmph," Dekker muttered under his breath. He dropped the unopened files back inside the box and looked up. "Sarah, we have a situation, and we want to ask your help."

"What? Really?" She snickered. "You've got to be kidding. My help? After the way I've been treated?"

Dekker nodded.

"You bring me in here and threaten years of imprisonment, claim I'm part of a group of diamond thieves, and use the word terrorist in connection with the ITA flight and then ask for my help."

"You're right. Forget it."

Dekker started for the door, the officers following.

The notion struck Sarah that everything Dekker had said and did up until then was a setup. He wanted her help from the beginning but needed to scare her first. They needed to make her pliable.

Before Dekker shut the door, Sarah said, "Wait."

The door stopped, then started to open again.

"What kind of help?" she asked.

Dekker almost looked like he was going to smile as he stepped back inside the room. He waved the officers away and closed the door.

With his back against the wall, he crossed his arms and placed a foot on the wall.

"There's a criminal element interested in our red light district. We've been working to root them out for years, but it's never-ending."

"Understandable."

"We have a few insiders—"

"Like your undercover diamond worker?"

Dekker nodded, not missing a beat. "Like him."

"Go on."

"Of the most organized criminal activity in the area,

glorified pimps run over seventy percent of the girls in the windows. The girls are legal in the Netherlands. But human trafficking, the victims who aren't there willingly, is something we're always fighting."

"It's a problem the entire world faces."

"Right. Well, the Netherlands has been labeled as the top destination of victims of human trafficking, and we aim to do everything we can to stop that."

"What do you need from me?" Sarah asked.

"Your unique history revealed how you dealt with a major organization years ago that operated out of crypts."

"I remember it clearly. It started in Budapest, then Italy, and then to Esztergom, Hungary, where Armond Stuart was killed."

"That's what I'm talking about. Didn't you chase him throughout the United States as well?"

She nodded, her bladder begging for release.

"The man we're looking to take down is Sven Spaans. He's not just a trafficker of women, he is a murderer, but we can never gather enough evidence to make a case."

"How can I be of help?" She held up a finger. "Wait. Before we go any further, I need to use the toilet."

Dekker pushed off the wall and opened the door. He called for the female officer and ushered her inside.

"Please take Miss Roberts to the toilet and return her here." He turned to Sarah. "When you get back, is there anything you need?"

Sarah started for the door. "Another coffee would be good."

"Done. See you back in five."

The restrooms were remarkably clean, the white walls

sterile looking. The female officer waited outside in the hall. When Sarah was done and breathing easier as her bladder had ceased protesting, she was escorted back to the interview room.

A steaming cup of coffee in a proper mug was at her spot. Dekker sat in a chair in the corner.

Once seated, the female officer exited the room and closed the door behind her.

Sarah took a sip from her coffee, inhaled the aroma, and relaxed as she knew their angle now. It had all been for the deal. She would be released to do some menial task, and then she could get that damned black book and leave for Toronto.

And she had to call Aaron to make sure he got her message.

"As I was saying, Sven Spaans is public enemy number one in Amsterdam. Is that how you say it in America?"

"Something like that."

"We have a meeting set up with him for seventeen hundred hours this afternoon."

"What do you need from me?"

"Sven has been informed that he has a runner."

"A runner?"

"Yes, a girl under his control has taken off. According to our contact, someone Sven trusts, this runner was picked up at the airport and released to his care. When they meet at the warehouse at seventeen hundred, the runner is supposed to be handed back to Sven."

"Who is this runner?" Sarah asked but suspected that was the role they wanted her to play.

"There is no runner. We want to use you. When Sven swoops in to pick up his runner, we'll be waiting to nab him."

"With one look, won't he realize I never worked for him?"

"He has approximately one thousand girls under his control. He has soldiers who run things for him. His boss is the man we're really after, but if we bring Sven in, we are one step closer to the boss."

"Who's the boss?"

"A Chinese man who runs torture clubs in Moscow, Athens, and Toronto. That's what sparked our interest as we saw that the Torture Club in Toronto was recently raided. When I called Detective Marina Diner, the name you gave us, we heard you were responsible for ceasing their operations recently."

"And you put two and two together." Sarah crossed her legs. Something about this was too convenient, but she was excited as it seemed everything was falling into place.

"We have confirmation that the Chinese man we're looking to apprehend arrived this morning in Amsterdam on an earlier flight."

And he's got a certain black book of mine.

"Is there any way to locate the Chinese man?" Sarah asked.

Dekker shook his head. "All we have is Sven for now. And we have him at the warehouse in an hour. But we don't have a girl. We don't have a runner. We hope that you'll be that runner."

"In exchange for what?"

"All the charges against you dropped here in Amsterdam. You'd be free to go. It would be as if we had never met. When Sven is handcuffed, we will take the wire off you and bid you farewell."

"The wire?"

"Can't let you go in without a wire. We would need to record everything he says, get his voice on tape, asking why you ran. You respond that you will not be a part of his human trafficking machine or something like that. We'll always have two dozen officers within seconds of your location. Nothing can go wrong. You'll be completely safe. But we need your answer immediately as we're low on time."

"I want one thing from you."

"What's that?"

"The name of the Chinese boss."

"James Wong."

"That's it? Just James Wong? Doesn't sound very threatening."

"Believe me, he is. With connections all over Europe, Canada, and the United States, this man is powerful, and he's here in Amsterdam today. Not only that, he's suspected of dealing with the Mexicans recently."

"The Mexicans?"

"Laundering drug cartel money through his North American operations. We stop Wong, we stop a lot of traffic, human and otherwise."

"I'm in, but no wire. If Sven even detects a wire, I'm done for."

Dekker got up from his chair and walked across the small room. Sarah had momentarily forgotten her coffee.

He opened the door and talked to an officer just outside her hearing range.

He turned back to her. "The wire is a necessity. Sven won't find it. Even if he did, we'll have snipers in place.

There's nothing he could do fast enough that we won't be faster. You'll be completely safe. Trust me."

"Famous last words …"

Chapter 14

SVEN JAMMED THE GEARS of his BMW, driving faster than he should on the narrow roads.

"What was so important that you needed to talk to me right away?" he asked.

Amber lowered herself into the front seat and tried to remain calm. The disease in her blood roamed her body, knowing it would eventually win, reducing her to dying of a common cold one day. How was that justice? How was that for a wasted life?

"I'm a bit moody today," Amber said. "I want to discuss a few things, but not while you're busy. Deal with your runner, then buy me a coffee at a café, and we'll talk."

She pushed her purse between the seat and the door, so Sven wouldn't see it. The weight of her gun calmed her. There would be no more beatings. She would explain what she had and how he also got a death sentence, and then she would kill them both.

It was the only way. Not only was she prepared to do it, but it was also the right thing to do.

"You know I don't like to *talk*." He said the last word with such disdain she felt nausea whirl in her stomach.

Sven hated to talk. All he ever wanted to do was fuck. Make money, count money, and fuck. Never talk. Too bad. Today he won't just get fucked; he'll get fucked over.

"After the runner," she said, barely above a whisper. "Our talk will be short. Don't worry."

"I don't worry, Amber. I never worry. What's pissed me off is that Wong is in town today, and I have to deal with a runner. He doesn't like that sort of thing. Bad for business. That's why I'm dealing with it myself. That's why"—he leaned across her, flipped open the glove box, and pulled out a black gun—"the runner will die in that warehouse. She will explain herself first. I want to see her cry and beg for her miserable life. I want you to use your cell phone to record me putting the gun in her mouth and blowing her brains out." He held up the gun. Amber cringed away from him. "I have to make an example of this girl so the rest of you retards never think of doing the same thing. I need to show Wong that I got this. And now that you insisted on me picking you up, you'll help kill the runner."

Amber looked out the window to avoid him seeing her tears. Another innocent girl, in pain, running, trying to get home to her family, was killed and buried in the canal with the rest of them. How many girls did Sven kill per year? How many more had to die?

She wiped at her eyes and committed to herself that Sven would not kill any more innocent girls if she had anything to do with it. She would make sure of it. The only two people that would die were Sven Spaans and herself. No more innocents.

After all she had done over her short life, she was not innocent anymore. Not by a long shot. Killing Sven wasn't murder, it was just cause. Killing him was the right thing to do.

She inwardly smiled. It would be a pleasure.

The BMW raced recklessly toward the warehouse.

Chapter 15

SARAH LOVED THE MICRO technology Dekker's team brought out and now believed that Sven Spaans would never detect the wire. It was a fake clip-on belly button ring. Nothing more than costume jewelry. She wouldn't be required to take off her shirt, but no one would bat an eye at a belly button ring even if she did.

They were in a police van heading toward the warehouse. Dekker had supplied Sarah with a document absolving her of any crimes on Netherlands soil. She had figured out that everything about her being held at the police station was contrived to get her to agree to help them in their sting operation.

But how did they know she was coming to Amsterdam in the first place? Casper? The American government? The Canadian authorities? There had to be survivors who praised her actions after what she did on that doomed plane. Fifty or more people were moved to the rear of the airliner. All those people are alive today.

Inspector Dekker had lied to her because he had a plan from the beginning, a grand plan. Once she met with Sven Spaans, incriminated him, and waited for the Netherlands authorities to swoop in and make their arrests, she would exit stage left.

They weren't counting on her leaving with Sven as her prisoner. Dekker had no idea that Sarah was hunting James Wong and that Sven could lead her to him.

Inspector Lars Dekker had, unbeknownst to himself, offered James Wong and his black book on a silver platter to Sarah by setting up this little meeting with Sven Spaans.

She needed to locate James Wong and end her time in Europe. Every minute away from Aaron without confirmation he got her message was freaking her out.

"Okay, we're almost there," Dekker shouted over the sound of the van's engine. "You ready?" he asked.

Sarah nodded. They had supplied her with a soft pink, collared shirt. Easier on the belly button microphone, they had said. She still wore the jeans Aaron had brought her before heading to the airport hotel in Toronto the day before. Her shoulder ached from her injury at the Torture Club, but it wasn't flaring too bad.

If everything went well, she would be sipping a cappuccino at a canal-side café within the hour.

You around, sis?

Vivian had been strangely quiet again. Vivian was always there, lurking in the shadows, but if Sarah were walking into something altogether dangerous, Vivian would need to be there to walk her through it. A little reassurance went a long way.

"Remember the lines," Dekker said. "Get him to confirm you're a runner from his human trafficking ring. Let him intimate that he wants to take you back to your job." He used air quotes on the last word. "You'll never make it inside his car as we'll swoop in and arrest him."

"Who will deliver me to him?"

"Our inside man. He's on-site already."

Sarah nodded. "What's his name?"

"Doesn't matter. He won't know you, either. Better that way. He will take you to Sven, then leave. He's a good cop, but don't let on you know that."

She nodded again. "A gun?"

"What?" Dekker frowned.

"I need a weapon of some kind. What if things go bad fast? I won't like it if this Sven character starts slapping the shit out of me."

Dekker moved closer. "Sit down," he said.

Sarah sat.

"This is an undercover operation. With your cooperation, we could put Sven away for a long time. We could effectively free dozens, if not hundreds, of girls who the system has abandoned. Do you understand?"

"Of course."

"That means you cannot show up armed. You cannot be one of his girls who tried to run and return armed. You are a lowly sex servant in his eyes. He hits you, we'll be there. He attacks you, we'll be there. He pulls a gun, our snipers will disarm him. You are safe. I can't guarantee he won't strike you, but you won't be hospitalized." Holding onto a piece of metal jutting out near the van's roof, Dekker leaned closer.

"So no, you don't get a weapon, least of all a gun."

"Thought that would be your answer."

"Let's test the wire."

One of Dekker's men placed headphones on and motioned for Sarah to turn around. She stood up, Dekker easing out of her way, and turned her back to them.

"Now speak," the man ordered.

"My name is Sarah Roberts. I'm here against my will. I've been coerced into being a guinea pig—"

"That's enough," Dekker cut in. "We got you loud and clear."

Sarah turned back around, her face pensive. Before she left the van, she needed Dekker to know she was aware of what he had done. As far as she understood it, this Sven guy was a real badass. Short of him wanting to jam a knife inside her, she had no idea how fast these guys would respond to her distress call if something went wrong in that warehouse. Her life may very well depend on the men around her and the men in the second van. When you put your life in someone else's hands, you don't want false pretenses.

What they wouldn't count on is how fast she could be. Disable the undercover cop by breaking his leg, attack Sven, and lead him out of the warehouse before they could stop her. It would be a challenge, but Sarah was up for it. James Wong's black book was that important, and she intended to get it.

"Are we good?" Dekker asked. "You ready?"

"I'm ready." Sarah smiled, staring into his eyes.

Dekker looked away to check his watch. "We have ten minutes." He turned to the driver. "Pull up to the corner and let her out." He turned back to Sarah. "Our contact is a tall, good-looking agent. A Matt Dillon lookalike. You can't miss him."

"He knows what I look like?"

Dekker nodded. "He's been briefed."

"Will he be armed? If this goes south, will he be the first one to stop something?"

"He's armed with blanks. And no, he will not be on our side. When we rescue you, word on the street will be that our guy barely made it out alive. He needs to remain undercover."

She would have no friendlies close by and only seconds to escape with Sven as her prisoner. Aaron could do it. Had he trained her enough to handle it on her own?

I'll find out shortly.

"How close will you be again?" Sarah asked.

"Seconds away."

"When you say seconds, how many exactly?"

"Ten to twenty."

"And I'll be watched by snipers?" Sarah asked.

Dekker nodded. "Snipers are already in place."

"With orders to shoot to kill?"

"No," Dekker said, shaking his head. "We want Sven alive."

"Thought so."

The van stopped, and the side door was ripped open. The Matt Dillon lookalike stood in the afternoon sunshine, his hand up for hers.

"Let's go," he snarled.

With one last look at Dekker, Sarah moved through the men, jumped out of the van, and was led away by Matt Dillon's doppelgänger.

This does not feel good at all, sis. We cool here?

Vivian remained silent.

Chapter 16

Sᴠᴇɴ sᴛᴏᴘᴘᴇᴅ ᴛʜᴇ ᴄᴀʀ half a block from the warehouse.

"Stay here," he said. "Don't move. I will walk around the building and ensure there are no surprises. If I don't come back in ten minutes, take the car back to the apartment."

"Why wouldn't you come back?" Amber asked.

His grimace was one of disgust. "How stupid are you, Amber?" He wiped his face and looked out the window. "Do you know how I stay alive in this business? How I stay free to roam the streets? How I run my business?"

She shook her head, afraid to speak. He looked back at her. She was sure the venom in his eyes was hatred, and it was directed at her.

"I stay alive because I'm smart. I'm always one step ahead of those other assholes. You know, the ones who get caught and serve time." He smacked his forehead for emphasis. "Don't you see that this could be a setup? I have every reason to believe this is on the level and a few reasons to believe it isn't." He opened his door slightly. "So I'm going to check it out. Then I will kill the runner, and we will go have dinner and do your little talk shit or whatever the fuck you want to do. Then you work tonight. You work hard because, looking at you, your days in the window are numbered. You hear me, bitch, numbered."

Amber just nodded. When he worked himself up, it was better to stay quiet.

"I'll be back," Sven said as he opened the car door the rest of the way. "Be ready. Make sure you have your cell on video, and it's ready to record. Now, ten minutes. Give me that. If I'm not back, take off."

He bounded out of the car and shut the door quietly. Then he crouched down and ran for the corner of a brick building ten feet away, disappearing behind it.

Amber jumped at the chance to pull his black gun from the glove box. With one last look through the windshield to ensure he wasn't returning to the car, she unclipped the magazine, emptied the bullets, and then put the gun back together. Another look out the window before she shoved the gun back inside the glove box, hoping she placed the handle exactly the way he had left it.

A side zipper on the inside of her purse was a perfect spot to stash the unused bullets. After that, she checked to ensure her gun was loaded and ready. One zip and the purse was closed and slipped down between the door and the seat.

She was ready. Maybe the girl in the warehouse would live through this, maybe not. But Sven wouldn't live through it.

Amber Dijkstra had a solid reason for believing that, and

that solid reason was resting in her purse, waiting for her finger's pressure on the trigger.

With the HIV virus, things didn't work out. Sometimes things just don't work out.

For Sven, she would make sure things would not work out.

Ever again.

Chapter 17

AARON WOKE BLIND IN a moving vehicle. His kidnappers had covered his head with a burlap sack and tied his wrists and ankles. His tongue flopped around his arid mouth, not a drop of saliva available. How long had he been out? How long could he go without a drink?

He tested the bindings on his wrists and discovered they had cut off his circulation, and his fingers were ten lumps without feeling. His feet were about the same. How long could his extremities go without proper circulation?

"Hello," he said through the sack, his voice cracking and sounding foreign to him. "Hello?" he tried again, louder.

Someone moved nearby. He detected someone getting closer. The vehicle bounced and jostled along what felt like a dirt road littered with potholes. With each crunch of the suspension, his teeth clattered, and his butt ached.

How long has it been?

Someone was closer still.

White lightning filled his inner vision as something smashed into his face from the side. The violence of the hit laid him out flat on the seat, gasping.

"Keep your mouth shut," a man said. "Maybe you'll live through the day."

Aaron remained on his back as blood trickled from the corner of his mouth. He had taken hits before. As far as hits go, that one wasn't so bad. Not seeing it coming was what hurt more.

He had no idea where he was, who these people were, or where they were taking him. But he did know that he was kidnapped to get to Sarah. And for that alone, he would do what he could to thwart their plans, even if it meant he had to die.

He had been shot and close to death before as a result of his search for his beloved sister. They would never get to Sarah through him. Whatever they thought, he would make that fact clear, even if his life depended on it.

Chapter 18

Sven returned to the vehicle eight minutes later, worrying Amber that she would have to leave without him. He opened her door and yanked her out of the car. As she stumbled and fell, he grabbed his gun from the glove box.

"Get your phone out." He moved beside her. "Come on, come on. Let's go. Faster. They're already here, waiting inside."

Without getting off the ground, Amber pulled out her cell phone, doing everything she could to keep the inside of the purse away from Sven's eyes. It was stupid of her to leave her phone in the purse after Sven had told her he wanted to record the shooting. She should have pulled it out when he wasn't beside her.

Stupid, stupid, stupid.

She produced the phone, turned it on, and punched the camera button as she got to her feet. Then she flipped it to video mode and showed Sven she was ready. By that time, he had slipped his gun into the back of his pants.

Maybe it was good to have forgotten to have the phone ready. It distracted Sven from looking at his gun. She had run the risk of Sven checking to make sure it was loaded. What would she have said if he asked her—accused her—of taking the bullets out? She had been the only one in the car.

He would never have made it to see the runner. She would have had to shoot him where he stood. But he didn't question her because he didn't know his gun was empty.

Empty? Shit!

She'd left a bullet in the chamber. Sven had one bullet. But it was only one.

Say goodbye to the runner, then, because she wasn't going to tell him about her HIV and shoot him in the forehead until his gun was empty. Otherwise, he would turn it on her.

One bullet. One more dead girl. What did it all matter anyway? If it weren't Sven, it would be Sven's boss or some other douchebag pimp. The girl was dead already, no matter how today turned out.

Sven ran for the corner of the brick building, waving Amber after him. Nerves frayed, Amber followed Sven with weak knees, hoping her legs wouldn't give out until they were both dead.

But what if, at the last moment, she couldn't do it? Killing Sven would be a pleasure. She knew she could do that. But eating a bullet would be a lot harder. Maybe she would just kill Sven and learn to live with her disease in Australia or Canada, or maybe she would move to Iceland and forget everything and everybody.

But who would pay for the trip? Where would she get the money? She was broke. Sven took everything. She had no future, no family that cared about her, and no bank accounts. She had no kids that loved her—Sven ensured she had abortions every time he got her pregnant. She probably couldn't even get pregnant now if she wanted to.

All because of Sven.

No, the pleasure of killing Sven had been a long time coming.

She followed Sven through a metal door at the back of a large building. Just before entering, she thought she saw someone retreat behind a dumpster. She leaned back out the door to see if her eyes were playing tricks on her. Nothing moved.

"For the love of shit, *come on*!" Sven pleaded. "Stop wasting time."

He dropped down a flight of stairs, traversed a short hallway, and opened a door that led to a cavernous room. Amber followed a few feet behind.

She entered the large room, taking it all in. The ceiling was at least forty feet high and covered in steel girders and sheets of glass. Huge shelves lined the far walls where she assumed forklifts would store supplies all the way to the roof. She idly wondered what this building was once used for.

Near the back wall, where two chairs held open a set of double doors, a man stood over a pretty blonde girl who rested on her knees, her head down, chin on chest.

Sven strode across the dirty warehouse floor toward them, looking back only once to gesture for her to hurry up.

She turned her back to him, pulled the gun from her purse, and before turning back around, slipped it into the rear of her skirt. Then, with her purse over her shoulder, lighter now, she raised her cell phone, hit record, and started after him.

It was finally ending. All the customers could go to hell. Sven could go to hell.

Today she took back control of her life.

Amber Dijkstra was in charge now.

Her strides across the warehouse floor held more purpose than at any other time in her life.

Chapter 19

THE MATT DILLON LOOKALIKE had guided her through a back alley, down a bike path, and into the back of a warehouse.

"We both know why we're here," he whispered. "Do your job, and I'll do mine, and we both walk out of here alive to see another day. If you're upset about the way I handle you, I'm sorry. Everything has to appear real. Sven Spaans could be watching as we speak. This is the last time we talk as if we're on the same side. Got it?"

Sarah nodded.

He propped two doors open with chairs he'd found in the corridor and came to stand beside her.

"On your knees," he said.

"What?"

"You heard me." He turned to her. "On your knees. You're submissive. Ask for forgiveness for running. Cry. Beg. Do this right, and you'll get an award."

"I don't want an award, dickhead."

He snapped his head toward her, fury on his face. "This isn't a game. Don't dare talk back to me in Sven's presence."

"You gonna be able to protect me if he decides to shoot or stab me? You gotta gun?"

"Ankle holster," Matt Dillon whispered. "Don't worry. He needs his girls. He won't come all this way to kill you."

They remained that way for ten minutes, Sarah on her knees with Matt standing beside her.

A door clicked on the other side of the warehouse.

A tall man, well over six feet, with blond hair and the face of a Norwegian, entered the warehouse, followed by a woman in heels, a tiny skirt, and bad hair. They whispered something to each other. The man had to be Sven. Sarah had no idea who the girl was.

The woman following Sven did a full turn, pulled something from her purse, and then Sarah lost sight of one of the woman's arms as she fixed her skirt from behind.

Or jammed something in her back.

The woman hiked her purse strap high on her shoulder, raised her cell phone, and walked toward them as if she were recording.

Sven made it to them first.

Sarah made herself appear sheepish by looking down at Sven's shoes. They did not fit with his image. Loafers without socks. It reminded her of that eighties show, Miami Vice.

Then Vivian entered her mind. Not words this time, only feelings like emotions rolling in with dark clouds.

Vivian was afraid. Vivian felt fear.

Sarah was afraid now.

What's going on, Vivian?

Chapter 20

AMBER STAYED BACK FAR enough so Sven couldn't have time to lunge at her when she pulled her weapon. She only hoped her first shot entered his forehead as she had planned. If not, he'd have a chance to grab her. Maybe the second shot would be true, but getting off more than two shots would be a gamble with Sven's temper.

She aimed the cell phone at the girl on the ground. Not your average hooker. This one was a looker. Maybe she was new and not used up yet. That made sense. Sven's girls didn't try to run once they got to know him.

Sven pulled out his gun and waved it around.

Amber moved to the side so her camera would pick up all the action. Once the first bullet came out of Sven's gun, his weapon would click empty. That was her cue to drop the cell camera and shoot him between the eyes. What did it matter if he died without knowing he had HIV? Maybe it would be better for everyone if he died without knowing.

It would all work out.

She might die by his hand if her plan fucked up, but that wasn't so bad. If Sven didn't kill her, she would.

Then something strange happened.

The girl on her knees yelled one word.

"Stop!"

Chapter 21

VIVIAN RAMBLED ON FOR a full minute.

Sven wants to kill you. The man beside you isn't a cop. He's an informer. The wire in your belly button isn't a wire. The girl's suicidal. Sarah, try to survive. Be fast. Break his nose—

"Stop!" Sarah yelled at Vivian. The voice inside her head dimmed, faded, then died.

Sarah raised her head to look at Sven. The gun in his hand stopped moving back and forth. He smiled down at her. With the knowledge Vivian imparted to her still rolling through her mind, she wasn't afraid. The professional side of Sarah, the one that fought and made it out of countless scrapes with assholes like Sven, honed in on her nerves and settled her. She was ready. And she was angry.

"What do you want me to stop, little girl?" Sven gestured at his gun. "This? You want me to stop waving this in your face?" He laughed a short burst, stopped suddenly, then pulled his lip back in a snarl. "Or maybe there's something else you want me to wave in your face." He grabbed his crotch and bucked his hips in a weak imitation of Michael Jackson, then let out a high-pitched squeak as if Michael ever sounded like Sven.

"No, asshole," Sarah mumbled, her bangs covering her eyes. *The ankle holster.* She needed Matt Dillon's gun. She needed something. Inspector Dekker had set her up. He had left her here to die. They weren't listening in with the wire in a van just outside. There were no snipers in place and no backup. If anything, Dekker was already heading home for dinner, where he would wait for the report of a female American tourist shot in a warehouse. She was on her own and in the company of thine enemies.

"When I said stop, I want you to stop thinking you're all that." She lifted one knee and placed a foot on the ground. Matt Dillon shuffled his feet beside her. "I'm tired of dealing with narcissistic assholes." She lifted her other knee and placed that foot on the ground as she slowly stood to her full height. "You know," she said as she stared Sven in the eyes, "the world is overrun by parents raising narcissistic kids. Telling them they're so important without dressing them down when they need it. Well, today, I'm here to dress you down."

Sven's snarl deepened. He stepped closer to Sarah. "I like the lip on this one. I bet you give a mean blowjob. Those pretty lips wrapped to my base. Man, how come I never met you before?"

Matt shuffled beside her. "Hey man, we cool? I can go?"

Sven turned to him. "This runner, your bitch?"

Matt nodded. "I brought her back. You can have her. Don't need her anymore. I hate runners."

"Gee, thanks." He looked at Sarah. "This guy says I can have you. Like you're meat. A doll. A fucking rocking chair. A piece of furniture he's discarding." Sven moved to the side, raised his weapon to Matt Dillon's face, and fired. It happened so fast.

The weapon's roar was loud and immediate. The woman Sven came with let out a short yip as Matt's handsome face imploded, and what was left of his brains exploded out the back of his skull.

His gun's empty now, Vivian whispered. *You're good.*

Out of reflex, Sarah stepped away from Dillon's falling body. The brain and skull fragments sprayed past her.

"Nobody, and I mean nobody," Sven shouted at Dillon's convulsing body, "tells me what I want or what I don't want. She's always been mine, you piece of shit. And when she dies, she'll still be mine. I'll own the fucking corpse."

Sven turned back to Sarah. The woman behind Sven held the cell phone up, but now her hands visibly shook.

The hopeful part of Sarah wondered if Dekker was on the up and up. Would armed men storm the building now that Sven had committed murder and the woman's cell phone recorded it?

Sven brought his weapon up and placed it under Sarah's chin. She tried to swallow, but the tip of the gun blocked it.

"Now, about you running." He looked over at his woman. "You close enough? You getting this?"

The gun had better be empty, Vivian. Sven is my only way to get to James Wong.

"Come closer," Sven whispered through his teeth, jaw

muscles pronounced. "I want her brains on camera as they leave her skull." Sven turned back to Sarah and edged his face so close to hers that she could smell his last meal. "No one runs from me and lives to tell the other girls about it."

"You really are a narcissistic piece of dog shit, aren't you?" Sarah whispered to him.

With Sven as close as he was, he couldn't see when Sarah raised her knee. It hit his crotch square, lifting Sven a clear foot off the warehouse floor. When he came down, bent slightly at the waist, his finger was rapidly depressing the trigger of his weapon, but the gun didn't fire.

Only seconds passed before Sarah brought her hand up, open-palmed, and jabbed at the base of his nose, instantly breaking it with an audible crunch of cartilage. He moaned, dropped the empty gun, teetered to the side, and fell curled up in a ball, one hand on his crotch, the other covering his nose as blood seeped through his fingers.

The woman continued to record, but her hands seemed steadier now. She was also smiling.

Sarah couldn't pass up the chance to offer a solid kick to Sven's stomach for all the girls he'd abused, for the man he just killed, and for being such a prick of a human being.

"You," she said with kick number one, "will take me to meet James Wong," kick number two, "whether you want to or not." Sarah turned to the woman with the cell phone. "And who are you?" she asked.

The woman lowered the cell phone. "My name is Amber." She stepped closer and stretched out her hand. "Pleased to meet you."

"Sarah."

They shook.

"Thanks for doing that," Amber said. "It's been a long time coming. Nobody ever touches Sven. He needed his ass kicked. But don't get any blood on you."

"Why not?"

"Sven probably has HIV."

Sven moaned on the floor and tried to look up at them. "HIV?" he rasped, his voice nasally.

Amber addressed him. "That's right. I got my test back, and it's positive. Whether I picked it up and gave it to you or you gave it to me doesn't matter. We both have it. We both have a death sentence."

Sarah checked for blood on her hands. Remarkably she was completely clean of any of Sven's bodily fluids. A quick scan of the warehouse revealed no help, no task force coming in to save the day. Nothing.

Vivian, that was crazy close. He had one bullet. I could've bought a first-class ticket to come to see you on the other side.

But you didn't ... Vivian's voice was soft and velvety.

Sarah saw the weapon in the back of Amber's skirt.

Shit!

She stepped forward as Amber rambled on about how Sven had ruined her life. The second before Sarah got to the gun, Amber jerked it out, aimed it at Sven, and fired. Sven barely had a chance to squeak out a protest before the top of his head exploded.

Amber fired again, then again.

Sarah stepped back to put some distance between them, ready to run if Amber turned toward her. But Amber continued firing until her weapon clicked empty, and Sven's death convulsions had ended.

Amber tossed the gun aside and surveyed her work, still filming with her phone.

"Not bad," she said, almost too casually. "That's a lot of holes in one body. About as many as you tried to fuck in me. Now I just fucked you." She spit on Sven's corpse. "And turned you into a woman." She laughed out loud. "Don't rest in peace, you prick. I hope you burn in a lake of fire in Hell."

Amber turned to Sarah, her face calm, resolute. "Sorry about that. Got a little carried away."

"No problem. It's just, you killed my only chance of finding James Wong. I needed Sven alive."

"No, you didn't."

"What do you mean?"

"Come on." Amber started walking. "Oh, and bring Sven's empty gun. I've got the bullets for it."

Sarah grabbed the gun off the ground and followed as Amber shut off the video on her phone.

"Why don't I need Sven?" Sarah asked.

"I know James Wong. I know where he stays and the girl he fucks when he's in town. One of the girls is my horrible roommate, Nikki de Haas." Amber looked at her phone. "It's almost dinner time. I'll take you back to my place. Wong might even be there right now." Amber looked over her shoulder and smiled. "Thanks for hurting Sven. That was the most fun I've had in years."

"Yeah, um, no problem. You're pretty wild with that gun."

"Oh, that was nothing. I needed to kill him. I'll kill myself later."

"Kill yourself?" Sarah asked as they stepped outside into the fading light of the sun.

"It was supposed to be a murder-suicide. I won't fade away and eventually die of AIDS. Not me. Not this girl."

"Then why aren't you dead? What stopped you?"

"I decided to wait until you nail Wong. After the skills you used on Sven, I can't wait to see you maim Wong." She sounded like a schoolgirl with glee. "Oh boy, is this ever gonna be good."

"Yeah, real good."

Sarah reached under her shirt, yanked the fake wire out of her belly button, dropped it on the cobblestones outside the warehouse, and crunched it under her shoe.

Fuck you, Dekker. When it's your time, you won't see me coming.

They turned a corner and stopped. A blond man stood about seventy feet ahead, clapping his hands.

Casper.

"You could've helped back there," Sarah shouted at him as she strode his way. "And stop clapping. Makes you look like a pompous ass."

Casper lowered his hands. "I didn't know where Dekker dropped you off," he shouted back. "I just arrived. He said you'd be dead by now."

Amber followed as Sarah began to run at Casper.

"I'll be seeing you soon, Sarah," he shouted. "And try to stay breathing. I need you in Mexico. Actually, Aaron needs you in Mexico."

Then Casper stepped behind a building.

Sarah got to the corner seconds later. When she rounded it, Casper was nowhere in sight. The canal bridge in front of her was empty.

"Where could he have gone?" she asked between breaths

as Amber shambled up to her.

Out of breath, Amber panted. "He could … be anywhere … by now."

"Dammit!" Sarah slammed a fist into her palm. "I'll find you and learn what you're up to. Watch your back, ghost man."

Amber put an arm around Sarah's shoulders.

"Us girls have to stick together. Come on. Come to my place. I'll make us dinner and give you a place to stay until you meet Wong. My only deal is you hurt Wong badly when you meet him. Cool?"

Sarah nodded. "Fine. I can't guarantee Wong lives through his ordeal."

"I would prefer he didn't."

The girls walked up the side of the canal, turned a corner, and continued by another canal, the whole time Sarah watching their backs.

What did Casper mean when he said Mexico? And why would Aaron need her in Mexico? Dekker also mentioned Mexico. How did Mexico tie into all this?

She needed to call Aaron. She had to make sure he was okay. Failing that, she had to contact Parkman so he could look in on Aaron.

If anything happened to Aaron, she would go insane.

If anyone hurt him, she would stop at nothing until they were all dead.

Every last one of them.

Chapter 22

AMBER STOPPED IN FRONT of a cozy-looking building that slanted to one side.

"This is where I live. Second floor."

"The building's on an angle," Sarah said, raising her hands to demonstrate by keeping her left higher than her right.

"In Amsterdam, tilted houses are called Dancing Houses. This city is built on over 11,000,000 wooden poles, about fifteen to twenty meters long. They keep the houses and buildings out of the water and mud. Over the centuries, some sink in places more than others. We have Dancing Houses all over Amsterdam."

"What's wrong with us that we just walked away from a murder you committed, and we're chatting about Amsterdam's history as if we're tourists?"

Amber smiled. "Nothing's wrong with us. We did the

world a favor. C'mon. Let's get something to eat."

"Why not."

Inside Amber's apartment, magazines were strewn all over the coffee table and sofa. An armchair was clear, so Sarah picked that one to sit in.

"Sorry about the mess. Nikki thinks she'll be a runway model one day and studies all the American glamour magazines, does her makeup their way, and poses in the window she works at downtown like she's Kate Moss or Miranda Kerr. I can't stand Nikki. We don't get along. I hate the men she chooses. They creep on me when she brings them home. She was supposed to move out months ago."

Amber hurriedly closed magazines, cleared the sofa, took the ones off the coffee table, piled them together, and dumped them on the floor by the TV.

"There. Now I'll fix us something to eat. You hungry?"

Sarah nodded. "A little. But what I need to do is use your phone to make a call to Toronto."

"Go for it. The phone's right beside you on the table there. Is there any food you're allergic to?"

"Nothing," Sarah said with a shake of her head.

"Then we'll have Caesar salad, bread, whatever else I can find in the kitchen, plus wine. Red okay?" she asked as she headed for the kitchen.

"Red's preferred."

Sarah picked up the phone, dialed the international exchange, and typed in Aaron's home number. When it went to the machine, she tried his cell phone.

Nothing.

Then she tried Parkman's cell, hoping he was still in Toronto. He answered on the second ring.

"Who's calling?" he asked, no doubt not able to recognize the number.

"Sarah."

"Sarah," he breathed, the relief in his voice evident. "I've been hearing terrible things about you. Are you okay?"

"What have you heard?"

"That the plane you were on skidded off the runway, and the media announced a female was in custody. Someone leaked a name. It was you. Tell me what's going on. Are you calling because you need help?"

"I do need help, but not in the way you think."

"Tell me."

"Call Aaron. Make sure he's safe. Meet up with him. Give him a message for me." Sarah told Parkman what her sister had said about beating up the student and then lying low for a week. "It might not be too late. Get to him. Make this happen. I'm worried. He isn't picking up his phone."

"I haven't heard from him since we dropped you off at the airport. How did you know I was still in Toronto?"

"Lucky guess."

"I'll call Aaron, and if I can't reach him, I'll head to the dojo. Maybe one of his teachers can tell me where he is." He paused. Sarah guessed he was moving a toothpick from one side of his mouth to the other. "But you're okay, right?"

"Yeah. The authorities over here lied to me. I need to figure out why. They set me up, too."

"Who lied? Who set you up? What's going on?"

"Too much to tell right now. I'm safe. I'm tired, and I need to figure my shit out. I've got help." Sarah looked up as Amber approached with a tray. On the tray was a bowl piled high with salad, a plate with bread, and a tall glass of red wine. "Listen, Parkman, get in touch with Aaron. I'll call your cell tomorrow."

"I'll do what I can and watch for your call."

"Ciao." Sarah hung up. "This looks amazing. I didn't realize how hungry I was until you set this tray in front of me."

Amber reclined on the sofa with her own tray. "Eat up. We'll talk for a bit, but you need rest to deal with the jet lag. If Nikki hasn't come home by the morning, I know where to find her. We'll get to Wong. Don't worry."

Sarah took a bite of the salad and moaned. "This is so good."

As she ate, she thought about Casper. What could his role be in all this? She thought about Inspector Dekker, too. He had to be a real cop. Otherwise, how could he access interview rooms at the police station? But if he was a real cop, then how could he send her into that warehouse without protection? Unless the Matt Dillon lookalike—an informant—was supposed to be her backup. No, too dangerous. Something must've gotten fucked up along the way. She refused to believe Dekker sent her to that warehouse to be killed. If it weren't for Amber pulling Sven's bullets out, Sarah would've most likely been killed by him.

That made Dekker an accessory to murder, which made Dekker her enemy. As before, Sarah didn't differentiate whether or not a man wore a uniform or what kind of job he had. A man was simply a man. If he broke the law or put her life in danger, cop or not, she made him pay for it.

There was no menu when it came to Karma. Everyone, cop or not, got served what they deserved, and based on Sarah's information, Dekker had a large Karmic meal coming his way.

As she finished the salad and half the wine, she turned to Amber.

"I'll need Sven's gun tomorrow or the day after. I've got a score to settle with a certain inspector Lars Dekker."

"Sure," Amber said as she lowered her head and smiled conspiratorially. "Can I ask what for?"

"I need to send a message to him. I've decided to abduct a police officer and hold him hostage at the back of one of the bawdy houses in the red light district."

Amber dropped her fork and began clapping with glee.

Sarah was starting to like Amber. More than she thought possible.

"I've got just the place," Amber screeched. "Ohh, how exciting."

Chapter 23

"TOOK YOU LONG ENOUGH," Dekker shouted into the phone. "Where are you?"

Special Agent Buck Schaffer of the CIA, as the Dutch authorities had come to know him, held his breath, waited, then released it in a long torrent. Upon exhaling, he said, "A fuck up like this could end a man's career."

"Are you threatening me?" Dekker shouted. "In my own country? Who the hell do you think you are?"

"I might ask you the same thing. Sarah was supposed to be *watched*." He spoke the last word from the back of his throat, making it come out like a growl.

"She was. We had a man with her inside the warehouse."

"The one with the movie star looks."

Dekker's breath sounded like it caught in his throat on the other end of the line. "Where are you?"

"Inside the warehouse."

"Where's Sarah?" Dekker asked.

"No idea."

"Don't leave. I'm in a restaurant two minutes away."

Dekker clicked off.

Buck walked the crime scene. He counted four people by the disturbance in the grit on the steel floor of the warehouse. Two exited through the back doors, and two lay dead on the floor.

Sarah and that girl he saw running alongside the canal. But how did they do this?

One guy still had his gun. The weapon that killed the Scandinavian-looking guy was missing, as was the gun that had fallen by his feet. Buck saw a definite imprint of a weapon in the dirt. As far as Buck's trained eye revealed, it appeared that the Scandinavian man shot Dekker's guy. After that, a scuffle of some sort happened that explained the blood drying around his nose. Then someone emptied a gun into his body. Since Dekker left Sarah unarmed, he had to assume Sarah's friend killed the Scandinavian. Unless Sarah was able to beat him, steal his gun, and then shoot him with it.

Sarah Roberts was a lot of things, but was she that good? Without U.S. Army training? Without guerrilla warfare training? Images of a female Rambo flitted through his mind.

And who was Sarah's friend? How did she come into this, armed and ready to murder people to save Sarah?

Buck shook his head. Momentarily, he entertained the idea Sarah was delusional. Possibly a danger to herself. He didn't believe Sarah was that good. Sarah had help, and she would always need help.

This little test was supposed to go over more smoother. Set Sarah up with—he could never remember names—

Seven, or Seve, or Sven, and let her lead them to James Wong. Then he could fly her to Mexico. His last communication with the HQ revealed Aaron Stevens was across the border and already being held in Tijuana, Mexico.

Kidnapping Aaron had been planned expertly. It would be enough to incite Sarah. But the brains behind all this didn't know her like Buck was beginning to. She was weak, fragile, and gullible. Dekker had her on the ropes back at the police station, and Sarah had no idea what she was walking into at the warehouse.

Psychic? Dead sister helping her?

Buck didn't think so. Sarah was just a lost little girl in over her head with incredible luck and strong friends. She'd be a worthy ally but dead in a minute if needed. No dead sister could stop a bullet. Sarah was still flesh and blood.

Leaving Dekker to manage Sarah's hand-off to the Scandinavian was Buck's mistake. He wouldn't make that mistake again.

The back doors burst open. Dekker strode through, followed by about a dozen officers. Dekker stopped over his fallen man. He breathed loudly, everyone waiting to see what he would say.

"I want Sarah Roberts found and arrested for murder. Go. Now."

Officers shuffled their feet and started for the doors.

"Wait!" Buck shouted. Everyone stopped. He turned to Dekker. "You want this guy's murderer?" he asked, gesturing at the man on the ground. "Look no further." Buck pointed at the Scandinavian.

"Why would Sven shoot one of his own?" Dekker asked, then curled his lower lip under and bit down on it.

"You'd have to ask him yourself. But since I'm confident he would plead the fifth, let the evidence speak for him."

Schaffer described the scene as he saw it, all the attending officers listening in as if this was police college and they were being lectured on a day in the life of a detective.

When he finished, Dekker rubbed his chin in thought.

"So, Sven Spaans kills my informant, and some girl kills Spaans? Then Sarah and this mystery girl walk away together? Is that what you're trying to say, Schaffer? Are you telling me that a sick fuck like Sven just shot my guy, and he didn't shoot Sarah, who he thought was a runner?"

Buck hadn't told Dekker that he had seen Sarah and the girl on the street. The desperation in Dekker's eyes told him he needed to watch his step. Inspector Lars Dekker didn't want to believe what was right in front of him. What he wanted to believe was that the CIA was covering something up to protect an American. Buck had a lot of pull, but the Americans could not tell the Netherlands authorities how to police their own land. He could ask for assistance, even advise Dekker, but that was the extent of it.

"The evidence is clear," Buck said. "Read it however you like, but Sarah entered this warehouse unarmed. Your guy still has his weapon. Now Sarah is on the run. She's scared and not sure which way to turn. But she's no murderer of cops."

Dekker moved closer to Buck.

"I see things differently. Sven Spaans has a broken nose that bled. His heart was still beating to pump that blood out. He received that injury before he died. Sarah's a fighter. She attacked ITA's senior flight crew member with a knife. Sarah's tough. You're underestimating her. That's your mistake. So here's how I see it." Dekker pointed at Sven. "Sarah knew she would be shot and figured out we weren't listening in on the wire she was wearing as we didn't swoop in when guns were pulled. Our GPS tracker was found broken into pieces just outside those doors." Dekker pointed. The room was silent as he schooled every officer there.

"When Sarah saw her situation was futile, she attacked Sven and broke his nose. He dropped his gun to grab at his nose, which accounts for that mark there." This time Dekker kicked at the dirt. "Since our man wasn't helping, Sarah shot him and then shot Sven with what was left in the gun." Dekker cleared his throat, then bit down on his bottom lip again.

"You've got it wrong," Buck said, loud enough for only Dekker to hear.

Dekker brushed the hair out of his eyes. "You are welcome to stay in Amsterdam, Mr. Schaffer. Take a canal tour. Drink wine. Find a café and smoke up. I don't care. But you're not an official advisor in any capacity. I agreed to your terms." Dekker wiped his nose, which had started to run. "I agreed to scare Sarah even though half the passengers on that flight called her a hero. I agreed to bring her to this warehouse to help the Americans locate James Wong. I understood from your assurances that my people were safe. I understood that Sarah was willing to be bait. Evidently, I *mis*understood." Dekker turned away from Buck and waved his arms high. "Find that American girl Sarah Roberts and arrest her for the murder of one of my informants. I want every available officer on the streets of Amsterdam to look for her until she is caught. Go! Now!"

Men ran in all directions. Dekker walked by Buck so fast

that he brushed his shirt sleeve and bumped his arm.

"And clean up these bodies. I want to prepare for this man's funeral." He looked back over his shoulder. "And I want his murderer behind bars before we bury him so he can rest in peace."

Dekker pulled out his cell phone, clicked something, held it up to his ear, and disappeared outside.

"Dammit," Buck whispered.

He, too, got on his phone and dialed his office.

Maybe someone higher up would need to contact Dekker's boss. They had to lay off Sarah. He needed her for Mexico. Losing Sarah now would cost too much.

Too much would be lost.

Like maybe *his* career.

Chapter 24

THE EMPTY GLASS REMINDED Sarah that she had fallen asleep in the armchair while nursing the wine. When the adrenaline had worn off and the wine settled in over her system last night, she had been a victim of sleep.

Now the sun rose over the city of Amsterdam and beamed into the second-floor apartment's front window. She rolled to her side to avoid the sun in her eyes, but that was too uncomfortable.

Amber emerged from the hall and entered the kitchen.

"Ahh, you're awake," Amber bellowed. "Coffee?"

Sarah straightened herself in the chair. "Coffee sounds great. It's early. I didn't think you'd be up yet."

Amber banged something in the kitchen. Then a kettle started up.

"Nikki didn't come home last night," Amber yelled from the kitchen. "I checked her bedroom door, but it's locked."

Sarah got up from the chair, stretched, and yawned. "Does she stay out all night often?" Sarah asked.

Amber stuck her head out from the kitchen. "Many times. When we first started living together, she told me those things. Common courtesy shit. But not anymore."

Sarah nodded. "I need the bathroom."

"You want a bath?" Amber asked.

"Well, no, maybe a shower. But just the bathroom now."

"Oh, you mean you need the toilet? Or the WC."

Sarah frowned. "Oh yeah, they called it a water closet in Hungary, too. I forgot about that."

Amber smiled as if she knew what Sarah meant from the beginning but was making her spell it out. "It's just down the hall."

When Sarah was finished in the toilet, Amber had placed a French press on the coffee table with two cups.

"Just the way I like it," Sarah said. "But I have to ask you, what's that smell by the bathroom?"

"Smell? What smell?"

Sarah headed back down the hall. Amber followed. At the bathroom door, she breathed in. Amber did the same, then scrunched up her face.

"That's disgusting," Amber said. "What is that?"

Sarah shrugged. "At first, I thought it was the sewer backing up. But I have a suspicion it's coming from behind that door."

Amber pivoted in the confined space. "Nikki's room." She approached the door and placed her nose by the crack. When she turned back around, she nodded. "Definitely coming from Nikki's room."

"We need to get in there."

Amber knocked. "Nikki, you home?" she asked. "Nikki?"

"Do you have a key for this door?" Sarah asked.

Amber shook her head.

"Step aside, then."

When Amber moved, Sarah rushed the door with a side kick, aimed two inches to the left of the door handle. It took two kicks to crack the door and buckle in the locking mechanism enough to pry the door open the rest of the way.

Cautiously, Sarah entered the room. Inside, the smell intensified. She had to cover her nose to breathe. A small desk sat in a corner covered in magazines and cutouts from magazines. It made Sarah think of a collage in progress. On the hardwood floor, piled a foot high and running the length of the wall under the window, were magazines like Elle, Glamour, Vogue, Lucky, and Allure. The only other furniture was the bed, made up of frilly pink sheets, pillows shaped like hearts, and two teddy bears. The room of an adult female who grew up but kept the special, fun part of being a girl ever-present in her life.

At the foot of the bed, a soft, small feminine hand stuck out. It was easy to see the blood under it.

"You sure you want to see this?" Sarah asked.

Amber nodded. "I have to see for myself."

It was Sarah's turn to move aside as Amber stepped past her. At the end of the bed, Amber gasped and held a hand up to her mouth. Amber ran from the room. Retching sounds came from the bathroom a moment later.

Sarah moved forward until she looked down at the corpse of a once-pretty girl in her mid-twenties. Whoever did this had to be angry. The blade was still embedded in the girl's neck, all the way to the spine. The girl's head had been almost cut clean off. She resembled a human Pez Dispenser. Defensive wounds were evident on her hands.

Without touching the woman's body, Sarah knelt and examined the fingernails. It looked like she had collected human skin under her nails. Investigators would have a lot to go on. Rigor mortis had just set in. Time of death would be easy to establish as well.

It probably happened within a few hours from when Sarah and Amber returned from the warehouse last night.

She got to her feet and left the bedroom. In the living room, she took a few deep breaths to clear her lungs, poured the coffee, and waited for Amber to collect herself and return.

They needed to gather their things and leave as soon as possible. Find another place to stay. A dead body would complicate things unnecessarily for them. Once James Wong was located and dealt with, they could see if there was a connection between him and the body in the other room. At least try to match his DNA to the skin under the dead girl's fingernails.

She took another sip from her coffee. Anxiety built in her stomach every second because they were still in the apartment where a murder had occurred.

The bathroom door clicked.

When Amber appeared from the hallway, she held up a purse. "This isn't Nikki's." Amber's eyes were rimmed in red. She had been crying but tried to hide it.

"Do you know whose it is?" Sarah asked.

Amber was nodding. "Mila Visser's."

"Who is Mila Visser?"

"She's the other girl Wong sleeps with when he's in

town. They came here. He killed Nikki and ran with Mila. She must've left her purse."

"Find Mila, find Wong." Sarah set her cup down. "Sounds reasonable. Do you know where we can find Mila?"

"Yes. And Wong, too. It's a half-hour walk, maybe longer."

"Then let's go. We can't stay here."

"I agree. Let me get my things."

"Amber," Sarah said. Amber turned back to her. "I'm sorry."

Amber nodded. "I hated Nikki, but I didn't want her dead. I just wanted her to take her shit and live with someone else. Now I have to carry that guilt."

"Don't punish yourself. It's not your fault." Forgetting the coffee, Sarah said, "Now let's go. Don't forget the gun and bring your cell phone. We may need that recording from yesterday. If the police think we had anything to do with Sven's death, they'll hold us for Nikki's murder."

"That's probably the reason Nikki was murdered here," Amber said from the other room. "In my apartment."

The authorities would come to Amber's apartment if that were the case. They could be on their way right now.

"Amber, we have to go."

Amber appeared in the hall. "I'm ready."

Sarah had her shoes on and was standing by the apartment door when someone knocked.

"Open up. Police."

Chapter 25

SWEAT RAN INTO HIS eyes. The heat was unbearable, but they did nothing to relieve it. Since they'd attacked him in his apartment in Toronto, they hadn't given him anything to eat or drink. He was so thirsty that his salty tongue felt like a dead weight. They kept him in a room fashioned from bamboo. It was too strong for him to break through, but with his energy dwindling, he wouldn't be able to break out of an origami prison cell.

Weakened by lack of food, tired, and eternally thirsty, Aaron lay out on a bed of straw. A hole in the corner served as a toilet. He had stopped yelling hours ago. No one listened to his pleas. No one came to check on him.

There had to be a reason they'd taken him and brought him here. Whatever that reason, it wasn't to allow him to die a slow death. Eventually, he would be given water and food.

He opened his eyes and turned his head slowly toward

the door. The sun crept under the door and through a few cracks in the walls. It was the sun that was killing him now. The heat made him sweat, losing liquid that wasn't being replenished.

Maybe they knew more about him than he had previously thought. Being a black belt in Shotokan karate meant he could be lethal. The no drink and no food treatment had to be a formality to weaken him so he wouldn't be able to fight back. Hopefully, they wouldn't wait until death's door to offer him some kind of nourishment.

A fly alit onto his arm. Not wanting to expend energy by jerking his arm to scare it off, he felt it crawl in a zigzag until it flew off at the sound of footsteps approaching outside.

He tried to get up, but couldn't without too much effort, so he rested his head back down.

A chain rattled outside the door, and a lock clicked. A moment later, the door opened, and four men entered. Aaron turned away and raised his hands to ward off the sun's heat as it bore down on him.

"Get up," one of the men ordered in a Hispanic accent.

Aaron moved slowly and rolled to the side to push off in his attempt to rise, even though he wasn't sure he'd be able to remain standing.

The two largest men moved to either side of him and grabbed his arms. They lifted him to his feet so fast, stars swam in his vision, and his weakened neck couldn't support his dangling head. There wasn't enough energy in his body to hold himself up on his own two feet, so the men had to support him.

"Do you know why you're here?" the leader asked.

Aaron tried to shake his head. "No," he muttered.

"Bait." The man grunted. "Like a worm on a hook. That's all you are, a fucking worm."

Aaron opened his right eye and focused on the man talking. He resembled a warrior of some kind. Like someone out of a video game. Bronze skin, muscles bulging everywhere, thick shoulders, thick neck. His tank top was crisscrossed by a belt loaded with thick bullets. A large machine gun was strapped to his back, and three handguns were holstered, two on his waist and one on his right thigh.

"Why?" Aaron managed to ask.

"We want your girlfriend."

"Sarah—"

The man slapped Aaron's face so hard he wondered if he would lose consciousness as his head dropped forward, chin to chest.

"We need to send a message to her," the man said. "How do you suppose we do that?"

Aaron focused on his breathing. Keep it regular. Keep awake. He decided to not lift his head. There was no point in wasting energy.

"Don't," he said, then added, "know."

"That's not good enough. You're her man. Where has your woman gone? Tell us, and we will make life easier for you."

Easy? This was easy? He would hate to see difficult.

Whatever they wanted with Sarah, he couldn't help as he had no idea where she was. Even if he did, he wouldn't help. There was no way he would be a part of having Sarah meet the likes of these men.

Not wanting to talk but still needing to send a message, Aaron rolled his tongue around inside his mouth and tried to muster up enough saliva to spit. The minute amount that he gathered wasn't worthy of spit material, so the sound alone would have to suffice.

He lifted his head a few inches, puckered up, and spit toward the leader's shoes. As expected, nothing came out, but they reacted to the sound, to the disrespect.

Another slap across the face. Then another. His eyes closed, he didn't see the fist until it crashed into his stomach.

The arms holding him up on either side let go. He crumpled into a ball on the dirty prison cell floor, gasping for air.

After a moment, the leader told his men to get him up again.

They lifted him up and dragged him out of his makeshift prison. He tried to open his eyes and take in his surroundings, but the sun bit down on his irises when he lifted his eyelids. Another squint away from the sun revealed baked earth, cacti, and a huge mansion a hundred meters away.

It was like he was at a tropical resort. The house was so beautiful. The cars out front gleamed in the sunlight. A Benz, a Porsche, and what he thought was a Rolls Royce Phantom. There was money here. A lot of it.

To the left, a tall fence topped with barbed wire lined the property with intermittent signs that read High Voltage.

They came up to a stone stairwell built into the terrain. On the right was a stable for horses. Behind that, another building looked like a barn. Without a word, the men led him to the barn. As they drew closer, the door opened from the inside. Aaron tried to count how many men were present but lost count at a dozen.

They entered the barn, the sting of the blazing sun

gratefully left outside as the coolness of the barn wrapped around his limbs. He breathed easier. Maybe they were transferring him to the barn for good. He could survive in this cool climate. At least it wouldn't add to his thirst as much.

A table with restraints was set up by the side wall. As the men turned that way, he understood that as the destination. Should he fight back? *Could* he fight back? What damage could he do in his current state against over a dozen armed men?

They levitated him, dropped him, and spread his limbs out on the table. They secured his wrists and ankles to the table to the point where circulation was cut off immediately. A short, sharp yelp escaped his lips.

"Are you thirsty?" That leader's voice again.

A newfound strength allowed Aaron to squirm. He fought the restraints while the men around him laughed. He looked at them. An animal instinct to fight overcame him, adrenaline flowing. He scanned each face, each man in order, wanting to never forget their look, their eyes.

If he walked away from this, each man in this room would regret their laughter. Each man would be hunted, and Sarah was the best hunter he knew.

They didn't have to go looking for Sarah. Sarah would come looking for them.

Then the barn went dark as a cloth was draped over his face. Something must have secured the cloth to the table because it forced his head back, leaving him unable to lift it.

"He's thirsty," someone shouted.

A few of the men spoke in Spanish. Aaron gritted his teeth and pulled on his restraints. More Spanish. He breathed in deeply and tried to lift his head, but the cloth remained unforgiving.

Suddenly, a nightmarish amount of water cascaded over his face, and his breath was cut off. The water covered his mouth, nose, and eyes, flooding down his throat and igniting his gag reflex. Aaron's stomach convulsed and clenched as water reached his lungs. It was unavoidable as water reached his lungs. He was virtually drowning on the table. He needed to not breathe, but everything in him yearned to take a breath.

His body worked against him as vomit responded to the gag reflex. During this time, the water cascading over the cloth didn't stop. The men shouted around him as if they were viewing a cock fight, the betting high, while terror enveloped Aaron's body.

His stomach released and forced its contents upward. He gagged in an attempt to breathe. Water continually filled his mouth and nostrils. Then the bile from his abdomen filled his mouth along with the water, and he inhaled into his lungs, the liquid mess of what he thought were his final moments.

His eyes bulged. The ceiling of the barn came into focus, and then the realization that the cloth had been torn away. Someone shoved his face sideways. Fingers pulled his jaw open as someone poked the back of his mouth with something like a stick. He vomited again, but the stomach contents, mixed with the water, pooled beside his head and not back inside his mouth or esophagus.

His lungs begged for air and finally got a little. Then a moment later, on the next breath, they got more. Gracefully, more after that. The air was sweet, divine.

Men moved away. Some laughed. His face was soaked. His mouth wasn't so dry anymore. It tasted of bile. Eyes still wide, he looked at the man who spoke to him with a Hispanic accent.

"What was that"—he coughed—"for?"

"Where's Sarah?" the man asked.

Aaron dropped his head back and breathed. The beams on the roof of the barn reminded him of a barn he had played in when he was a small boy and still with his parents—before they had abandoned him and his sister. When his sister was murdered, and he had hunted her killer, he'd almost died. Aaron had survived a lot in his two and a half decades, but he wasn't sure he would survive this place. He didn't know where Sarah was and wouldn't tell them if he did. What would they believe? How long would they torture him to get to Sarah? Until he died?

His host moved closer. "That's called water torture. Water torture goes back to the Spanish Inquisition." He grabbed Aaron's jaw and twisted his head, so Aaron was looking at him. "It's painful, eh? The drowning, damage to the lungs, and sometimes even brain damage. There's usually lasting psychological damage, too. When you vomit, you risk sudden death because you're breathing in your own spew. Crazy, eh? It's how your gag reflex can kill you." He released Aaron's jawline. Aaron focused his gaze on the ceiling and maintained his breathing, which had improved considerably. "Tell us where Sarah is, and all this goes away."

"I have no idea where she is."

The leader backhanded Aaron's face. "Wrong answer. Are you stupid? Tell us what you do know then."

"I dropped her off at the airport in Toronto."

"To go where?"

"Europe."

"Specifically?"

His hands and feet were numb. He couldn't feel them anymore. He needed to be untied. His hot prison cell was suddenly better than this.

"I know her plane landed in Amsterdam, but she was supposed to transfer from there." He turned his head and looked at his host. "You'll never find her in all of Europe."

The host smiled, revealing a wretched set of teeth, one capped in gold.

"We have special abilities even governments of small countries don't have. We'll find your bitch with you alive or dead." He nodded. "We'll find her."

The cloth covered Aaron's face again.

Then the water came rushing in, cutting off his scream.

Chapter 26

"WHAT'LL WE DO?" AMBER whispered as the police knocked on her apartment door again.

"I'll hide," Sarah whispered. "Find a way to get rid of them. They're only here because they found Sven's body, and people know you're his girl. Act surprised. Try to cry. Then get rid of them."

Amber nodded her understanding, adjusted her shirt, and whispered, "I got this."

Sarah ran the length of the hall and decided on Nikki's room, as it would appear justified if that door were locked. She held her breath, opened and closed the door quietly, then set the lock. What if they want to search the place and find her with a dead body?

Shit. Maybe this was a bad idea.

She put her ear to the door and tried to hear what was happening. Amber was speaking. Something about not letting them in. A man's voice, authoritative, asked where she had been at a certain time. A door slammed in the apartment. Footsteps hammered their way down the hall. Then a soft knock on the door.

Sarah unlocked and opened it a crack.

"He's gone," Amber said.

Sarah locked Nikki's door behind her. "What did they want?"

"They wanted to know where I was yesterday. Asked me about my boyfriend. It was weird. He asked about Sven as if Sven was still alive."

"They were trying to see what you knew."

"You were right. Bastards didn't even tell me he was dead."

"They're probably watching this place. Is there a café where we can meet?"

"Meet?" Amber asked as they made it to the apartment door.

"I'll go first. You follow a few minutes later. We separate and reconvene at a café."

"Yeah, okay, two blocks up. It's called Café Americain. You can't miss it. It's got large black umbrellas and a big fountain beside the tables and chairs."

"Okay, I'll head there now. See you in ten minutes. Let's have a cappuccino, and then you can take me to Mila."

"Agreed."

Sarah peered through the peephole in the door. The hallway outside was empty. She nodded at Amber, stepped out into the hall, and made her way downstairs and outside. She found the café without trouble and located a table at the edge of the seating area so no one could disturb them.

When the waitress brought out a menu, Sarah told her she was waiting for someone else.

Approximately ten minutes later—Sarah had no way of telling time—Amber shambled up to the café and sat down opposite her. The waitress noticed and came to take their order of two cappuccinos and two croissants.

"Everything work out?" Sarah asked. "You all right?"

Amber nodded as she hooked her purse on the back of her chair and turned to face Sarah. She shrugged. "I guess so. On the way here, it just hit me. Sven's dead. I'm free. And Nikki's dead, too. So much has happened so fast. It hasn't hit me yet. I must be in shock."

"You're free? You weren't free before?"

Amber shook her head in the negative. "Sven picked me up when I was seventeen. Wined and dined me. Within a month, I was sleeping with his friends"—she used air quotes on the last word—"his customers. By the time I turned eighteen, I'd been beaten, had broken my right arm twice, was raped several times, and sodomized—oh, and lost a tooth, all in the name of love. Sven loved me, and if I loved him, this was how I showed it—making money for us. I was supposed to be an artist." She looked down and fumbled with the corner of her shirt. "I lost my dad when I was two. Never knew him. My mother hated me. Always told me I was useless. She didn't want me. I ran away from home too young and discovered what love really was, I guess."

"You went from one abusive relationship to another."

"I know that now, but I could not stop it then. Once I was in, I couldn't see a way out." She looked down and brushed her finger at a black mark embedded in the tabletop. "Over the years, I never saw much of the money, but I had a place to stay, and I wasn't with my mother anymore."

"Where's your mother now?" Sarah asked.

"Over that way, about six miles."

"What's over there?"

"Her grave."

"She's dead? When?"

"Two years ago. Just after my twenty-fifth birthday."

"How did you feel at the funeral?"

"Don't know." Amber met Sarah's eyes. "Didn't go. She didn't deserve my presence when she was alive. She definitely didn't deserve it when she was a corpse. In the end, I now understand that she led me into the life I have through conditioning. I read books now. She was my primary caregiver when I was little. She programmed me like a computer. I have faults, defects, and more issues than Nikki's Glamour magazines. I could learn to live with my baggage, heal some things, and try to be a better person, but I can't change what's in my core. So I accepted my life. I accepted Sven. I even started to like the sex. Kept me detached emotionally, but I felt loved in a strange way. People wanted me. Desired me. For a long time, that was enough. And it felt good."

"What's changed?"

"HIV. A death sentence. When the test came back positive, I decided to take care of the people who killed me before I died. Since my mom was already dead, I wanted Sven dead, then myself. At first, I was just going to tell him about the HIV, but he'd beat me or find a way to do it without getting blood on him. It was hopeless. So killing him instead just felt like the right thing to do." She fidgeted with her hands. "No one knows what he's put me through."

"And now? You still want to kill yourself?"

Amber watched the tourists passing by on the other side of the fountain. "Not sure yet. Ask me that again tonight. Maybe tomorrow." She faced Sarah. "I need to think about it. Now, let's change the subject."

Sarah crossed her legs and leaned forward on the table. "Then tell me about the cops here. Do you have a good knowledge of the Amsterdam Police?"

Amber chuckled. "Of course I do. It's part of my profession. What do you want to know?"

"I don't know Amsterdam like you." Sarah leaned in farther so no one would overhear her. "Earlier, I mentioned I was going to abduct a cop. Where can I stash him? I need a place to make a trade. And before we establish all that, I need to know what the police carry."

"Carry?"

"What's standard issue? What weapons do they routinely have on them?"

The waitress meandered through the tables toward them. Sarah nodded toward the waitress, so Amber knew she was coming and leaned back in her chair. As the waitress set their drinks and croissants down, Sarah looked around, making sure no one was watching them. The sun was already heating the city. Camera-toting tourists were filling the streets in droves as the morning wore on. Bicyclists beeped their tiny bells as unsuspecting foreigners stepped in their way. Another day in Amsterdam. If only this were a vacation and Aaron was here to enjoy it with her.

The waitress finished and headed off to serve other tables.

"Okay," Amber flapped a sugar packet back and forth,

tore the end off, poured and stirred it into her frothy cappuccino. "Let me start by saying I love you."

Sarah arched her eyebrows and offered a mock look of surprise.

"Oh, well, I, hmm, love you, too," she stammered.

They laughed. It felt good to be here, laughing with Amber. Maybe when this was all over, Amber wouldn't kill herself. There was so much left to live for, so much left in her life to do. She would need to make changes, but Sarah was confident she could do it.

"I have a place in mind," Amber said, "where you could hold your victim. Also, I have friends. Friends who don't like the police. As long as you're doing all the dirty work, there are girls in my trade who'll keep a watchful eye on the premises. No one will get in or out without us knowing."

"Things are looking up," Sarah said as she bit into her croissant. Part of the flaky pastry crumbled onto her lap. It was so delicious she ignored the mess and took another bite.

"Standard issue for a cop here is handcuffs, pepper spray, a short baton, a gun called a Walther, and a radio."

"It's what I thought," Sarah said after swallowing. "Basic stuff. I'm going to want his gun and pepper spray." She sipped her cappuccino. "How do you know their gun type?"

"Do you know how many cops I've slept with over the years doing what I do? Now, you tell me. What cop are you after? Anyone specific?"

Sarah shook her head. "Random."

Amber rubbed her hands together. "Ohh, this is going to be great. I haven't had this much fun in forever. And I've got nothing to lose."

"I need to get Dekker's attention."

"Who's Dekker?"

"The inspector who set me up at that warehouse. I learned long ago that pleasing everyone is almost impossible," Sarah said. "Pissing people off is a lot easier. So I stick with that. I get better results."

Amber stopped chewing her croissant and looked at Sarah with a deadpan expression. Then she broke into laughter that took a full minute to rein in. Amber's laugh was infectious, and Sarah laughed along with her.

"I love it," Amber said as she got herself under control. "Pissing everyone off. Classic."

They finished, and Sarah paid the bill.

"Come with me, my newfound friend," Amber said, taking Sarah's arm. "I will take you to where I work. Then we will go find Mila."

"Sounds good to me."

As they approached the canals, Sarah noticed what looked like a houseboat moored to the side. But this was more a house than a boat. It had a back deck and flower pots spaced out evenly along it. From what she could tell, the flowers were freshly watered.

"Where do those boats sail?" she asked.

Amber turned to Sarah. "They don't sail. That's a house on the water. It has its own address and everything."

"What?" she asked, surprised.

"Yes. There are over 150 canals throughout Amsterdam, with over 2,500 of these things lining their banks. As like this one," she pointed at the blue-sided one they were passing, "they usually have a terrace and a garden. It's a permanent address. They don't move. They're moored as if built there."

"Fascinating. I see a ton of bikes everywhere, too. Not

just people riding them, but bikes locked to fences, grates, and the base of trees. Bikes everywhere. The Dutch must be huge cyclists."

"They are. Here's a statistic you may not know. Approximately 850,000 people live in Amsterdam, and there are approximately 880,000 bikes. That's more than one bike per person. Each month they estimate a few thousand bikes fall into the canal. We have a crane that works every day dragging the bottom of the canals, pulling up to a thousand bikes out of the water monthly."

"It's such a different culture than in North America. We should be riding bikes more. Maybe it's because things are farther away back home, more spread out. Who knows?"

They walked along another canal, staying in the shade as the sun worked its way up to offering a scorcher of a summer day. They passed a sign on a building that read *Anne Frank Huis*.

"Is this the actual house where Anne Frank lived?" Sarah asked.

"The very one. Tourists come every year to view it. The lines can get pretty long."

"I imagine so."

Soon they had traversed canals, seen more homes moored to the banks, and watched tour boats take their charges expertly up and down the canals, maneuvering in and out of little tunnels under small bridges. It was a unique and wonderful experience.

"Amber, tell me a bit about the red light district. Are there torture gardens or torture clubs here?"

"Oh, Sarah, there's anything you want here. The district has four live sex theaters where people pay to watch sex acts."

"Sex acts? Real ones?" Sarah asked.

Amber was nodding. "Yes, real sex, as in intercourse on the stage. There is a torture garden here, just like in the U.K., but it's more of a fetish club. Wong runs an underground torture club, but he moves it around the city every few months. I'm not sure how he does it or why, but for some reason, Wong stays under the radar. And Sven did whatever Wong told him to. Sven was tough, feared by many, but he was Wong's bitch."

Amber's voice changed. Sarah leaned forward to catch a glimpse of her face. She was wiping away a tear.

"You okay?" Sarah asked, placing a hand on Amber's shoulder.

"Yeah, just thinking about Nikki back in my apartment. She was a crazy bitch, but she didn't deserve that."

Sarah rubbed Amber's shoulder. "I'm sorry."

"Me too, me too."

They walked on in silence until they entered the red-light district. It was easy to distinguish the difference. Even though the sun was high, purple lights lined the tops of the windows. Inside some of the windows, the lights illuminated girls who were starting early. Other windows had curtains drawn.

On the other side of the canal, Sarah caught a glimpse of two police officers. They were looking at her. She nudged Amber's arm.

"We have observers. Two cops at three o'clock."

Amber's eyes followed a tour boat as it moved down the canal, then stopped on the cops.

"They're looking at a piece of paper," Amber whispered.

Sarah found a window where the officers were reflected.

They looked at the paper, then at Sarah, then back at the paper. One nodded and started away. The other followed. They were headed toward a bridge that would bring them to Sarah's side of the canal.

"Shit," Sarah snapped her fingers. "We have to go. They're coming. If that's my picture, they've made me."

"Stay close."

Amber picked up her pace. As they turned a corner, Sarah took a quick look back. One of the officers was on a radio.

"They're calling it in," Sarah said. "We have to get off the streets."

"Half a block up."

Amber broke into a run with Sarah close behind. They turned another corner. All they needed was to get inside somewhere and wait unless the backup consisted of hundreds of cops surrounding the area. Then Sarah was out of luck, and her search for the black book would come to a screeching halt.

"In here," Sarah said as she got to a building where a door was slightly ajar.

"No," Amber said over her shoulder as she passed the door. "My window is two doors down."

Sarah followed Amber fifteen more feet, then bounded inside a building behind Amber, almost stumbling into her. She stopped to catch her breath and looked back outside. No one had followed them.

"Looks like we got away in time," Sarah said, trying to catch her breath.

Amber closed and locked the front door. "Let's go to the back, out of view of the street. You can meet the other girls.

They're getting ready to start the day shift."

Red light basked the front room. The sofa against the wall was probably beige or cream, but the red light made it impossible to tell. Even the dark-colored carpet could be brown or black but became a deep purple because of the light.

Amber led her down a narrow corridor lined with doors. It made her think of a miniature version of a hotel.

"These are the rooms the girls take their customers to," Amber explained.

At the end of the hall, Amber typed in a code on a keypad, and the door beeped. When she opened it, sound burst through. Women in various stages of dress or undress sat around a long wooden table, eating and smoking. At the sight of Sarah, the din quieted. The girls were trendy, all but one of them with straightened hair and good makeup. The sixth one had curly hair and olive skin, like an Italian. One girl had a pink bra and panties on and a tube top. Three of them had breast augmentation as they were larger than proportionate to their bodies. The only disconcerting image about any of them was their facial skin. The elasticity had faded years ago except on the youngest girl, but she was working on it, a cigarette in her hand. Definitely, two of the girls had done hard drugs in their time, their half-lidded eyes taking Sarah in as if she posed a threat. None of the girls gave off a nasty scent. They were all drenched in perfume to the point where the air in the room had been stolen and replaced by the air hovering at a Woman's Fragrance Exhibition.

By the time Amber approached an older woman near the back of the room and whispered something to her, the room was dead quiet.

The old woman nodded. "But first," she said. "Hand this to her."

Amber took a piece of paper from the woman's hand, looked at it, then passed it to Sarah.

A passport photo of Sarah was featured in the center of the paper. Below that were instructions to contact the police if anyone saw this person. The Dutch alarm number 112 was written on the bottom. Sarah was described as armed and dangerous. She was wanted for murder.

That's why those cops ran after us. If they know I'm here …"

"It's okay. Madam said it's okay for now. She wants to hear your story."

"I'm putting all of you at risk by staying here."

"Not in this room, you're not," Madam said. "You're safe here. Think of it as a sanctuary."

"Okay." Sarah steadied her hands. They had started to shake as she read the paper. People had died in Toronto last week. She thought she would never be able to escape a murder charge. And now, in Amsterdam, they were hunting her for murder. Who did they think she killed, though? Was this Casper's handiwork? Something to bring her in and start interrogations again?

When it dawned on her, her eyes lit up enough that Amber noticed.

"What?" Amber asked.

"They think I killed Sven and that informant back in the warehouse."

"Oh shit," Amber said, covering her mouth with her forearm. "I killed an informant because I didn't empty Sven's chamber."

Two girls at the table clapped.

They must really hate cops here.

"You have no idea the trouble the law gives us," Amber said. "And they want free fucks to leave us alone. And get this, what we do is legal. Can you believe it?"

"We have to get to work," Madam said. "Tell us why you're here, Sarah. Maybe we can help."

Sarah took a seat at the table and told Amber, the Madam, and the other girls her plan and how Inspector Dekker duped her. Once she had Dekker, she could go after James Wong.

Madam lit a cigarette, blew the smoke out slowly, and nodded.

"We can help. I want to help. Because of Wong. His crew has made a bad name for our district. We will do what you need." The girls around the table were nodding. "There's a room downstairs for the S&M clientele. Take your prisoner down there. No one will hear a thing."

"Are you sure?"

Madam nodded.

"And Sarah." Amber touched her arm. "When you're done with Dekker, I will give them my cell phone. The video is proof you didn't kill anyone."

"But you'll get charged with murder."

"The way I see it is, Sven shot the cop, and I shot Sven in self-defense. We ran from the warehouse because we were scared. It'll all work out. Come on, let's go downstairs to the dungeon so you can familiarize yourself with all the whips and chains we keep down there."

Amber sounded like a little girl having fun at summer

camp.

"I need to make a phone call. When can I do that?"

"In my office," Madam said. "Amber, go with her and block my number."

"Let's do the phone call first and get it out of the way."

They headed out of the room and down the hallway toward the front office, Sarah's stomach doing flips at what Parkman might have found out about Aaron.

She only hoped Aaron was safe, or she might lose her mind.

Chapter 27

BREATHING WAS A CHORE. With every intake, every exhale, a rattle vibrated somewhere in his lungs, making him want to cough. He'd coughed so much over the past hour since they had brought him back to his cell, each spasm more painful than the last, so he tried to repress it. Residual liquid in his lungs surfaced when he lay down, forcing a cough, sometimes as violent as gagging, but then short breaths in and out calmed things back to normal.

Enduring water torture had been hell. Defenseless, tied to the table, no options for escape available, nothing he could do but lie there and gag and drown. The horror of it, the thought that this was the end, panic in the brain that death was imminent, caused him to shudder uncontrollably when he was brought back to his baking hot prison room.

When they had tossed him onto the hard-packed floor, an outburst of coughing eventually left him moaning.

Where was Sarah? Was she safe? Why did these people want Sarah? How many days had it been?

He would watch the rise and fall of the sun. He would mentally log the days. He had seen most of the property except near the big house. He needed a mental account of everything he could get. But whatever happened, he needed to think smart, play smart, and stay alive.

Sarah would come. She would bring help.

When he realized he was waiting to be saved by his girlfriend, he didn't know if he should laugh or cry.

Someone approached from the outside. Aaron had propped himself up against one of the outer walls near the back of the room to keep his lungs elevated. He brought his lower legs in until he sat cross-legged on the floor.

He fought off another cough as the lock was worked on. Then the door opened. The sun was almost down, and only a yellowish, orange dusk was left in its place. Aaron idly wondered if this room was strategically placed on top of a little hill where the sun would wreak havoc on the inhabitants throughout the day. Were they coming to ask more questions about Sarah? More torture?

Three men entered, two of them holding another man up. There was enough light left in the sky to see the man clearly. He wore a mask of blood and mucus on his face. He breathed through his open mouth as his nose was broken.

They let him go to the center of the room, where he flopped down and remained still. The third man tossed a bottle of water to Aaron and something in a brown bag, then the trio exited the room and locked the door.

Feverishly, Aaron opened the brown bag at the smell of bread. He hadn't eaten since lunch on the day they had taken him. By the time the bag made it to his hands, he could already smell its contents. Ravenous, he bit into the sandwich and felt like he was eating sunshine. He uncapped the water and drank so fast it spilled down his chin and into the back of his throat, which caused a spasm. Aaron choked back the water, spit out the bread, and gagged again. Violent coughing overcame him, and he almost tipped the water over, spilling its contents when he rolled to the side to cough.

After a minute, he got himself together, breathing slowly, and chanced another small bite of the sandwich. Ham and cheese. It had never tasted so good. He watched the immobile man in the center of the room while he took small sips from the water bottle. During the rest of his first meal in Mexico, he didn't cough again.

Once the sandwich was gone and half the water, he realized he should've asked his cellmate when was the last time he had eaten. The man still hadn't moved. He was bone-rail thin. His clothes were too big for him, the pants tied with a rope instead of a belt. It almost appeared as if the man lost weight while wearing the same clothes and never went shopping for new ones.

Aaron never thought that drinking water again, as much as he ached for it, would ever be such an issue. What about swimming? Could he ever dive, put his head underwater, or *swim* underwater ever again?

One step at a time. At least now he was drinking.

The man on the floor grunted.

"Hey, you okay?" Aaron asked. "You speak English?"

The man moved. He tried to roll over but couldn't do it. He grunted and didn't move again. Only the loud breathing told Aaron the man was still alive.

The sandwich felt heavy inside his stomach. Maybe after not eating for days, or however long it had been, he should've started with something lighter like soup. Not that he had any options here. His stomach grumbled. He drank the rest of the water without a thought of saving any for tomorrow's heat, rolled to the side, and tried to support his head with straw.

The man in the center of the room didn't move. The light seeping in from the outside slowly disappeared. Aaron closed his eyes. Tomorrow. He would do something tomorrow. He would steal a weapon and attack one of the men. The food and water would give him strength. He was too much of a fighter to sit idle on his hands.

Tomorrow he would kill some of his Mexican captors.

Tomorrow he would leave this place.

Aaron fell asleep with hopelessness on his mind.

Chapter 28

Sarah sat behind Madam's oak desk and waited while Amber dialed the numbers that blocked the line. When Sarah dialed Parkman's cell from memory, he answered right away.

"Sarah?"

"Tell me you've got something."

"I do."

Sarah dropped her head to the desk. "Oh, what a relief."

"I've got something, but I don't think you'll like it."

She raised her head slowly. "What is it? Tell me."

"Aaron's not answering his home phone or his cell. Nothing. I went to the dojo. Daniel and Benjamin were in. They told me about a Mexican student—"

"What? Mexican?"

"Yes, does that mean something to you?"

"Casper said something about Mexico and how Aaron would need me in Mexico. This is freaking me out,

Parkman."

"Wait a sec. Are you calling Vivian 'Casper' now?"

"It wasn't Vivian. Forget it. Go on."

Casper had a lot of explaining to do. He knew a hell of a lot more than he was letting on. He had to be toying with her on the plane. Standing a few streets down when she and Amber came out of the warehouse, blaming Dekker for his not being there. Always near, always watching. And he knew about a Mexican connection to Aaron. Casper was fucking with her family, her people. Casper had some serious explaining to do.

Parkman's voice brought her back to the call. "Daniel told me about the student who was causing a disturbance at the dojo and how Aaron gave him back his month's fee and explained that they weren't prepared to continue teaching him. Before the guy left, he said he was looking for you. Said he'd get in touch with me, too. Then he threatened Aaron and said he'd see him again very soon, according to Benjamin."

"How did Aaron take that?" Sarah asked as she tried to work out the details.

"He told the guy to leave and never come back. Once the dojo closed that night, no one has seen Aaron since."

"Oh, man." Sarah felt weak. She needed the desk to lean on. How could she keep going if she lost Aaron because of someone she pissed off or something she did? "Anything else, Parkman?"

Amber had moved to the other side of the office, where she pulled the curtain back and peeked out at the street.

"The boys have a key to Aaron's apartment. They took me up. Nothing seems out of place. So I went into police mode and started knocking on the doors of Aaron's neighbors. Got Daniel and Benjamin to help."

"Where was Alex all this time?" Sarah asked.

"On a date."

"Okay, did you learn anything?"

"One of Aaron's neighbors thought she heard a commotion and looked out her peephole in the door. Two tall, well-built Mexican men escorted Aaron out of his apartment. The neighbor said Aaron didn't look himself. She thought he was on drugs. I called it into a few friends on the force here in Toronto and even got Detective Diner to look into it, but nothing has turned up so far. Absolutely nothing. No ransom notes. No calls, nothing. It's like Aaron disappeared into thin air. I'm sorry, Sarah. I'm on this. Twenty-four, seven."

Sarah bit down on her knuckles to avoid crying. "I know, Parkman, I know. Just keep looking. I'll do what I can from here. I know of someone who might have inside knowledge of what's happened to Aaron. I'll get back to you if I learn anything over here."

"Stay safe, Sarah."

"Watch your back, Parkman. This doesn't look good."

"It'll all work out. If someone snatched Aaron to get to you, they know not to hurt him. That would only piss you off. They need proof of life. If it's the Mexicans, they know that better than anybody. We'll get him back, Sarah."

"Okay. Hey Parkman?"

"Yeah?"

"You know I love you, right?"

"Of course, Sarah. I love you, too."

"Let's get my man back. Okay?"

"My first priority. I've dropped everything for this."

"Okay, stay safe."

She hung up and dropped her head onto her forearms to cry. Amber moved around in the room, her footsteps getting closer. Her hand rested on Sarah's back.

"I'm sorry," Amber said. "Sounds like you're having a bad day."

Sarah lifted her head and wiped at the tears. "Let's get this show on the road. I need to get to Dekker and find that man from yesterday, the one with the white hair. He knows about Mexico, and if he doesn't tell me what he knows, I'll kill it out of him."

"Uh, Sarah, you can't kill something out of someone. If you kill them, then they're dead. Boom. No more information."

"I'll find a way to get the information and then kill him or do it the other way around. Doesn't matter to me as long as he's dead." She shot up from the desk, wiped the last of her tears, rubbed her hands on her jeans, and grabbed a Kleenex off the desk. "Nobody fucks with my family. Nobody. It's time to start hurting people." She gritted her teeth.

Amber clapped and hopped on the spot.

She was beginning to like having Amber around.

Chapter 29

A LOUD CLANGING JERKED Aaron awake. The doors to his hell hole ripped open, and the morning sun filtered in, basking the center of the straw-covered floor in an early morning orange. The drowsiness of sleep passed in seconds when Aaron realized where he was.

Thirst was the first ache of the morning. It dismayed him that he had to pee. He didn't want to release any more liquids than necessary.

The guy in the center of the floor hadn't moved all night. He still lay on the floor, face down, breathing raggedly, but now with the doors open and the sun streaming in, it looked like he had a celestial spotlight pointing right at him. Aaron remained in the shadows near the back wall.

The same men who took him from the room yesterday stepped inside. Thoughts of being tied to the table poured in. Too much water. Gagging, unable to breathe.

His throat tightened, and he focused on breathing regularly. He would be more careful asking for water in the future. And that sandwich last night hadn't been enough. His stomach was empty and growling.

The men moved inside the room slowly and stopped over the prisoner sprawled out on the floor.

"Lift him up," the leader said.

As if he weighed ten pounds, the men grabbed the prisoner's arms, twisted him into a sitting position, then dragged him to his feet, his head lolling as far as his neck would allow.

The leader lurched forward with something in his hand and placed it in the prisoner's face. Seconds later, the prisoner gasped and jolted his head back, his breathing worse now that he was awake.

"What?" the prisoner mumbled. The one nasal word sounded like he spoke through his broken nose. "I've told everything I know. I didn't do it."

The leader offered a lopsided smile and tilted his head. "I don't believe you."

Aaron's strength was severely limited, but his mind played out a scene. He would get to his feet, snap the first guy's knee from behind, spin and break the leg of the other guy, and then lunge for the leader. In his best physical state, he was sure his odds were high. Currently, his odds were less than ten percent. He probably wouldn't even be done with the first guy before the leader shot him. And how could he be sure he had the strength to break anything?

"I swear!" the prisoner pleaded.

The leader pulled out a knife, at least eighteen inches long, from a brown sheath hanging off his belt. He twisted it back and forth in the air so his prisoner could see the sun glint off its deadly steel.

Aaron moved to get his feet under him. He couldn't sit idly by and watch a man get stabbed.

It caught the leader's eyes. "You want some of this, too?" he asked Aaron. "I'll cut deep." He jabbed the knife in the air once, twice, and thrice. "I'll cut you deep if you get up."

His attention drew back to the other prisoner, who was sniveling now, saliva dangling from his mouth.

"Please. I've told you everything."

"You've told me nothing, and you disrespect me."

The knife was fast. In and out. Then in and out again. Aaron was sure he was only taunting the prisoner as the blade didn't enter the man's body, and no blood painted the blade. But the man groaned as if he'd been cut.

Then the blade came again, and the man jerked and spasmed each time.

"You like the show?" the leader asked. "Turn Hector around. Show Aaron what his fate will be."

The men holding Hector twisted the man, now crying and moaning loudly, so Aaron could see better. The sun filled the room with enough light that Aaron saw the slashes. The man's cheek had cuts, his neck was bleeding, and three cuts crisscrossed Hector's upper chest. The blade wasn't going in far, just enough to open the skin.

Death by a thousand cuts.

"Turn him back around."

When Hector was facing forward again, the knife flashed half a dozen times.

"Stop!" Aaron yelled.

The knife stopped.

"What is this?" the leader asked.

The men released Hector. He fell in a bloody clump and instantly started crawling for the open door.

"What is this?" the leader asked again. He stepped forward. "This is the end of your life, Mr. Stevens. This is the end of Sarah Roberts's life. This is the end of everything you know. And this," he pointed at Hector, "is a demonstration to show you what happens when an employee, someone who has been faithful to the family for ten years, decides to steal. If we do this to a thief, think about what we will do to someone who hurts our business to the tune of millions of dollars like your Sarah did. For theft, only Hector pays." The leader turned his attention back to Hector. "But business interruption and loss of income, Sarah's entire family pays." He met Aaron's gaze. "But Sarah will pay the most. When she gets here, she will know what Hell is whether she's religious or not."

The leader turned away, dropped to one knee, and jabbed the knife in and out of Hector's back as he crawled. Aaron covered his face. He felt shame at not helping. Disgust and fear mixed in his stomach. He wanted to kill them all but didn't have the strength to cross the room.

How could he warn Parkman and Sarah's parents? Who were these people? How did Sarah upset Mexicans?

A hand dropped on his head, startling him out of his thoughts. A clump of his hair was pulled, and his head twisted to watch what the leader was doing to Hector as Hector's screams reverberated against the room's walls.

The knife had made a bloody mess of Hector's back, his shirt in tatters. The leader flipped Hector over and lifted his hand. One of the men came and held Hector's arm.

The leader glanced at Aaron. Hatred fueled a light behind the leader's eyes as he began to cut. Blood squirted forth, some landing on the leader's right cheek. Hector screamed until he passed out.

Aaron tried to look away, but the hold on his hair was too tight, so he closed his eyes. The second his lids dropped, a fist smashed into the side of his face.

"Eyes open," the man who held him shouted.

The side of his face numbing, Aaron watched as the leader removed Hector's fingers one by one.

"The Bible says to cut out the tongue if it's used in sin," Hector said. "Cut off the hand of a thief. Cut out the eye of one who covets thy neighbor's wife." He shrugged as if this were a game and he had made a bad move on the board. "Oops. I cut off his fingers." Hector remained unconscious at the leader's feet. "I was supposed to cut off the hand of the thief."

The leader started in on the hand. Aaron closed his eyes and received another blow to the side of the face. Maybe he should keep his eyes closed. Then perhaps one of the blows to the face would mercifully knock him out. The image of smelling salts came to mind. They'd just wake him back up as they did to Hector.

He opened his eyes as the leader tossed the hand aside.

"Now his eyes," the leader said.

If they didn't stop and dress the wounds soon, Hector would bleed out and die. Even though he didn't want to admit it to himself, Aaron knew the leader wouldn't stop.

One of the leader's men moved in place to hold Hector's head with both arms. The leader leaned in close with the knife, glanced at Aaron to ensure he was watching, then flicked the tip of the knife inside Hector's right eye, twisted it as Hector's body went into a seizure, and pulled outward. The eye popped out and dangled from his cheek, mixed with blood and a jelly-like substance. Lastly, the leader opened Hector's mouth, yanked his tongue out, and severed the tip off with one swipe of the knife.

"There, all done." He got to his feet. The helper released Hector. "He got off easy," the leader said, pointing at Hector with the bloody knife. The hand holding Aaron's hair let go, and the man walked across the room to stand by the leader's side. "You won't be so lucky. But there is a way to avoid a messy death."

In his shock, Aaron remained silent.

"I thought you'd never ask," the leader said. "Here's how. Tell me where Sarah Roberts is. When we bring her here, you get a bullet. Die in seconds. A much better investment than what we have planned for you. So, what do you say? Tell us where she is."

The leader handed the knife to the man on the right, who began cleaning it with a cloth he'd brought with him.

"Sarah," Aaron said. "Is on her way here."

The leader began clapping.

"You don't need to go after her," Aaron said. "She will come to you."

The leader stopped clapping and lowered his hands. "Do you joke here?"

"No. By now, they know I'm missing. Your man threatened me in front of several witnesses at the dojo. They will soon learn I'm in Mexico and fly down here. In time, you will see Sarah Roberts, but it won't be on the terms you would hope for."

"How's that?" the leader asked.

"She will be angry. That doesn't make for a good house guest. Then she will kill all of you. I will ask that she leaves you for me."

"Very kind of you," the leader said. "And ballsy."

He grabbed the clean knife back from his assistant, stepped forward, flipped Hector over, and jammed the blade into Hector's stomach. Slicing sideways in an arc, he opened the stomach up and pulled back on the flap of skin he'd made.

Aaron didn't want to throw up, but he couldn't watch the horror in front of him any longer. Yet his eyes were glued to the leader.

Hector's intestines were being pulled out and tossed aside like ugly, dirty sausages as the leader laughed a maniacal tune.

Hector was clearly dead now. The leader stood back up, handed the knife off, and moved toward the door. The other man immediately began cleaning the knife again.

"You will die here, Aaron Stevens. As will Sarah. We have an army of soldiers defending our family. We're stronger than the mafia. We're stronger than the president. He's afraid to even come down to this part of Mexico. We kill the police in the dozens just to send a message. We hang men and women, civilians, from highway bridges to send a message. How delusional are you that you think one little girl will hurt us? You see, Hector. That's you in a week, maybe two. Enjoy your stay here. I'll be back this afternoon to ask you where Sarah is. You had better have an answer."

The two men followed the leader outside, then closed and locked the door.

They left Hector's body on the floor of the prison cell.

The flies were already gathering as Aaron vomited what little he had in his stomach.

Then he wept.

Chapter 30

"TELL ME AGAIN HOW this will work," Sarah said.

Amber reclined on the couch with Melissa, one of the other girls who worked dayshift in the front window. Two other girls, Gabi and Porsche, leaned against the wall. Madam listened from behind her desk.

Porsche had brewed a pot of tea. They all sipped chamomile and ate ginger snaps while Amber reviewed their plan for the third time.

Tall, thin Melissa was a regular with a few Dutch police officers on their days off. According to Melissa, one of two cops would come today to be her customer.

"During Melissa's shift," Amber said. "If she's visited by one of her cop regulars, she'll notify Madam, and the rest of us will take up our positions."

"Which are?"

"Gabi will lock the door and flip the closed sign. Porsche

will draw the curtains. Melissa will lead her cop to the dungeon. By this time, Madam will have notified you and me." Amber smiled. Sarah worried Amber was having too much fun. "Melissa will strip down and make sure her cop is naked. When all other customers have been escorted out, you smash through the dungeon door with your gun out and kidnap yourself a cop. Melissa will act the part," Amber winked at Melissa, who winked back, "of a scared little girl, gather her meager clothes, and run past you."

"Then I will announce that I have locked down the building, and I'm holding him hostage."

"Exactly," Amber said, slapping her hands together so hard that Porsche jumped.

"Sorry," Amber whispered.

Porsche brushed it off.

"So now we wait," Sarah said.

"And get back to work," Madam added.

Gabi, Porsche, and Melissa took their tea and a few cookies out of the office, leaving Amber and Sarah to stare at Madam.

"You're sure about this?" Sarah asked. "You don't mind staging a kidnapping here?"

Madam shrugged one shoulder. "We're innocent. You took over the whole place. I should be asking if you're sure."

"Never more sure about it. This has to be done. I need to do something that'll make Dekker listen. I need to force his hand."

Madam nodded. "Then my place is yours to use. With Sven gone, things will be a lot smoother around here. You're to thank for that. This is me showing my appreciation."

"Well, I'm not sure it was all my doing—" Amber kicked

her and gave her a be-quiet face.

Madam held up the paper the police had left behind with Sarah's face on it.

"Looks like it to me. They want you for his murder." Madam shrugged again. "Doesn't matter. He was a horrible man. My girls will be happier."

Use the phone ... Vivian whispered.

Without thinking, Sarah muttered, "Um, I need to make a call again."

Madam got up from her seat and headed for the door. "Go ahead. We have all day to wait for a cop visit. Be my guest." She opened the door and stopped. "Amber, block the number first."

"Of course," Amber said as the door closed behind Madam. "Who do you need to call? Someone in America?"

"I don't know."

Amber frowned. "Oh ..." She slurped loudly from her tea cup. "How's that? How do you not know who you want to call?"

"It's a long story." Sarah got up, pulled the curtain back, and peeked out the window. "One that involves my sister."

Amber didn't respond or ask for more. After a moment, Sarah heard Amber bite into a cookie.

"Why are you guys helping me?" Sarah asked. She turned back to look at Amber. "Don't misunderstand me. I'm grateful, but there's a lot of risks involved."

Amber wiped a crumb from her lip. "No risk, really. You're doing all the crazy work."

Sarah let the curtain fall back in place. "You can't deny kidnapping a member of the Dutch Police Force won't come with risk."

"Normally, I wouldn't deny that. But what you're doing, how you've set it up, we're just collateral. Is that how you say it in English?"

Sarah nodded. "But why? You could've told me to take my issues elsewhere."

"Come, sit down."

Sarah headed back to her chair.

"You didn't know Sven. I was his girlfriend for ten years. However, I wouldn't use the word *girlfriend*. Victim is a better word. With Sven gone and people thinking you killed him, half of the red light district in Amsterdam would host you."

"But there's something else here," Sarah said, feeling it in her gut.

Amber averted her eyes. After a moment of staring into her tea, she looked back up at Sarah.

"I didn't want to tell you, but … Madam is my mother's sister. My aunt."

"What? Really?"

Amber leaned back on the couch and rested her arms along the top. "My aunt swore I would never end up in this business. When I met Sven, I didn't know where that relationship was headed. Within a year, I was a regular call girl. Since I was already in, Madam told Sven that I had to work here so she could keep an eye on me. It was that, or she would report Sven to the authorities. He beat her up for that threat—a couple of times—but after a year or so, he agreed to let me work here. In this business, he owned me like you might own a dog." She blew air through her lips.

Amber was holding something back, but Sarah couldn't put her finger on it. There was a depth in Amber's eyes. A haunting, a knowing. Like a deep family secret. Or maybe it was just Sven and his evil ways. But why? Now that Sven was dead, they could all move on. Why join Sarah now? Why go deeper into the fray? Something wasn't adding up.

A number echoed through Sarah's head. She jerked forward, grabbed a pen off Madam's desk, and jotted the number down.

"What's that?" Amber asked.

"A phone number. The one I have to call."

"You just remembered it?"

"No." She set the pen down and turned to Amber. "It was just told to me."

Amber frowned. "*Told* to you? How's that?"

"My sister. She talks to me. From the other side."

"Really?"

Sarah nodded.

"Creepy."

"Not really." Sarah pulled up a chair. "Here's the short version." Sarah told Amber about Vivian and why she was there. What had happened in Toronto and why she was after James Wong. "Dekker sent me to that warehouse to be killed. At least, that's what I think. The guy that I chased outside the warehouse is Casper. I think he was supposed to be there to stop them if things went bad, but he didn't show up in time. I'd probably be dead right now if it weren't for you."

"Wow, that's some story. But I can't take the credit."

"Why not?"

"If Vivian is so powerful, she would've either not allowed you to enter that warehouse or would've saved your life once inside."

"She did. She knew you were coming. She always has an

out that I'm not aware of."

They sat in silence for a moment, the tea cold. Amber reached for another cookie.

"I better make this call," Sarah said.

"Yeah." Amber got off the couch. "I'll block the number." At the desk, Amber held the phone and stared at Sarah. "I was wondering how you were a runner. It didn't add up." She tapped the desk twice with her open palm. "I'm so happy I emptied his gun before we entered that warehouse. I forgot the bullet in the chamber, but once he used it, we were both safe."

"Crazy close call. But we made it, and we're going to make it through this as well."

"Who are you calling?" Amber asked.

"Still don't know. Just got the number. Supposed to call it. So I do what I'm told. It always works out."

"I gotta see this."

Amber dialed the call block number and handed the phone to Sarah, who then dialed the rest of the numbers into the phone. She moved around to sit at the desk and waited while the phone rang. Amber sat on the corner of the desk beside her.

A man answered the phone.

"Hello?" Sarah whispered tentatively.

"Who is this?" a gruff voice asked.

"I think I've called a Billy Goat," Sarah said to Amber.

"Sarah Roberts?" the voice on the other end of the line asked, obviously surprised.

"The one and only, live tonight, never before seen in such a theater as the grand stage in Amsterdam …" Sarah stopped. This wasn't a joke, but she had no idea who the man on the other end of the line was and why they were on the phone.

"Where are you?" the man asked. His voice had grown stern, deeper.

The tone was familiar. That stern voice resonated in her head until she got it.

Inspector Lars Dekker.

Why call him, Vivian?

Vivian explained in seconds why Sarah had Dekker on the phone.

"Dekker?" Sarah said.

"What?"

"You know those cranes that drag the bottom of the canal for bikes?"

"Yeah? So?"

"Move them two blocks north of the Wine Cat Brothel, by the corner of the bridge there."

"Why?"

"One sec." Sarah didn't know why yet. She waited.

"Tell me why, Sarah," Dekker prodded.

"You're trying to trace this call, aren't you?"

Amber didn't look concerned. She mouthed the words, *it's okay.*

"You're wanted for murder," Dekker almost shouted. "And you call me to drag the canal. I want to know why."

"Because you need to trust me." Sarah said it as Vivian instructed. Then more came. "Because I will call you back later today with more instructions. This is the first base. Later we'll make it to second base. If you're a good boy, we'll continue to third base. But I must warn you, don't strike out when the bases are loaded."

"What the fuck are you talking about?"

Sarah jolted as more information permeated her consciousness.

"James Wong. He has taken out the garbage."

"You're not making sense," Dekker shouted.

"Two blocks north of the Wine Cat Brothel. Drag it."

"Why should I waste my time?"

"Because your life depends on it."

He was silent for a heartbeat. "Are you threatening me?"

Sarah jolted again as Vivian offered more. She felt the color leave her face. Amber leaned forward and touched her shoulder. Then the floodgates opened, and tears streamed down Sarah's face.

"Oh no, oh no …"

"What is it?" Dekker shouted. "Why are you crying?"

"Because—" Sarah tried to say. She grabbed a tissue, wiped her eyes, sniffled, and steeled herself for what she had to repeat. "Drag the canal. You will find five girls that Wong has disposed of. One as young as fifteen. He killed these women before breakfast and wrapped their bodies in chicken wire."

"I don't believe you. How would you know something like that if you're not in league with him?"

"I have an alibi. But that's not important right now. You know about me. Whether you want to believe it or not, Vivian speaks through me, and she's telling me to tell you to drag the canal."

"Why chicken wire?" Dekker asked.

"The tight wire cuts the skin of the bodies as they begin to bloat with gases. That releases the accumulating gas. The bodies won't float if they're wrapped in chicken wire." Sarah sniffled at the image in her mind. Five prostitutes, five women, and five girls with moms, dads, and brothers and sisters died because Wong was done with them. Wong was tired of them. Dumped from a garbage truck at five in the morning off the edge of the bridge. Wong couldn't be allowed to live after this, black book or no black book. When she killed Wong, she would find chicken wire, wrap him up and toss him into the sea for fish food. James Wong had gone too far.

"Drag the canal, Dekker," Sarah whispered. "This is my first call today. Be ready for my second call."

She hung up as Dekker protested further.

Then she lay on the couch with a box of Kleenex and cried for the abandoned girls, the lost ones. She grieved their loss but now knew they would receive a proper burial.

At one point, Amber left the room quietly to leave Sarah alone with her remorse.

Chapter 31

Lunch was delivered when the mid-afternoon calm came to the brothel. By two in the afternoon, only one customer was in the back being serviced by Porsche. Sarah had seen massage parlors in Toronto and Kelowna and completely understood what was happening in Madam's brothel. How aloof she had become didn't surprise her. The thought of random men entering the premises and ordering sexual favors like one would order a meal at a restaurant bothered her, but there was no stopping this industry. As far as she could tell, these particular girls weren't being forced to work here, and Madam ran a clean and well-organized place. Amber had told her that Porsche and Gabi had kids at home waiting for them. They chose to work dayshift so they could be home when school let out. Gabi was married but brought home triple what her factory worker husband earned. This made him happy, as long as she didn't come home with a disease. They were as close to a regular working couple as one could get.

Lunch consisted of two pizzas, one margarita, and one Italian sausage. The women split them evenly and ate quietly around the lunch table in the back room, all lost in their own thoughts. Sarah understood that everyone was probably on pins and needles, waiting for a cop to enter the premises. Melissa assured them that one of her two regulars would come later in the afternoon. They had decided to try again tomorrow if neither one came.

After lunch, Porsche and Gabi cleaned up and then headed to the front windows to gyrate for potential customers. Amber and Sarah moved to Madam's office while Madam was out. She was strolling along the canal to where Sarah told Dekker he'd find five bodies. Within the hour, she would return with an update on whether Dekker showed or not and, if he did, what they were up to.

"Something's really bothering me," Sarah said as she plopped down on the couch.

"What's that?" Amber asked. She stood by the window, watching the street through a crack in the curtains.

"Vivian told me to get a message out to Aaron. I did, but I can't tell if he got the message. Then Casper mentions Mexico and how Aaron would need me. Dekker talked about Wong's money laundering operation for the Mexicans, and now Parkman said Aaron's missing. A neighbor saw him leave with men who appeared to be Mexican. I know that sounds confusing, but that's it in a nutshell."

"That is a lot. I don't think it's all coincidences."

"Exactly. I'm worried that Aaron needs me, and I've abandoned him to go after Wong."

Amber turned from the window and walked over to sit on

the edge of Madam's desk. "Call Parkman. It ought to be about nine in the morning in Toronto. See if he has any updates."

Sarah got off the couch. "You're right. I will."

Amber got to the phone first, dialed in the block feature, and handed the phone to Sarah.

After the seventh ring, it went to voicemail. He would always answer even if he were sleeping.

"That's odd. Parkman is glued to his phone. When he sees Private Caller, like yesterday, he would assume it was me."

She tried again and got voicemail.

"Shit." She looked at Amber, her eyes watering. "I hope nothing happened to Parkman. I need him."

"I'm sure he's all right. Everything will work out. Stay focused. Let's do this cop thing right. You can be on a flight to Toronto by tomorrow."

"Yeah, if everything works out."

She held the phone in one hand, the corner of the desk in the other. Immobile, with nothing to do until a cop showed up at the brothel. She hated being this idle, but she couldn't leave the building. She wouldn't make it ten minutes outside unless she were in disguise.

The word, *parents* flitted through her mind in Vivian's voice.

"Do that line block thing for me," Sarah snapped.

Amber typed in the numbers and nodded at Sarah to go ahead. She dialed her parents' number in Santa Rosa. It had to be around six in the morning over there, but she was sure her father would be awake.

On the third ring, he answered. "Bit early, isn't it?"

"Dad!"

"Sarah?"

"Who did you think it was?" she asked.

"Telemarketer. Didn't recognize the number. How are you? Where are you?"

"In the Netherlands, working on something."

"Baby girl, are you staying safe?"

It was so good to hear his voice and the cheerfulness of his laugh. He hadn't called her *baby girl* in years. It was a term she never tired of. He was the only man on earth that had this effect on her. She never realized how much she missed her parents until she called them.

"I'm led around by my sister, Dad. I'm safe. She doesn't let anything happen to me."

"Yeah, well, that stuff in Toronto hit our newspapers, too. It worried your mother. You know how she can get."

"Sorry about that. But I'm fine. Listen, have you heard from Parkman?"

"Yesterday, I think. He wanted to know if we'd heard from Aaron."

"Had you?"

"Nope. Nothing. Is everything okay?"

Sarah glanced at Amber across the room. She was lying on the couch, engrossed in a magazine.

"It should be. Look, if you hear from Parkman, can you let him know I called—"

"Hold on. There's someone at the door."

"Dad," Sarah yelled. "Wait!" But she was too late. The clunk of the phone being set down was followed by his short footsteps to the door. He must've grabbed the phone in the main foyer when she called.

She heard the lock click and the door open in Santa Rosa.

"Mr. Roberts?" a deep male voice asked.

"What's this all about?" her father asked.

"Is Mrs. Roberts here as well?"

Sarah heard her mother's voice from a distance.

"What's all this noise at just after six in the morning?" Amelia asked. Then her tone changed to one of surprise. "Who are you guys?"

"Ma'am, you and your husband must come with us."

"Nooo!" Sarah shouted into the phone. Amber started on the couch and glared at Sarah. "Who's at the door, Dad?"

"I'm going to have to see some ID," Caleb said.

Silence accompanied the line that spanned thousands of miles. Sarah panted but kept her mouth away from the receiver so it didn't interfere with listening.

"The CIA?" Caleb asked. "What's this all about?"

"We'll inform you once we're on our way. But we have to leave now, sir."

"What's the rush?" Amelia said. "We haven't even had coffee yet."

"Please, ma'am. We've got coffee at the base. I'm afraid I'm going to have to insist. We can't waste any more time."

"Dad!" Sarah yelled into the phone.

Amber had set the magazine down and was standing by the desk now.

"Let me say goodbye to my daughter," Caleb said. "I was on the phone when you knocked."

The phone clunked as it was picked up.

"I'm afraid I can't let you do that, sir."

Sounds of a struggle ensued.

"Dad! Mom!"

Grunts, groans. A loud metallic sound, like the phone dropped.

"Sarah, we're being taken by—"

Then the line was cut off.

"Nooo," Sarah muttered.

She tried the line again. It rang and rang. Frantically, she hung up and dialed again. Nothing. Then again. Nothing.

Amber touched her shoulder, but Sarah brushed it off.

"I have to get through to them." She began dialing, punching the buttons hard enough to vibrate the phone's base on the desk.

"Sarah. Set the phone down and explain what happened."

The phone rang on the other end of the line. Sarah waited. The machine picked up. She slammed the phone down.

"Sarah!" Amber shouted. "Stop."

The office door burst open as Sarah clenched her jaw and tightened her fists. Madam walked in and came up to the desk.

"What's going on?" Madam asked.

"Something happened to Sarah's parents while Sarah was on the phone with her father."

Madam turned to address Amber. "I have questions for you."

"Okay," Amber said, then glanced at Sarah as if unsure where this was going.

"When did you first meet Sarah?" Madam asked.

"At the warehouse. We've been over this."

"Have you two been separated at all, even for a few minutes since the warehouse?"

Sarah focused on Madam. "What's going on?" she asked.

"Amber." Madam's eyes didn't leave Amber's face. "Answer me."

"No, not a single second. Sarah came to the apartment. We found Nikki dead and left. We stopped at Café Americain and came here."

Madam turned her steely gaze upon Sarah. "So it's true."

"What?" Sarah nearly shouted, her patience slipping away.

"The police found five bodies in the canal about twenty minutes ago. I saw Dekker there. He was supervising the extraction. They had the entire area roped off."

"So what's true?" Amber asked.

"Sarah *is* psychic."

Sarah looked away, her parents on her mind. All she could do was hope that the men at her parents' door were actually from the CIA. But what would the CIA want with them?

This had to be connected to Casper. He knew about Aaron, the Mexicans. He said he was with a group similar to the CIA. Or did he say he was actually with them?

Amber tapped her shoulder.

"Sarah, we've called your name twice."

"What? Sorry. Daydreaming." She felt better. Vivian had whispered *parents*. Sarah had called. It was all timing. It must've been so Sarah would know her parents were safe. Why else would Vivian do that? To torture her?

She just needed to get to Casper. Learn what he knows. Find out what's happening to everyone back in North America. Then life would settle down.

"Sarah?" Amber whispered.

She looked up again. Madam was gone. The door was

closed.

"What's going on?"

"Shhh." Amber jammed a finger against her lips. "Melissa's cop just showed up. She's taking him down to the dungeon right now. Madam has gone to empty the place of customers. They've already hit the closed sign on the front door and pulled the curtains. You're up."

Sarah pulled the gun from the back of her jeans, got to her feet, and headed to the door.

"Here comes second base, Dekker," she said.

Amber clapped her hands quietly behind Sarah as she exited the office.

Chapter 32

AARON BAKED LIKE A basted turkey in the prison cell most of the day. Hector's smell as he slowly decayed in the heat was quickly becoming unbearable, but he could do nothing about it. There was no breeze to speak of, no way for him to sit upwind, and the men didn't seem interested in removing the body.

He faded in and out of consciousness throughout the day as his thirst intensified. Interestingly, he wasn't starving as much as he was thirsty.

Maybe his captors would come back today. What torture had they designed for the next session? He wondered how much he could handle.

He hadn't been this weak since he was a preteen, and his parents had abandoned him and his sister Joanne like unwanted pets. Through years of determination and strength, he had forged a new Aaron and made something of himself.

Where had all that gone? Weakened by a lack of food and water? There had to be some inner resolve, some fight left in him. But to fight here while an army of men surrounded him didn't offer great odds. He had to wait until the time was right. Wait until their guard was down—if it ever was.

The door opened. The sun blasted him as it set in the west. He hadn't heard the chain, the lock. Maybe he'd been dozing again. He tried to sit up, blinking rapidly but fell back down.

Conserve your strength.

He kept one eye half-lidded as he watched the men enter and wrap Hector in a large plastic roll. They were so efficient he could tell they'd done this several times. What kind of life was this for the soldiers? All in the name of making money?

The men walked out, Hector's plastic-wrapped body under their arms like they were carrying a carpet roll. Only a dark red splotch of blood reminded him that Hector had been here, had died here, right in front of him. And he had done nothing to stop it.

But if he had tried to stop them, he would likely be dead.

The men reentered the room, strode across to him, grabbed his arms, and hauled him to his feet so fast his head spun.

"Wait," Aaron mumbled. "Where are you taking me?"

The men walked him out of the prison room without a response. He was guided along in front of the horse stables, along the dirt road, and into the barn from yesterday. The barn where they offered him too much water.

"I don't need another drink," he said, even though his lips were turning a salty white. "I'm fine."

The man on his right laughed as if Aaron had made a

joke.

The inside of the barn was dark. As they guided Aaron toward the back, he counted six men standing around a wooden table. The leader was there.

"Enjoying our weather?" the leader asked.

"Could really go for a swim in the ocean," Aaron said. "Maybe you could arrange a drive down there tomorrow? After all, I am a guest, and a decent measure of hospitality would dictate—"

A fist slammed into his stomach from his right side. He was still too far from the leader and the rest of the men at the table to expect the punch, nor did he see it coming from the guy holding him. All his breath was expelled from his lungs, and he couldn't breathe for a moment. His body urged him to curl up on the floor.

"Look at him," the leader shouted. "He looks like a grounded fish." The leader opened his mouth in an O shape and pantomimed breathing difficulties.

They dropped Aaron at the leader's feet and stepped away from him. A minute amount of air seeped through to his lungs. His stomach felt like it had clenched to the size of a raisin. Then more air forced its way in. Panting and gasping, he tried to collect himself.

"Get him up," the leader ordered.

Hands forced him to his feet.

"Only one chance today. Where is Sarah Roberts?" The leader stepped closer, the knife from yesterday in his right hand. Aaron marveled at how clean it was. "This is your only chance to save yourself. Once I start cutting, you will never recover from the damage I will cause."

Aaron understood that he would probably die among

these heathens in this dirty barn just because he was underfed, malnourished, and outnumbered.

He found his voice. "Your best chance to save *your*self," he said in the most authoritative voice he could muster, "is to release me now. Put me on a plane, send me home, and forget the name, Sarah Roberts. A steak dinner with all the trimmings and some red wine as an apology would suffice. This, and only this, will be your saving grace. Do this, and maybe, just maybe, all of you will live to fuck your girlfriends or wives or each other's girlfriends or whatever the fuck you inbreeds do to each other." He turned back to the leader. The Mexican's face had reddened, his eyes narrow. "Think about that. Think on it. Your days are numbered. Not mine so much."

The leader landed a solid punch on Aaron's cheek. His reflexes moved to block it without thought, but his sluggish arms were far too late. The floor got close, but he didn't meet it as the man on his right arrested his fall.

"Get his arm on the table," the leader shouted.

Aaron was dragged across the floor. Men gathered around, staying close. Someone yanked on his right hand, stressing the rotator cuff in his shoulder. His arm was forced flat on the table as panic entered Aaron's system. His face had numbed where the fist had made contact.

"Hold him," the leader ordered. "I need something," the leader said, "for Sarah to see you're still alive and that I have you. This will only hurt a little."

Aaron twisted into a position where he could watch what the leader would do.

The large knife glinted in the single bulb that dangled over the table.

Then the knife's blade came against his skin at the big knuckle of the index finger, and Aaron knew what the leader was about to do. His life would never be the same. His fighting career, his dojo.

Hopelessness engulfed him. Anger, hatred, fear, and pain filled him as the leader began slicing his finger off.

Aaron screamed and wailed. He cried out. He called to God for mercy until he passed out.

If losing consciousness could be called merciful, then God answered his call.

Chapter 33

"LADIES," MADAM SAID AS Sarah approached the lunch room. "Everyone, take your positions. I want you two upstairs watching from the windows above. Shout down if you see something we need to know about. Amber, follow Sarah to the dungeon in case Sarah needs help."

The girls scattered to all parts of the building. Amber stayed close to Sarah. It wasn't the first time Sarah wondered why they were helping her kidnap a cop. Nor why Amber seemed so happy with the notion. Something didn't add up for Sarah, but she wasn't about to grill them on why they were helping now.

Madam nodded subtly toward Sarah, glided out of the lunch room, and started up the hall toward her office, where she would stay behind the locked door for the remainder of the ordeal.

The oldest profession in history was alive and well in

many cities worldwide. Nothing would ever stop it. But Sarah could put a dent into what was reported as a $150 billion industry of human trafficking. Locate Wong, recover the black book, deal with Dekker, and meet up with Casper all in the next day, and she could hurt the industry. Even though the odds were against her, she had no choice but to move forward.

Sarah checked the clock on the wall. Melissa had had enough time. The cop would be handcuffed by now or at least disrobed.

She headed for the dungeon door, Amber's gun clammy in her grip.

Vivian hadn't advised whether this was good or bad. Obviously, it was bad, but if it produced the results she wanted, it would be good.

She hesitated outside the door to listen. Voices mumbled, whispered, indiscernible. Amber stayed close behind her. Slowly, Sarah wrapped her free hand around the doorknob, turned it, and looked back at Amber. She mouthed the word *okay* and received a nod from Amber.

Without making a noise, she pushed the door open a crack, then wider. Melissa's back was to the door. She wore a G-string, her bra already off. The man only wore underwear. His right wrist was secured to the wall with a handcuff.

Sarah moved inside the room. The cop's eyes were locked on Melissa's breasts as she slipped a thumb inside the rim of his underwear and began lowering them.

When his head shot up, he saw Sarah with the gun.

"Hey, what's this?" he shouted.

Melissa jumped back and released his underwear as she stepped away, covering her ample breasts.

"Get your clothes," Sarah said to Melissa. "Then get out. Leave the building."

Melissa had been briefed that this would look like a random act of violence perpetrated by Sarah so the brothel would be protected when it was all over. Ordering Melissa out of the building and having her act surprised was all part of it, and Melissa was turning out to be a fine actress.

She quickly grabbed her meager clothes scattered about the floor, gave Sarah a wide berth as if she had a disease, and ran for the door, almost barreling into Amber on her way out.

The performance was encore worthy.

"What about me?" the cop asked.

"You stay," Sarah shouted.

"What is this?" he asked, looking over Sarah's shoulder at Amber. "Some kinky fuck game?"

"You only have the kinky part wrong," Sarah replied as she lowered the weapon. He was cuffed and still in his underwear, his clothes in a heap beside him.

Sarah glanced back at Amber. She shut the door but remained inside. She was supposed to leave the room and stay on the other side of the door. Now she looked like an accomplice.

The cop was young. Easy early twenties. His right eye twitched. He showed fear. Sarah was sure he would do what he was told.

"So, we still gonna fuck?" he asked.

"Oh yeah, someone will get fucked, but not you or me."

"Then who?"

"Where's your radio?"

He stared at her for a heartbeat. "You know me?"

"Where's your radio?" Sarah asked again.

"Fuck you, American," he said. "I'm a member of the Dutch police. You're in a lot of trouble, Miss."

Sarah strode over to him, jammed the gun into his belly button, and brought her nose to his, tip to tip.

The twitch in his eye increased. He was scared. She just became unpredictable. How long had he been a cop? How often had he had a gun pointed at him, much less jammed into his stomach? For a moment, she wondered if he would piss himself.

"I wouldn't worry about me right now," Sarah whispered. "I think you're the one who is in trouble." She pulled away enough so that he couldn't head butt her or raise his knee into her crotch without her seeing it. "A cop caught with his pants down in the dungeon of a brothel in the red light district. You're the one fucked now."

"This is legal," he pleaded.

Sarah ignored him and turned to Amber. "I need a disposable phone. Can you get one down here? Any of the girls left one before I ordered them out of the building?"

"I'll go check." Amber disappeared out the door.

Sarah roamed the room, examining the adult toys and paraphernalia. There were chains attached to the walls at various places. A large sex swing hung from the ceiling in one corner. Sarah sat in it, adjusted the piece that supported the back, and eased down into it. It looked like she reclined in a floating La-Z-Boy without armrests. She avoided the ankle straps for obvious reasons.

"What's this all about—" the cop cut himself off as his eyes widened. "Hey, wait a second. You're that girl from the poster."

"What are you hunting me for?" Sarah asked.

"You murdered a cop's informant in a warehouse," he answered.

I knew it.

He still looked surprised, but his fear was showing through. He had to be contemplating that if she was a murderer, and now she had him, a cop, as a hostage, what was next for him?

"That's right. You found me." She pushed with her feet to start swinging. "You're a cop. What's to stop me from killing you?"

His lower lip began to quiver.

"How long have you been a cop?" Sarah asked.

"Second week," he managed to mutter.

"Oh shit, sorry. You may quit after this." She swung harder. "I mean, if you live through it. What's your name?"

He didn't say anything at first.

"Don't make me come over there and beat it out of you. Just tell me your name before you piss me off."

"Police Patrol Officer Prins."

Amber bounded through the door and handed Sarah two phones.

"Take your pick," Amber said.

Sarah grabbed the Vodafone and dialed the Dutch alarm number 112. When the dispatcher came on, she was ready.

"My name is Sarah Roberts. I'm the American girl you're looking for. Contact Inspector Lars Dekker and inform him that I'm willing to talk. Do it now. I'll call back in thirty minutes. When I do, have Dekker there, or I'll disappear."

Sarah turned off the phone and addressed Prins. "You better hope Dekker's there."

Sarah turned away from Prins, met Amber's eye, and winked at her.

The plan was working, but she couldn't stop thinking about Aaron. What had happened to him? Where was he? And what could Casper know about Aaron? Should she still be running after James Wong or going home to see what had happened to her man, Parkman, and her parents?

So many unanswered questions. The biggest one of all was where Vivian could be in all this. What were her thoughts? And when was she going to start sharing them?

Why so much silence, sis?

Sarah kicked her feet and swung higher in the sex swing as the cop in the corner glistened with sweat.

Chapter 34

THIRTY MINUTES PASSED QUICKLY in the dungeon. Madam had tea sent down. Along with the tea was information. The girls upstairs watching the streets had reported officers out front of the Wine Cat Brothel fifteen minutes ago. They had reported that the officers were still doing routine walkabouts looking for the girl in the poster that had been posted all over town. So far, no one had found it odd that Madam's business was closed mid-afternoon. Sarah figured she would be finished with the dungeon in the next few hours, and then Madam's business could go back to normal.

"Time's up, Prins," Sarah said. "Let's hope Dekker is at the other end of this phone."

Amber had stayed with her and now stood by the door. Sarah had had a chair brought down when the sex swing became uncomfortable. She rose from the chair, the gun in the back of her jeans snug and tight, and turned the cell phone on.

Once she dialed out, it rang at the other end.

"Is this Sarah Roberts?" the female dispatcher asked, probably recognizing the number.

"Where's Dekker?"

"I have Inspector Dekker available by cell phone. Dekker's on the road. He is waiting for your call." The dispatcher offered the number, and Sarah hung up immediately after.

Sarah dialed Dekker's number while it was still fresh in her mind. It looked slightly different than the phone number Vivian had her call when she told Dekker about the women in the canal wrapped in chicken wire.

He answered before the first ring ended. "Sarah?" he said, almost sounding glad to hear from her.

"The women? The canal? Was I right?"

"Yes." He paused and took a deep breath. "Where are you?" he asked.

"That's not why I called."

"Then why?"

"Another body."

"What?" He paused and cleared his throat. "Where? Wait a second. I can't spend all day running around Amsterdam collecting bodies. What the hell is going on, Sarah?"

"James Wong is scared. He's on the run. He's taking out the trash before he's incriminated on too many charges to ever see the light of day."

"Our intelligence suggests Wong has fled the city," Dekker said.

Sarah's hands shook with anger. After all she had done to get here. Leaving Aaron behind, alone, in Toronto. She couldn't raise Parkman on the phone. Her parents detained by government officials. All she sacrificed to nail Wong, and now he up and left the city.

"He had better not have fled the city. For your sake."

"For my sake?" Dekker's voice rose. "What the hell does that mean?"

Sarah breathed in and out twice, calming breaths.

"You still there?" Dekker asked.

"How well do you know James Wong?"

"We have a fair amount of intel on him. Why?"

"Nikki de Haas. Ring a bell?"

"Yeah, one of his floozies. Why?"

"Do you know where de Haas lived? You have an address?"

"I can get it. But I won't give it to you."

"Nikki's dead," Sarah said, then glanced at Amber to see how she was handling it. She seemed fine and even nodded back at Sarah to keep going. "Wong killed her in her apartment."

"How do you know all this?" Dekker asked. "And the girls in the canal. Were you there? Are you in touch with someone who was there?"

"If I told you I was psychic, you wouldn't believe me. So read about me online. This is your second base. Third base is coming."

"What the fuck are you talking about, Sarah? This isn't a game. People are dying here. Since you arrived, Amsterdam has turned into a bloodbath."

"This isn't a game?" she repeated. "What was your fake interrogation for then? To get my cooperation to go to the warehouse? I was supposed to die there, wasn't I? You sent me to die, Dekker. This is a game for you. You rolled the dice first, and I hate losing. I'll call back in half an hour. Make sure you've located Nikki's body by then. It's in the bedroom of the apartment. I can see it clearly. She's behind the bed. When you enter the room, at first, you'll just see her wrist sticking out from behind her bed. She's into fashion magazines. I can see them lined up against the wall under the window. Go, Dekker. Find the body. Then I have one more body to tell you about." She looked at the cop handcuffed to the wall. "After that, we meet."

"I'll go now. Give me half an hour."

Sarah disconnected the call, popped the battery out of the cell, and stepped on the phone.

"I'll use the other phone for my last call to Dekker," she said to Amber. "When this is over, I can replace these phones."

"Don't worry. They were gifts to you. You know how much these girls make?" Amber shook her head. "It's insane. They can afford it."

"Can you cover for me?" Sarah asked.

"Cover? What do you mean?"

"I have to go somewhere. I won't be long. Watch him." She pointed at Prins.

"But Sarah, you can't show your face on the street. You'll get picked up."

"Disguise me, then."

Amber studied her for a moment. "Come on. I've got just the thing."

At the door to the dungeon, Sarah turned back to Officer Prins. "I'll be back."

He started to protest as she shut the door, cutting off his

voice mid-sentence. The dungeon was almost one hundred percent soundproof for the few customers that preferred to be whipped. Madam didn't want other customers put off by the wailing and crying coming from the basement.

Upstairs, Amber offered Sarah a couple of quick fixes to disguise her appearance, and after fifteen minutes, Sarah was out on the streets of Amsterdam, makeup done and a wig in place, headed to the warehouse where she wanted to meet Dekker later.

The same warehouse where the bodies of Sven Spaans and the undercover cop had already been removed. Where police tape still hung, cordoning off the area, billowing in the soft breeze.

The same warehouse where she would set her trap for Dekker.

Chapter 35

Desperation filled Sarah's stomach with acid as she walked, further agitating her frayed nerves. The not knowing was the worst. Not knowing what had happened to Aaron. Not knowing how Mexico was related to it. Not knowing what had happened to Parkman and her parents. It was harder to not know than to have answers.

She needed Dekker and his knowledge of Wong to get to Wong. She needed to finish what she had started. It was the only way. And the way things were going, before long, she would be on a flight to wherever Wong fled, or she would return to Canada and look for Aaron and Parkman while making calls to the government in search of her parents.

She hurried along to the first sports store she could find and tried to find baseball bats. She bought two cricket paddles when she was told that baseball wasn't a very popular sport in the Netherlands and that she would be hard-pressed to locate a bat.

At the warehouse, she crouched under the police tape and snuck in the back through the same doors she'd exited with Amber. At the center of the warehouse, she stopped, closed her eyes, and breathed in the quiet atmosphere. This would work. Three exits. Walls lined with shelves. Enough light came in through the small windows that rimmed the roof's edge about thirty feet up. With the summer sun lasting into the early evening, they wouldn't need flashlights if she could get Dekker here before dark.

Sarah felt Vivian close and let her in. After a brief internal exchange, Sarah placed the cricket paddles where Vivian told her to—safely away and out of sight—and exited the warehouse the same way she had entered.

On the way back to the brothel, she felt eyes on her. Like someone was following her. The wig Amber had given her, and the eighties gaudy leather jacket with Michael Jackson zippers everywhere made it hard for anyone to see her true identity. The boots were a size too big and didn't match the jacket. She stood out, but not in a good way. No one could look at the poster of Sarah Roberts on a light post and say this Joan-Jett-meets-Michael-Jackson wannabe had to be her. Impossible.

But she still felt eyes on her. Turning around to catch someone stalking her proved futile. Either it was all in her head, or her pursuer was professional enough to follow her without being noticed.

If that was the case, then it had to be Casper. And if it were Casper, he would reveal himself when needed. And when that time came, Sarah would get her answers from him. Consequences were funny things. Whether your intentions were good or bad, everything was bound by cause and effect. Casper had a lot of explaining to do. He knew more than he was letting on. She couldn't believe she hadn't seen it before. But nothing would get past her again.

Whether Casper meant her harm or was trying to help her, he had to be held accountable for his role in all this, whatever this was.

Not only was she determined to learn of his role, but she was also the one who wanted to mete out his consequences. Drawing first blood should be on her epitaph one day. With people like Casper, it seemed to be the only thing that worked, the only thing that got through to them.

And Inspector Dekker, too.

Thinking of Dekker, she quickened her pace and forgot about being watched as she ran back to the brothel to call him.

Chapter 36

AMBER GREETED HER AT the door. "Where have you been? We were worried."

"Worried?" Sarah yanked the wig off and undid the jacket.

"If you disappear, we're just another brothel with a cop tied up in our basement. Scary for the Madam and the girls. Doesn't bode well for business."

"Have you got the other phone?" Sarah asked, ignoring her last statement. Amber handed it over. "Come on. Follow me down to the dungeon. This is my last call to Dekker."

On the way down, she wondered what Amber had meant about it being scary for the girls. All they had to do was call the police and say that the American girl had locked the place down and kidnapped a cop. Their story would be that as soon as Sarah had left the premises, they had unlocked Officer Prins, and that would be it. So what would worry them? Why be concerned? Unless there was something else at play. The same something that caused Amber to be practically giddy when she heard the plan to kidnap a policeman to get to Dekker. Even Madam bought into it. Sarah figured she'd learn their hidden agenda soon enough, but for now, as long as they played along, she was fine with having them. This task would prove to be a lot harder without their support.

Amber unlocked the dungeon's door and stepped back. What if Prins broke his wrist or cut his skin, using blood to lubricate the cuff from his wrist? Then Sarah needed to be the first one in.

The gun back in her hand, she used her foot to nudge the door inward.

Officer Prins was where she had left him, his wrist firmly secure in the cuff attached to the wall.

"I need to use the toilet," he pleaded.

"Later. We're almost done here."

Sarah dialed Dekker's cell number from memory. He answered right away.

"Dekker here."

It was a new phone. He would have no way of knowing it was Sarah calling.

"Did you locate Nikki's body?" Sarah asked.

"We did. Just as you said, it would be. Now what?"

"We meet."

Dekker sounded like he exhaled pent-up breath. He was probably tired of racing around Amsterdam to dead body sites. Meeting Sarah and apprehending her was probably his primary goal. With it being her idea, he would be relieved. But he had no idea what she had in store for him.

"Where?" he asked.

Sarah stared across the room at Officer Prins. Each time she was on the phone, he didn't cry out for help. Smart man. He knew his predicament and what would benefit him and what would damage him.

"The warehouse."

"What warehouse? The same one where you shot—" Dekker stopped. "Where you met Sven?"

"The same."

"When?"

"An hour."

"Come alone, I presume? Is that what you'll say next?"

"I'd have it no other way."

"How can you trust me to not bring a hundred cops, surround the place and never let you leave alive?" Dekker asked.

"Because I've got one of yours."

"You've got what?"

"Listen." Sarah brought the phone up to Prins's face. "Say something, Patrol Officer Prins."

Prins identified himself, gave his badge number, and added for Dekker's benefit that Sarah was crazy.

"That's good enough, Prins," Sarah said.

When Sarah put the phone back to her ear, Dekker was already talking.

"… I cannot believe that. How dare you? Sarah, this has to end—"

"Shut up, Dekker."

He stopped talking. There was no sound on the other end of the line. No car engine, no wind.

Where is he? Still in Amber's apartment? Standing over Nikki's corpse?

"Dekker?"

"Yeah."

"Meet me. Answer a few questions. Then you can have your cop back. That's the deal. If I see one cop within a mile of that warehouse other than you, Officer Prins dies. I might decide to call you from the States to tell you where you can locate his body. Or maybe I won't. Who knows? Just come alone, so I don't have to kill another cop."

"Sarah, I don't have to tell you if you flee, we can arrange with the American authorities to have you brought back for trial—"

"Dekker," she shouted, cutting him off. His voice had been rising, anger getting the best of him. "You're forgetting who holds the cards. Shut the fuck up and listen. Be at that warehouse. Come alone. Be unarmed. Anything else costs Prins his life and possibly yours."

She clicked off, pulled out the cell's battery, and smashed the phone under her heel.

She whispered to Amber, "The girls know the drill. Let's suit up and head over to the warehouse. I suspect Dekker's still at your place. That's enough time to set up in and around the warehouse and wait and watch. But first, I need the phone with the recording of Sven killing the undercover cop on it."

Amber reached into her back pocket and handed it over.

"Perfect," Sarah said. "I'm right behind you."

Amber turned and disappeared upstairs.

Sarah checked the battery life on the phone—55%—then pivoted to face the cop tied to the wall. "You will stay here. When Dekker and I are done, and I have what I want, I will tell Dekker where you are. He can come and release you himself."

"Hey. Aren't you supposed to bring me to your warehouse to trade me for him?"

"If I bring you and Dekker betrays me, which I expect him to, then what do I have? So no, you stay here. Don't you see," she said in a kid's voice, "you're my bargaining chip?"

"When you're handcuffed in the police station, I'll be what you offer up for a reduced sentence. That's your bargaining chip. Nobody kills cops. Nobody."

"If a cop deserves to go, I'm glad to be the one to do it." She smiled. "Let's hope I don't need you to bargain with for a reduced sentence. I might only get a year shaved off my time. The court process is slow. It could take months to get to sentencing decisions. Who's going to feed you? Huh? You better hope Dekker does this right. Hope Dekker doesn't fuck up."

A look of despair and hopelessness crossed Prins's face. "Can I at least be tied up lower so I can sit? What about a pee break? Come on. Best case, I'm released in a few hours. I'm gonna piss myself in that time."

Sarah kicked the chair across the room to him. He caught the back of it with his free hand, straightened it, and sat down.

"Piss in the corner. Isn't that what they use this room for anyway? Golden showers?"

Sarah activated the camera feature on the phone and filmed Officer Prins in his chair, one arm handcuffed to the wall, and then left the dungeon, closing and locking the door. Upstairs in Madam's office, everyone waited for her.

"As long as Dekker plays ball, I meet him in the warehouse in one hour, but I want to be there early."

"Each girl knows what to do," Madam said. "Amber says

there are three entrances to the building."

Sarah nodded.

"Okay, we will have two girls per entrance plus one on the warehouse's roof. She'll watch the streets below."

Madam got up from her desk and walked over to a painting on the wall. She lifted it off to reveal a safe. After several turns of the dial, she pulled on the handle and opened the safe. Sarah watched as Madam removed a box about the size of two shoe boxes. She placed it on her desk, leaving the door to the safe ajar.

"You all know how to use a gun?" Madam asked.

The girls around the room nodded.

"I'm not asking you to shoot anybody. But we need to help Sarah. If you ever wonder or doubt what we are doing, remember Sven. Remember when he would rape Amber every week. Remember when he would take a girl of his choosing whenever he wanted? Just remember who he worked for. It's that man that Sarah is going after. With a little surveillance, we can help Sarah get him. The guns are for your protection. If you don't want one, I'll understand." Madam opened the box on her desk. Inside were Rugers, Berettas, and a few Walthers. "If you do want one, take your pick. They're all loaded."

As if ravenous for food and someone had stuck a loaf of bread on the desk, all the girls in the room grabbed the guns simultaneously.

"Easy, easy, there's enough for at least one gun per girl." Madam looked at Sarah and shrugged. "You never know when you need protection in here."

Once everyone was suited up, and Sarah had her jacket and Joan Jett wig on again, they left through the back door, secured the building, and headed to the warehouse in pairs, all coming toward it from different streets.

Sarah kept telling herself that this would work out, but something still felt off. Why would Madam join them? She didn't need to be here. Was leaving Officer Prins alone in the building a good idea?

Sarah had been hoping at least Amber would join her at the warehouse. Maybe Madam would send another girl to watch the back or side door. But to have six girls was a gift. Although, if anything happened to any of them, having their death on her conscience would be horrible. All she could do was hope it all worked out and everyone went home at the end of the day.

There was a nagging feeling that it wouldn't work out as planned. People were going to die, and somehow it would be Dekker's fault because he played by his own set of rules.

Sarah swore to herself, knowing it was too late to pull back now.

Something altogether terrible was going to happen at the warehouse, but they had passed the point of no return.

There was no going back now.

Chapter 37

A BLOCK FROM THE warehouse, Sarah turned to Amber. "Are you doing okay?"

Amber continued looking straight ahead. "Yeah. Why not?"

"You know, people live with AIDS much longer than they did before."

That made Amber turn her way. "How much do you know about my situation?"

Sarah waited until a British couple speaking accented English walked past them. "You *were* planning on taking your life once you killed Sven."

"I was. But didn't."

"What changed your mind?"

"You."

"How?"

"Your passion, purpose. I'm still not sure, though. I don't

want to live with what Sven gave me."

"You're sure you got it from him?"

"Definitely."

"The anxiety you're feeling about the future comes from trying to control the future, which you can't do. I've tried. It doesn't work. If I thought about the future and what was coming for me, I might shrivel up and become a troll under some bridge. Thinking about what Dekker might be up to or wondering if I could control what would happen in the next hour only scares me. So I don't think about it because I can't change it. I've made my decision. I'm going forward. I will meet him and deal with what comes as it comes."

"I get it," Amber nodded. "Deal with it as it comes. But in the end, what am I?" She kicked a stone on the ground. "I'm just a whore with HIV. My résumé is shit now. I have no skills unless blowjobs are a skill. I'm washed up and used. I just don't want to live anymore."

They walked in silence for a few minutes. The warehouse was in sight. Sarah kept an eye on their surroundings, unaware of Dekker's exact intentions. The sun was still high enough that this would be all over before the sun dropped for the evening.

"You," Amber said. "You changed things in me. I'm not sure if it's temporary or permanent. After tonight I'll know. When you're gone, I'll know. But as long as you're here, I will see this through to the end. I want Wong as much as you do for killing Nikki and all those girls."

"That's good enough for me." Sarah patted Amber's shoulder. "Just think about it. There's too much to miss if you peace out early. I once heard someone say, 'You were born. Finish what you started.'"

They moved to the left and entered the rear of the warehouse. When Sarah looked over at Amber, she already had a gun in her hand, held unobtrusively down by her thigh.

As far as Sarah knew, the girls were taking up their positions at that very moment. If police officers approached the warehouse, the girls were supposed to do whatever they could to delay them. Failing that, shoot out a tire, aim for a radiator, lie down on the road in front of the oncoming police vehicles, anything to keep them out of the warehouse while Sarah dealt with Dekker.

The girl on the roof was supposed to use the butt of her weapon to knock twice to warn if the authorities were approaching the building.

Without another word, Amber headed to the far corner, where she would hide behind a shelf.

Sarah didn't have to wait long. A door creaked open from the right of the warehouse, and Dekker stuck his head in.

"You alone?" he asked from behind the door.

The girl on the roof hadn't sent a signal, which probably meant Dekker was alone.

"Yes," Sarah said. "You?"

Dekker stepped inside the door; his hands raised chest high. "Of course. You killed one of my most valuable informants, and now you have a cop as a hostage. I wouldn't leave his life to chance by bringing backup."

Dekker started toward her.

"You, Lars Dekker, playing by the book," Sarah said. "Since when?"

"*Inspector* Lars Dekker."

"Bullshit. It's just a title."

"One which I earned."

"Fuck you. Inspect my ass. You set me up. You wanted me killed by that lowlife Sven. Tell me why."

"That wasn't me."

"Oh yeah? It must have been that other guy, Tom, Dick, or Harry." She shook her head. He was still fifteen feet from her. She kept her hands on her hips, close to the weapons in the back of her pants, in case he jerked one out himself. "Dekker, a recent statistic says that 54 million people alive right now around the world will die during the next twelve months. I was thinking about you and thought, hey, what's one more? Nobody would miss you."

"Very funny. I could say the same about you."

"You already did when I was in here the last time." He was ten feet away now. "You carrying?"

"Nope."

"Bullshit."

"I'm not." He stopped five feet in front of her. Not a single noise could be heard from outside. He raised his hands higher and turned in a circle slowly so she could examine his body. "Satisfied? Now what? When do I get Officer Prins back?"

"I want you to watch a recording on a cell phone."

"Okay."

"It's in my back pocket." Sarah started reaching for it. "I'll pull it out slowly."

"I'm waiting."

He seemed overconfident. Like she wouldn't attack him, or he had ample backup. He would never come here on her terms. To him, this was poker, and he had something up his sleeve to help him win. But as long as the girl on the roof didn't knock and there was no gunfire outside, she would keep going.

The cell in her hands now, she accessed the video file, pressed play, and slowly handed it to Dekker. While he watched the video of Sven shooting his informant and Amber shooting Sven, his face remained expressionless. Sarah listened to Sven's voice and the gun going off. When the video stopped, Sarah idly wondered if Dekker would try to erase it. He might think this was the only copy. Without that evidence, Sarah could be arrested and possibly convicted of the murder of an undercover officer. With that video, she would avoid being arrested. At worst, questioned at length. The video was clear about who killed the Matt Dillon lookalike informant. Sven had wanted it just so when he ordered Amber to film the execution.

"Swipe sideways to the next video," Sarah said.

Dekker did. Then he pressed play and watched Officer Prins sitting in his chair back in the dungeon.

"Hey, I know this place," Dekker said.

Sarah's stomach dropped a foot.

How could he know the place from that little five-second video?

"That's Madam's basement dungeon," Dekker said. He looked up into Sarah's eyes. "Madam's helping you with this?"

There goes the immunity plan for the brothel.

Dekker didn't touch the cell phone screen before he handed it back. When Sarah swiped the screen, both videos were intact.

"No one helped me," she said in a feeble attempt to distance herself legally from Madam's brothel. "I ordered the girls out, took the place over, and waited for Prins, a regular there, to come looking for a piece."

"Bullshit."

"Who is Nikki's roommate? Did you discover that when you located her body?"

"Amber Dijkstra," Dekker said. "Sven's girlfriend and well-known Madam employee. The girl who just shot Sven on that cell phone."

"Right. Making the connection here? After Sven died, Amber and I talked. She brought me back to Madam's brothel." She hoped this explanation would keep the brothel out of trouble when Sarah fled Amsterdam. "When I discovered that Dutch police officers frequented Madam's brothel, I hung around, waiting for one to show. When Officer Prins showed up, I had my leverage."

"You're missing something, Sarah." Dekker smiled and crossed his arms over his chest. "You no longer have leverage now. You just lost it. I know where my cop is."

It was time to change the subject. This was falling apart fast. But what really bothered her was how he could identify the dungeon from the little video footage.

The sun must've dropped behind neighboring buildings because the inside of the warehouse darkened somewhat. They were close enough to still see each other, but ten feet back was gray.

"Having seen that video, and you now know I didn't kill your informant in this warehouse, I want my life back. Take those horrendous posters of my face down and call in the army of cops looking for me to inform them that I'm in the clear." She'd almost forgotten the wig. A quick pull and Joan Jett's hair came off her head. "When I asked you earlier if you sent me here to meet Sven and to be killed, you said it wasn't you. What did you mean? Who was it, then? Your boss?"

"Really? Sarah, these are things you could've asked me on the phone. Why am I here?"

"Mexico. Tell me what you know about Mexico, and I want everything you have on James Wong. Then you leave, and I leave to go hunt down Wong."

"After that? Then what?"

"I walk away. You walk away. Your Officer Prins is released, and you never see me again."

"That's all I get in exchange, a cop's life? When I already know where he is?"

Sarah didn't offer an answer.

"And what if I say no? What if I arrest you right now? I could destroy that cell phone and have you on murder charges, kidnapping, and several other charges faster than you could say, 'I'm a stupid whore who thought I got one up on Lars Dekker.'"

"Tell me about Mexico," Sarah said, trying to maintain her cool. With that last comment, she almost shot the bastard just to watch him squirm. "We're wasting time. You'll either deal with some cards or hold onto what you've got. Waffling any further is pointless."

"You're right—" He dove forward so fast his body was a blur.

She reached back for the gun while protecting her face with the other hand. In doing so, she missed the butt of the gun sticking out of the back of her pants.

The fist that struck her left cheek made solid contact, whipping her head sideways. She lost her balance, twisted around, stumbled, and tried to right herself as she reached for the gun again.

Her fingers came up empty as the weapon was ripped from her pants. By the time she turned to face him, the gun she had in her waistline ten seconds ago was being aimed at her. Dekker's feet were planted, both hands on the gun in a classic cop stance.

"Tables have turned, Sarah."

She spit blood onto the dirty warehouse floor. Her teeth had cut the inside of her cheek where the fist connected. She chastised herself for being so careless.

"I can see that the tables have turned."

"Why the cop? Why Madam's brothel?"

"Don't worry, Prins'll be back on his knees in no time at all."

Dekker lunged forward and sucker-punched her again. The gun clicked in her ear as she tried to right herself. That second one hurt more. She moved her jaw to see if anything was loose.

There was nothing worse than being careless. After all the years of doing this, she thought she could handle one cop in a warehouse.

Vivian, anything?

"I'll ask again," Dekker said, keeping the gun against her ear lobe. "I've got lots of time. You can't outrun a bullet, and I'm a good shot. Why Madam's brothel?"

"Why the interest?" Sarah asked as she backed away, heading toward the shelves. "And how did you know from that little video whose dungeon it was?" Amber hadn't jumped out yet because she knew that Sarah's gun in Dekker's hands was loaded. Any sudden movement now would be answered with a bullet. Sarah was on her own. "I get it. You're a regular there. Tell me your secrets, Dekker. How often have you been whipped or pissed on or even shit on in that dungeon? Is eating shit a fetish of yours, Dekker? Have you done that one yet, *Inspector* Lars Dekker?"

"Stop backing away," Dekker shouted. He leaned down to his lapel and said, "All clear. Have the men come in. I have the suspect under control."

"You lied." Sarah spat blood onto the floor. "You brought backup."

"You're delusional if you thought I'd come here alone. The game is up, Sarah. Your goose is cooked."

Sarah kept moving. She was less than ten feet from the shelf where she stored the cricket paddle. The inside of the warehouse grew even darker as the sun continued its descent. If Amber stepped out from behind the shelves, Sarah thought it unlikely Dekker would be able to see her due to the lack of light.

"The game is up?" Sarah mimicked. "Your goose is cooked? Who says that anymore? You know what your problem is, Dekker. You're living in the eighties."

"Stop walking away and tell me what I want to know."

"I want a deal," she said, still eight feet from the shelves.

"No deal. The only deal you'll get, *murderer*, is to tell me why you chose Madam's place before I kill you."

"You saw the video. I didn't kill anybody."

"I'll delete it and break the phone. You're finished."

"You're going to kill me in front of your backup? How? I'm unarmed."

"Backup will take a few more minutes to arrive. I kept them far enough away so you wouldn't see them. That gives you about a minute to live, or longer if you tell me why you chose Madam's brothel."

Still moving backward but slower now, she kept her voice steady. "This sounds personal to you. Why? And how do I know you won't kill me once I tell you?"

"Either you will die in a minute or spend a very long time in prison here in the Netherlands."

"I disagree." Finally, she bumped into the shelving unit.

Dekker moved in close enough to touch her chest with the gun. She spread her hands out, fingers feeling for the cricket paddle.

"You disagree?" Dekker said, spittle coming out of his mouth. "I've killed whores for less."

"I get it," Sarah said as the fingers of her right hand wrapped around the handle of the paddle. "I finally get it."

"Get what?"

"You work for Wong."

His eyes gave him away. There was no protest on his face.

"You like the order someone like Wong and Sven give to the thousands of girls who work in Amsterdam. With Sven dead, order becomes chaos. With Wong pissed off, you're in trouble. Killing me restores some of that order. My death is the currency you will use to buy your way back into the fold with Wong."

"Something like that."

"How did it start? Look the other way for a grand? Or less? Did you take a few hundred?" She used a surprised tone of voice as if it couldn't be possible. "You sold out, didn't you? You whored yourself out. You're no better than the girls trafficked here in your city."

Two loud metallic bangs resounded throughout the

warehouse from the rooftop. The warning that the authorities were moving in.

Dekker looked upward.

Her hand already tight on the paddle's handle, Sarah swung for Dekker's leg while twisting away from the gun's barrel.

The instant the paddle connected with the side of Dekker's knee, the gun in his hand fired, the report momentarily deafening her. Sarah had pivoted so hard that she twisted her ankle, bumped the edge of the shelf going down, and hit the floor on her wounded shoulder blade, the injury from Toronto still raw. The gun in Dekker's hand fired again, but now Sarah was flat out on the warehouse floor, so the bullet missed by a few feet.

It was crazy how the brain stayed fresh at the moment. She heard the bullet ricochet at the other end of the warehouse and saw Dekker was down on one knee above her, the gun descending toward her position. Like watching from the side, she saw herself rise up, the paddle swinging around for another blow, this time aimed at Dekker's face. All of that registered. Then the paddle connected solidly with Dekker's nose. The crack of the paddle vibrated her hand to the point where she almost dropped it. But the gun didn't fire again. Dekker dropped it, his hands moving outward to break his fall as he fell in slow motion, Sarah watching it all, feeling it all, seeing it all.

It was a moment in Vivian's eyes. The overseer. Like déjà vu. A glimpse of time slowed. An overview that could only be captured when shown in slow motion on the movie screen. Yet Sarah saw, felt, and rode with it, even during her panic and fear of being shot.

It reminded her in that hundredth of a second that her sister was there, watching, making sure Sarah was okay and would stay okay. Vivian was always there. Even when she remained silent for long periods, she was there, observing, staying close, and ready to pop in when needed.

As Amber came into view above her and one of the doors in the far corner of the warehouse banged open, Sarah felt warmth envelope her. Vivian loved her and was here to protect her. It would all work out. Everything would work out even when she discovered the whole truth about this situation. When dark days came, Vivian would be there.

It will always work out, resonated in her head.

Then Vivian's presence ushered away like a fan blowing smoke down a corridor, leaving Sarah shaken up.

"Get on your feet," Amber yelled at Dekker.

Sarah rolled to the side and winced at the shoulder wound as she pushed off the floor and got to her feet. She dropped the cricket paddle when she saw Amber had Dekker under control.

Dekker used the shelf beside him to get to one knee but stopped there.

"My knee," he pleaded. "Aches like a bitch." He looked up. "Reminds me of you."

Amber kicked at him. Dekker grunted.

As soon as Dekker's backup arrived, they'd all be arrested. The only other person in the warehouse was Madam. She was walking across the floor toward them.

"How many cops are coming?" Sarah asked Madam as she stopped in front of Dekker. "Did you see them outside?"

"My girls have halted their approach."

"Impossible," Dekker whispered from one knee.

"I have to admit," Sarah said. "I'm a little surprised. Your girls are good."

Madam didn't seem to be listening. All her attention was on Dekker.

"Long time," she said to him. Her voice had changed. It was deeper, stronger. Like some dark memory had surfaced, and she was steeling herself to speak about it. "I see you've been up to your old ways."

"Don't be ridiculous," Dekker said. "You don't know me anymore."

As Sarah had suspected, something had been going on from the beginning. The reason Madam and Amber were willing to help was to get to Dekker. Kidnapping a cop to force a meeting with Lars Dekker hadn't scared them off. She should've dug deeper, but they were helping her when she needed it, so she went with it.

Now it was easy to tell that Dekker knew them and had a history with them. Madam and Amber had set this up, and somehow Dekker's backup was waiting outside. But how could girls who worked at Madam's brothel stop the authorities from entering the warehouse after their boss ordered them inside?

"What's going on here?" Sarah asked, her frown deepening.

"Inspector Lars Dekker," Madam said, "didn't make it to the top on his back. He did it with us on our backs. He loaned me money thirty years ago and, when things were tough, took it back in trade. According to him, I always owed money. My girls paid for that. When I refused him entry to the brothel, Sven brought him around. If it wasn't Sven trafficking the girls and raping whom he wanted, it was Dekker."

"Come on, ladies," Dekker said, one hand out. "It was only sex. You're females. That's what you're supposed to be doing. You enjoyed it. Admit it."

Madam's eyes watered in anger. Amber's gun wavered in her hands.

"Dekker, you might want to shut up now," Sarah said.

"Let me plead my case," he barked. "You have customers all day, in and out of that brothel. What's the difference? To you gals, I'm just one more cock. I mean, really, who cares?" He shook his head and looked down at the floor. Then he met Madam's gaze. "I get it. None of the girls liked bareback. But I told you, if I'm the only one doing bareback, nobody gets a disease since I'm clean. It's all fucking rational. Why don't you fucking whores get it?"

"Dekker," Sarah said, her voice urging caution. "Conjure up an image of how you look right now. On bended knee, pleading for your life, and you're egging them on." She turned to Madam. "He can't hurt your girls anymore. It's over. But I can't let you kill him. I need what he has on James Wong."

"Fuck you, Sarah," Dekker shouted. "I'll never give Wong to you. I've known him too long. And he pays better than the Dutch government. And damn, those fringe benefits." He glanced at Sarah and winked. "You can't beat them."

Amber fired at the second Dekker lifted a gun. The bullet exited the side of Dekker's head in a spray of brain matter, chunks of bone, and blood. Inspector Lars Dekker slipped sideways, tilted farther, then fell over and bled out onto the warehouse floor until his heart stopped.

Sarah gasped and jumped back. What now? She'd seen

enough people die to stay clear-headed. Madam and Amber hovered over him and watched Dekker die. His eyes remained open, unseeing. Madam stepped closer and spat onto his face. Thoughts of DNA ran through Sarah's mind and how Amber and Madam would face the consequences for the murder of an inspector with the Dutch police.

"Where did the gun in his hand come from?" Sarah asked when she found her voice.

"Ankle holster," Amber said. "We knew he had one there from when he spent time at the brothel. That's why he wouldn't stand up. He was waiting for his opportunity to pull it out. I was waiting, too."

"Obviously." Sarah swallowed and took in a deep breath. "You both planned this from the beginning." It was more a statement than a question. "You used me to get to Dekker."

"We didn't use you," Madam said. "Your agenda fit ours nicely. All we did was help each other find a common end."

"I've got nothing, though. No names or places on Wong." She pointed at Dekker's body. "He knew how to locate Wong."

Someone near the back of the warehouse began clapping. It was so dark now that even Amber and Madam's faces were hard to see. How Amber saw Dekker go for his gun in this gloom amazed Sarah.

"Who's clapping?" Amber shouted, her gun up at a forty-five-degree angle, both hands wrapped around the butt of the weapon.

Suddenly the back doors opened. Sarah spun around in a crouch. Men in riot gear and masks entered, pushing Madam's girls in front of them. Another door banged open along the side of the building, and more men filed in behind the rest of the girls.

Amber pointed the gun at the ceiling and slowly lowered it to the floor.

Hopelessness settled in over Sarah. They would be arrested and detained forever. Getting to Aaron was over. Learning who took her parents and why was a dream now.

Doing the right thing isn't going so well for me, sis. A little help here.

The clapping at the back of the warehouse started up again. Approximately twenty armed men escorted the girls to Madam, where they huddled close to Dekker's body. The men in riot gear surrounded the women, forming a semi-circle.

That clapping was maddening. Whoever was doing it seemed to be enjoying themselves all too much.

Out of the gloom, a man edged closer. He wore a white suit and white shoes. He stopped before his face materialized.

"Well done," he said.

Casper!

"You've saved me a lot of time," Casper added. "Death is often the easier way to go with my job." He moved closer until his face came into view. It would be completely dark in the warehouse within minutes. Without flashlights, everyone would have to leave by feel. "You know Sarah, I once thought it would be better for me if you were dead, too. But now that's not the best option."

Sarah advanced on Casper until she was a foot away from him. "It would be better for me if you were dead. Then you would match that nickname of yours. Although, maybe not. You're not that friendly."

"I've saved your life tonight, Sarah. You could be a little

nicer."

Sarah pointed at Amber and Madam. "They saved my life tonight."

Casper was shaking his head. "No. The American government has been investigating James Wong and many others in his criminal enterprise. Lars Dekker was just another pawn. My men, your countrymen, Americans, kept Dekker's backup out of the way while you frolicked around in here."

That answered her doubt about prostitutes holding the authorities back. It had been Casper's men from the beginning.

"And how did you know that I would survive? Or them, for that matter?" She pointed at Amber and Madam.

"Dekker has a history in Amsterdam. I knew his file inside and out. Dekker has abused Madam and Amber and these other ladies for a long time. When I saw you come to the warehouse earlier this afternoon in that terrible wig, I was sure you'd added enough insurance to certify a win against Dekker that I let you have your say with him."

"It was still touch and go."

"I'm sure Vivian would've pulled something out of her celestial hat if things got bad." He smirked like it was an inside secret. "Take Gabi, Porsche, Melissa, and Amber back to their place of business," Casper said to his men. "Madam, go with them. Put the guns away. Sven's dead. Dekker's dead. Wong's on the run. Go about your business. I don't think anyone will trouble you for some time."

Madam's nod was so subtle in the dark that Sarah almost missed it.

The semi-circle of beefy men in riot gear opened. Amber

walked away without so much as a look back at Sarah. The dark swallowed them up, and Casper and Sarah were alone a moment later.

She didn't know whether or not to kick his ass or listen to what he had to say. He knew something about Aaron and Mexico, and he knew much more about everything else than he was letting on. A lot of people were using each other and getting away with it. But so far, only the bad guys were ending up dead.

"Sarah, I find you very annoying sometimes," Casper said.

"Then stop finding me." She turned to leave.

"Where are you going?" he asked.

"To look for Wong."

"And then what?"

"I don't know. Kill him."

"You'll need me."

His footsteps echoed throughout the warehouse as he began to follow her.

"Why? I've gotten by well enough without you so far." She was almost to the shelf that held the second cricket paddle. It had gotten so dark now that she feared she'd walk into the shelving unit.

"I know where Wong has gone."

That almost stopped Sarah. She could get Vivian to tell her. If so, why hadn't Vivian already told her? It had to be because Sarah needed to work with Casper. If Casper worked for the government, like he said on the plane before it crashed, and government men took her parents, then he probably knew where they were. Taking her parents out of their house at six in the morning could only mean one thing.

Leverage.

The government wanted something from her. Something they didn't think she would agree to. She had been in this place before and didn't acquiesce then. Add Aaron, Parkman, and her parents into the arrangement, and things would change. She would have to listen to them.

Unless she changed things first.

"Come on, Sarah. There's more."

They materialized a second before she head-butted the shelves and jammed a knee into a lower one. In this part of the warehouse, there was a tiny bit more light from a street lamp that had turned on outside.

"Leave the paddle alone," Casper said. "I let you walk over here. I could've killed you at any time. Turn around with your hands empty."

Sarah saw the paddle, studied its handle, and felt her hand twitch. But if he had a gun, reaching for it was pointless.

She turned around. His hands were empty.

"Where's Aaron? My parents? Parkman? Tell me what you know of Wong. Give it all up because you have to convince me to keep standing here. So far, you've been an enigma." She was working herself up. At any moment, she would smack him, punch him, crush his balls with her knee, anything to see him writhing on the warehouse floor. "You let me walk into this warehouse with Sven Spaans. I almost died then. If it wasn't for Amber, I was a goner."

"That was a mistake. Dekker was supposed to inform me where the meet was set up for. I was late and two blocks away. Forgive me, that one. The plan was for me to swoop in and save you. Get you to trust me."

"You set me up on that plane and then helped me move those people. Why?"

"I didn't believe you were really psychic."

"What was that part about me being dead and how it might have been better for you? Why is that not the case anymore?"

"Can we talk on the way to the airfield? We're running out of time."

"Airfield?"

"I've got a U.S. military plane waiting to fly us to Athens, Greece. James Wong has fled there, and as far as I know, he's got his little black book with him. He took out the trash here in Amsterdam, and my intel says he will do the same in Athens. But we can stop him. Together." Casper started away from her in the dark. "Come on. We'll talk on the plane."

Everything in her being told her to go. But what if he was lying, and they were flying her to a laboratory that would make a Nazi doctor's lab pale in comparison? They could poke, prod and operate on her for years without anyone finding out. Maybe that was why they took her parents, Aaron and Parkman. So no one would come looking for her when she disappeared. Mexico was a good place to hide them.

"Sarah?" he called from the open door along the side of the warehouse. He stood silhouetted in the street light. "You coming?"

"I don't trust you. I don't trust anyone."

"I know where Aaron is," Casper said.

That sentence stabbed her. She felt lightheaded. Her fear of the unknown, what was happening to Aaron, was only suppressed because Vivian hadn't directed her toward him in whatever plight had befallen him. Vivian had warmed her earlier with the notion that everything would work out and be okay.

"I can help you bring him home," Casper said. "That's why I'm here. Your parents are safe. We have them in the witness protection program until everything settles down. Parkman was hard to pick up in Toronto, but we got him. Tell me, what is it with him and those fucking toothpicks?" Sarah smiled in the dark as Casper prattled on. "Don't let me leave you here in this warehouse with a dead Dutch inspector. You won't get Wong, and Aaron will die without your help."

Numbed by his words, Sarah had to decide. Amsterdam was a hotbed now. She was supposed to meet Dekker in a warehouse tonight. Dekker's dead now. She kidnapped Officer Prins, who was probably still locked up in Madam's dungeon. Even with Amber's cell phone video coverage of Sven's murder, the Dutch authorities would want to talk to her, with high odds that she would be charged with offenses that would take years of court to battle.

On the other hand, Casper was powerful enough to keep Dekker's backup at bay in Dekker's own city while the warehouse meeting took place. And he had a U.S. military plane waiting. Best case scenario, she ends up in Greece and can disappear from there, leaving Amsterdam behind. Worst case scenario, Casper's lying. In that case, she could just kill him. One more body. No one would notice.

Sarah stared at his shadowy figure in the doorway. Kill him fast and move on to find Aaron on her own. Vivian would help. At least, she hoped so.

Go with him ...

Vivian's now familiar voice echoed throughout her head. That felt better. Decision made. Easy.

Thanks, sis.

She put one foot in front of the other and started across the dirty floor toward the ghost at the door. Fatigue set in over her system as her stomach growled. When was the last time she ate anything?

She would sleep on the plane. When this was done, she would bask in the tropical sun of Greece. When this nightmare ended, she would steal away with Aaron, and they would vacation somewhere exotic. She needed time away from all this shit. It was starting to wear on her.

"I knew you'd see the light," Casper said.

They stepped out of the warehouse and into a waiting black SUV.

Sarah stared out the window and wiped a tear as thoughts of Aaron called her home.

Chapter 38

The plane was a C-5 Galaxy escorting NATO troops for routine exercises in Athens.

Sarah and Casper were seated near the front, already seatbelted in. When they had arrived, the nose cone was open. A ramp led down to the tarmac where troops were boarding. Casper explained that it would take them three and a half hours to fly the less than three thousand kilometers to Athens.

"This four-engine Lockheed Galaxy can carry over 120 tons at a cruising speed of over nine hundred kilometers an hour. Amazing, isn't it?"

"You sound like you know a lot about military aircraft."

"A side hobby of mine," he said, downplaying his excitement.

He produced a bottle of red wine from a bag on the floor. He pulled out a corkscrew from inside a small pocket in the bag.

Sarah lunged across him and grabbed the bottle.

"I'll open it." She held out her hand for the corkscrew.

"Don't trust me yet?" He dropped it on her open palm.

"I never will. Remember? I told you at the warehouse that I don't trust anybody." She applied the corkscrew to the cork and began twisting.

"You trust Aaron," Casper said, a smug look on his face. Something gleamed in his eyes, like madness lurking.

Sarah stared for a brief moment, then let it go. Casper was safe for now. Vivian had endorsed him.

"Glasses?" she asked.

He reached inside the bag and pulled two small water glasses out. "Best I could do. Anyway, in Greece, they use these kinds of glasses for wine more often than not."

Sarah frowned as she poured the wine. "Interesting."

With a glass of wine in her hand, she put her head back and closed her eyes. Sarah didn't think she'd be able to stay awake for much longer.

"We've been tracking a relatively new Mexican cartel near Tijuana for some time," Casper started. "The Enzo Cartel."

Sarah's eyes popped open. "A cartel?" she asked, turning to face him.

He nodded. "They're reckless, strong, fortified, and dangerous."

"What's that got to do with me?" Sarah drank from her glass.

"They have Aaron."

She spit her wine out. "What?" She wiped at her pants, but only a minimal amount had landed on them.

"When you went after Wong's business—his criminal empire in Toronto—you cut off many of his customers."

The crew had finished loading. The engines revved, and the plane began to taxi out as smoothly as if it was riding on air.

"Customers? A cartel was Wong's customer?"

Casper nodded as he sipped from his wine. "We suspected Wong laundered their money through his prostitution business. A lot of cash trades hands there. America watches cash at the borders, but Mexico and Canada aren't as touchy about it."

"And?" Sarah said, exasperated. She waved her free hand in a circle. "Keep talking."

"You hurt Wong's business. He fled Canada and came to Amsterdam. When you arrived, he got scared and cleaned a few loose ends up. Now he's in Athens. The cartel learned of your involvement, and now they have probably ten million in unlaundered money, with more piling up. It'll cost them."

"So they want me?" she asked, her wine forgotten for the moment. "Is that it?"

Casper nodded.

"And they abducted Aaron to get to me."

Casper nodded again and sipped more from his wine. "We've been monitoring them for some time. Had we known, I would have had men pick up Aaron to keep him safe." He shook his head in dismay. "We were too late. We got to Parkman and your parents in time. Everyone's safe and off the map until this is sorted out."

"Then why aren't we going after this cartel and getting Aaron back?"

"We are."

"When?"

"Right now."

"Casper, don't fuck around." The engines revved, and the huge C-5 Galaxy thrust forward up the runway. "We're headed to Greece while sipping wine. To an outsider, it looks like we're on a fucking holiday while Aaron is held hostage by thugs who behead people in Mexico and hang them from bridges. I read the news."

"Getting Wong and his black book is step one."

Her curiosity bloomed at the mention of the black book. "What's your interest in that book?"

"It doesn't just give up names in Toronto. It lists all his clients and customers. It's not some little book. It's his ledger. James Wong is a good businessman, and any good businessman keeps well-tended records, and they never leave his sight. Also, Wong got his roots as a mob accountant. He *is* the accountant, the business, the money, and the brains. Get Wong, hurt everybody attached to him."

"So all this time, watching me, waiting, you were letting me hunt him to see what I could get for you?" Her anger rose as she felt her cheeks flush.

The plane had taken off and climbed to cruising altitude almost without her noticing. If there were somewhere to set her wine glass down, she would have done so so she could strangle and pummel Casper for faster answers.

"Remember when I said I thought it might be better if you were dead?"

Sarah only nodded, afraid of what she might say.

"If you died in that plane crash when we landed in Amsterdam, the Mexicans might have given up, gone away. When they snatched Aaron, I knew you were needed alive."

"For what?"

"Bait."

Without hesitation, Sarah sat up straighter. "Fine. Send me in. When do we go?"

"As soon as we're done in Greece."

She sat back in her seat and loosened her grip on the wine glass. Then she drank the rest of it back to calm her nerves. She needed rest to be effective in Greece. They had Aaron. What could they be doing with him? Would they feed him? Would they beat him?

"Sarah," Casper said, his voice softer. "We've got a lot of intel on this cartel. Intel that comes from the NSA, the DEA, and the CIA. I'm here to help."

"Who are you with?" she asked.

"Black ops."

"Black? Really? Isn't that fictional? Something you watch on TV?"

"No."

"Who do you take your orders from?"

"My boss."

She looked at him. "Cocky bastard. That's a non-answer."

"I can't tell you. All I can say is that we are after the same people, and we will fix this. We aim to bring Aaron home in one piece."

She thought about the military plane taking them to Greece. Casper had a lot of clout, probably more than any government official she'd met. Maybe he was telling the truth, and maybe not, but she still feared for Aaron. And it was her fault. But how could she have stopped her assault on the torture club in Toronto? How could she have walked away?

Or was this all on Vivian? If so, and Aaron came home one day, then Vivian would see that as a victory. All the bad guys are taken care of with a few blemishes on their side.

But if Aaron died?

Sarah shuddered in her seat.

"You okay?" Casper asked.

Ignoring the question, she held her glass out for more wine. He poured it full. She drank it like water, gave him the glass, and closed her eyes, resting her head back.

"You ever hear of the twenty-million dollar cat?"

After a moment of silence, Casper said, "Can't say that I have."

"The CIA once spent twenty-million dollars on a cat equipped with equipment to spy on the Russians."

"What happened? How did it work out?"

"The cat got hit by a taxi and died. The project died with it. That level of stupidity, that much waste, is another example of why I don't trust you people."

"I'm not the CIA."

"Same thing."

"No, it's not."

"Shut up. I'm trying to sleep."

The plane hit turbulence over the French Alps, but Sarah didn't notice too much as she slipped into full REM.

Chapter 39

Sarah jerked awake when the plane touched down. Casper was still beside her, reading a backlit Kindle. He hadn't disappeared like the last time they were on the same plane.

She sat up and wiped a bit of spittle from her chin. Her cheek still ached where Dekker had punched her. She opened her dry, pasty mouth, lowered her jaw, and tried to crack the pressure out of her ears.

"What time is it?" she asked, then yawned.

Casper checked his watch. "Just after one in the morning, Athens time."

"Great. What's first?"

"Sleep. Wong's being watched. We know where he'll be tomorrow morning at eleven. So we sleep."

"Where?"

"A nice place. Don't worry. You'll get your own room, too."

The plane taxied up the tarmac and stopped. Sarah undid her seatbelt, stood, and stretched. Soon after, the nose cone rose, and they headed outside. Casper noticed someone and headed off to speak to them. Sarah watched as they pumped hands, chatted briefly, and departed.

When he was beside her again, she asked, "What was that all about?"

"Had to properly thank him for the lift."

Once through the airport, without entering any customs as they flew within the Eurozone, Sarah followed Casper across the busy lanes of cars, where even at this hour, people were pulling in, picking up, and dropping off.

Once across the lanes, she looked up at a towering white hotel.

The Sofitel.

"Nice place," she said.

"Thank the U.S. government. Come on. Maybe the bar's still open. Finger food and a shot of something before sleep."

They checked in, got to the third floor, and entered their separate rooms. A sign behind the check-in counter said this was a five-star hotel, and Sarah could see why. The room was gorgeous, with a cherry oak desk, a black leather desk chair, and at least a forty-inch TV. The bathroom was everything a girl could want on holiday. Pity, she would only use it to shower in the morning and then be gone.

When they holidayed in Greece, she would be sure to bring Aaron here.

After five minutes, Casper knocked on her door. "You coming downstairs?"

"Yeah," she hollered back and headed for the door.

Once seated in the bar/restaurant, a shot of Johnnie

Walker Black in her hand, Sarah asked, "Shouldn't we be a little more inconspicuous? It felt like the authorities in Amsterdam knew I was there before I landed. Are the Greeks aware we're here?"

"Wong told Lars Dekker about you," Casper said. He was drinking something that came with a little umbrella. Sarah had wanted to question his manhood as a joke but was too tired for the debate. "Wong has no idea where we are this time."

"How do you know that?"

"Because my sources confirmed it. I told you we're monitoring him."

"How does he not know?" she asked. Part of her was curious, but another part was just making exhausted conversation. She needed the rest of the whiskey, and she needed her bed. Tomorrow was another day. Tomorrow she would deal with whatever came and then go to Mexico with or without Casper.

"He doesn't know because we entered Greece on a military plane en route through Turkey and the north side of Syria to examine the ISIS situation there. Nobody gets access to that itinerary. Not even Greek officials. All they get is the flight plans."

Sarah enjoyed the feeling the whiskey offered. Her eyes closed, then opened slowly. It was late. The stress had worn her down.

"I'm going back to my room," she said.

"Go, get some sleep. I'll knock when we need to move out. You should be ready by six in the morning. I'll come to your door at six or six-thirty."

"I'll be ready."

She got up, downed the rest of Johnnie, and left Casper alone with his fruity drink and his Kindle. She idly wondered what he was reading and decided to ask him in the morning.

She entered her room, got undressed, and crawled under the covers, asleep before the clock's second hand did one full rotation.

Chapter 40

A LOUD BANGING, A knocking. Something broken. Screaming.

Sarah snapped awake and sat up in bed. For a delirious moment, she had no idea where she was. Sun forced its way around the cracks in the curtain where it was set back off the wall. The hotel. The five-star hotel. Athens. Greece.

The banging again. Someone was knocking on her door.

"Sarah?" Casper shouted from the hallway. "You awake?"

"Yes," she yelled back. "Thanks!"

"It's six-thirty," he said. "Breakfast time. Meet me in the restaurant. Shower after. Let's go."

When the voice at the door silenced, she dropped back onto the pillows and yawned. Best sleep she'd had in a long time. Guilt set in when she thought of Aaron and what his sleeping conditions were probably like. But she was fixing that situation by going after Wong. The cartel was next.

Yeah, all in a day's work.

She got out of bed, washed her face in the sink, dressed in yesterday's clothes, and headed down to the restaurant.

Casper was already eating. "Didn't know if you'd come down or fall back to sleep."

"Wouldn't miss breakfast on the government's dollar. Can't say this opportunity comes all too often."

She approached the buffet breakfast table. Once her plate was loaded with scrambled eggs, sausage, ham, and bacon, she grabbed a small yogurt and headed to Casper's table.

"What were you reading on your Kindle last night?"

"Your memoirs."

She had been pulling a chair out but stopped briefly, then sat down. "My memoirs?"

"Yeah, the series of novels on Amazon details your life with Vivian and how you've stayed alive all this time. You know, *Dark Visions* is book one and so on."

"Oh." She grabbed a strip of bacon and bit off the tip. "Maybe I reveal too much in those books."

"We need to talk about that."

"We do?"

"You can't put me in any book if you ever write about your trip to Amsterdam and Greece. No one can know of my involvement."

"Why not?"

He set his fork down, wiped his mouth with a cloth napkin, and replaced it on his lap.

"Because I'm so unofficial I don't even exist on paper. Black ops, remember. POTUS has no idea who we are. That's why I'm Casper. I'm a ghost and still reasonably friendly, right?"

"I know you exist. You're right in front of me."

"Sarah, that's not the point, and you know it."

Sarah cut a sausage in half, jabbed her knife into the next one, and looked up at Casper.

"Nail Wong," she said. "Get the ledger, and let's deal with this cartel. If Aaron's still alive and we all make it home, maybe I'll let this chapter of my life disappear. Maybe I won't write about it. Trust me when I say I don't want to relive this one." She tossed half a sausage in her mouth.

"It sounded like there was an *or else* in there somewhere," Casper said.

"Or else you're in book fourteen, and I'll write about *The Cartel* in book fifteen. Full disclosure. What I learn goes down as a public fucking record. There can be no lawsuits as long as I don't lie in the memoirs."

Casper grabbed his drink from the table. It looked like apple juice. At least it didn't have any tiny umbrellas today. When he was done drinking, he ate the rest of his eggs, moved his plate aside, and wiped his mouth.

"I need you," he said. "We meet Wong in just over three hours. We need you to get inside the cartel. We do it my way. I deliver as promised and you don't write about me. Deal?"

"Deal. But Aaron's got to be safe and alive. I get him back, and you deal with all the bad guys," she popped another sausage in her mouth, "and we have a deal," she finished saying around the food in her mouth.

"I can't guarantee the state Aaron will be in." He leaned back in his chair, joining his hands over his flat stomach. "You have to face the fact that this is a brutal group. There are odds with everything we do, and even though the odds are good, he's still alive right now, but that may change in the future. Especially the closer you get to them."

"Make it a condition, a caveat."

"What I'm saying, Sarah, is pinning Aaron's health on not mentioning me in a book isn't a deal. You just can't mention me."

"And if I do?"

"Don't test it. In my world, there is no *if*."

"What *if* you die during the operation? Who would stop me?"

"Good point. Let's hope that doesn't happen."

"Yeah. Let's."

Neither said another word until breakfast was done, and Casper charged the bill to his room. Once they were outside in the lobby by the elevators, Sarah turned to him.

"When and where?" she asked.

"I'll knock on your door by 10:45."

The elevator doors slid open. They got on, and Sarah pressed her button.

"Do I get a gun?"

"Nope."

"Why not?"

"You could shoot me. Accidentally, of course. No way. You're too risky."

"Good point. Better not give me a gun."

The doors opened on the third floor, and she exited before Casper could say anything more.

Chapter 41

Sarah waited in her room until eleven, but no one knocked on her door. She stood by the large window, looking at the highway leading into Athens.

Something didn't add up. Yesterday Casper had said they knew where Wong was and that they were going to pick him up or nab him around eleven this morning. Then why be ready for 10:45? How could they get to where Wong was that fast?

Her breath caught in her throat. Unless Wong was coming to them. Landing at the airport, maybe even staying in this hotel.

But then, where was Casper?

Someone knocked. "Housekeeping." She heard the key card in the door and bolted across the room. Just as the door was opening, she slammed her shoulder into it.

"Sorry, almost done." Sarah was careful to keep her body

to the side in case whoever was in the hallway decided to shoot through the door. But no bullet came. All she heard was a muttered apology as the maid walked away.

Sarah placed her ear on the door and listened. Ten seconds later, she heard another knock down the hall, and the same woman said *housekeeping* again.

She had to get out of this room unnoticed. She was an easy target stuck in the room with no escape. She opened the door slowly, looked up and down the empty corridor, and stepped out, the room keycard in her back pocket. Instead of the elevator, she hustled down the hall and took the stairs to the ground floor. She had her passport, a billfold loaded with a few hundred American dollars, and her bank card. If Casper abandoned her, she could hunt Wong and get out of Greece on her own. If he set her up as bait for the Mexicans without telling her the plan, she would have to kill him and then expose him for who he was.

On the first floor, she moved toward the restaurant, which meant crossing in front of the counter. The area was relatively empty, as most of the guests would've checked out.

"Good morning," a clerk said to her from behind the check-in desk. "Kaliméra."

She sidled up to the side of the counter and put her back to the wall to examine the lobby and the cars pulling in out front. There was no sign of Casper.

"What's Kaliméra mean?" she asked.

"It means good morning in Greek."

"Ahh, thanks." Then Vivian whispered a word in her head: *efcharistó*. Sarah had no idea what that meant but decided to repeat it verbatim.

"Efcharistó."

The clerk smiled. "Parakaló."

"What did we just say?" she asked, idly wondering how this looked to the clerk.

"You said thank you, and I said, you're welcome." His smile faltered for a brief moment. "What room were you staying in?" he asked.

When she told him, he typed it into the system. "Ahh, yes, Vivian Roberts. Buck Schaffer's covering both rooms for two nights."

"Two nights?" Sarah asked. Deal with Wong today and leave was the arrangement. Why two nights?

"Mr. Schaffer just changed it to two nights, not ten minutes ago. He left a message on your phone about it."

"Oh, didn't get it. Did you see Mr. Schaffer?" she asked.

"He had me call a taxi over from the airport." The clerk moved from the computer, bent down, and looked out the front doors toward the road. "He might still be standing there. He was when you walked up."

"Thanks … I mean, efcharistó." Sarah headed for the doors.

A taxi pulled in off the road and drove over to a man standing on the side as she made it to the doors. He carried a briefcase of some kind. Outside, the taxi's back door was just shutting, and then the taxi pulled away.

Sarah ran after the cab as it hit the road and sped away from her. But not before she caught a glimpse of the face of the man in the back seat.

It wasn't Casper.

It was a Chinese man. And he hadn't been carrying a briefcase. It was a large leather-bound book.

She had missed James Wong by seconds.

Another taxi was coming her way. She ran into the street in front of it, arms flailing until it stopped.

Thankfully the back seat was empty. She hopped in and said, "Follow that cab. The one that's about two hundred yards ahead of us."

"No English," the driver said. "Greek. Sygnómi."

Vivian filled her head. "What?" she said to Vivian out loud.

"Greek," the driver replied.

Sarah ignored him and listened to each word Vivian said. Then she repeated it to the driver.

"Ahh, you speak Greek," the driver said in Greek, with Vivian translating in Sarah's head as he spoke.

The taxi started away from the hotel so fast he almost left rubber behind.

"Where did you learn to speak Greek?" he asked, with Vivian whispering the English to her.

"I don't speak Greek," Sarah said in Greek after Vivian told her how to say it. "Just these voices in my head."

The driver glanced at her in the mirror, then looked back at the road.

What did I say to him, Vivian? What was that last part?

Vivian explained.

Great. Thanks. Now he thinks I'm insane. After a minute, Sarah said, *You're enjoying this, aren't you?*

Vivian didn't respond. The driver was gaining on the taxi with the Chinese man. It was all going down too fast. What had happened to Casper? Was this a trick? He said they had intel on where Wong would be and when. Why was she following Wong into Athens, a city she was altogether unfamiliar with?

At least she had Vivian, who suddenly knew how to speak Greek. Although that made sense. She's on the other side. Vivian could probably translate every language known to man for Sarah.

But where was Casper? She adjusted herself in the back seat, moving a little lower. Then she turned to look out the back window. Two vehicles with kids, a Mercedes driven by a man in a suit, and one other taxi made up the cars close enough to be following them. She turned back around and stared at the back of Wong's cab.

Maybe no one was following her. Maybe Casper was dead, and she was on her own. Maybe Wong discovered they were in Athens, killed Casper, and was now heading into the city to go about his business.

Or everything she thought was mere speculation, and the man in the taxi ahead of her was a Chinese man on his way to meet his wife after forgetting a leather-bound scrapbook at their hotel.

None of it made sense. Casper was probably back at the hotel wondering why Sarah took off.

Or worse still—this was an ambush, and Sarah was walking right into their trap.

But what else could she do but follow her instincts? Or what Vivian said to do? And since Vivian was currently silent on the topic, Sarah would continue to follow the Chinese man with the large book until this lead proved fruitful or turned into a waste of time.

She had to believe it was Wong. It was too much of a coincidence. Soon she would see Wong's taxi pull over somewhere, and he would exit the vehicle.

And she would be on him faster than a fly alights on shit.

Chapter 42

SOMEONE KNOCKED ON THE door so lightly that Casper almost didn't notice it.

"Housekeeping," a male voice said.

Before Casper had a chance to respond, a key card entered the door, the handle dropped, and the door began to open.

"Still here," Casper shouted. "Haven't checked out yet."

In a millisecond, he understood that the man entering the room wasn't housekeeping. In fact, the tall, well-built man in a black Hugo Boss suit didn't even work for the hotel. No, he had to work for Wong.

Casper dove over the bed for his shoulder holster. His right hand snatched it up as he rolled off the bed and onto the floor, stopping suddenly where the wall was.

Hugo Boss rounded the corner, aimed his weapon with its attached suppressor, and shook his head back and forth twice.

"Leave it," he ordered.

Casper had been about to yank his gun out of the holster but stopped. He had needed only two, maybe three seconds more. Imagine dying because of a few seconds. That would never go on his gravestone, but it should.

"Up," the man ordered. "Leave the holster."

Casper set the holster aside and struggled to his feet from a scrunched position in the corner.

"Now what?" Casper asked.

It was getting close to 10:45. Sarah would be wondering where he'd gotten to.

"Sit." Hugo motioned at the desk chair by the window.

Casper did as he was told. This was bad. They had him. Did they have Sarah? Could they capture her? Didn't she have a dead sister who kept her alive?

Once in the chair, he stared at Hugo. The man didn't waver. He didn't take his eyes off Casper.

"What's the deal here?" Casper asked.

"We wait."

"For what?"

"Shut up now."

"Fuck you now. Wait for what?"

Hugo flipped the gun into his left hand, approached the chair, and drove a beefy fist into Casper's face. It knocked him sideways so violently that his forehead bounced once off the top of the desk.

When he looked back up, rubbing his cheek, Hugo was standing by the bathroom door, the gun in his right hand again.

"That's a whole new meaning to *head desk*, eh?" Casper

said. Hugo looked at his watch. "You know what I mean? When someone says something inane on social media. You know, head meets desk."

Hugo lowered the gun. His arm was probably getting tired.

"You gonna talk to me?" Casper asked. "Tell me what's going on? Because I have to go soon. Got a lunch date with a hot Greek guy that wants it from behind."

"Shut up. Last warning."

"Unless you're into that sort of thing," Casper continued. "Hey, I know, we're already in a hotel room. No need to buy each other dinner." Casper got up from the chair, fear motivating him to move. If he were going to die, he would do it on his feet. There was zero chance he would allow himself to get shot sitting at a desk in a leather office chair. That was no way for a soldier to leave this life. "Come on. Take off your jacket. Stay a while, big boy."

Hugo's cell phone beeped. He read the screen. Then smiled.

"It's time. Sarah's in the taxi. She's as good as dead. Now you."

Casper ran and made to jump at Hugo, but the sound suppressor spit metal venom one after another, arresting his advance.

Casper hit the carpeted floor with what he counted as five bullets in the chest area.

It was odd that he thought of the hotel maids at that moment. What happened to the maid who would normally clean this floor? Did she die for the master key that Hugo used on the door?

What a waste.

Everything was such a waste.

Buck Schaffer, also known as Casper to his friends, stopped moving on the floor of the five-star hotel.

Chapter 43

"WHAT IS THIS AREA called?" Sarah asked the driver in Greek.

"Monastiraki," the driver said, still acting wary.

He hadn't spoken to her for the forty-five-minute ride into Athens. Sarah didn't care. He had a job to do and was doing it well.

After several backward glances out the rear window, Sarah ascertained no one was following them. It was only the Chinese man and Sarah, and now they were in Monastiraki.

The blinker on the cab ahead indicated they were pulling over to double park. Then the four-ways came on.

As if on cue, Vivian told Sarah how to speak the Greek words that Sarah was thinking.

"Pull over," Sarah said, but the driver was already doing it.

A horn sounded behind them.

"Sixty euros," the driver said.

Sarah pulled out an American fifty and a twenty and told him to keep the change. Up ahead, the Chinese man had exited his cab and was headed for the sidewalk.

"Wait," her driver said in English. "I only accept euros."

Sarah stopped and looked back at him. "You knew English this whole time?"

"Only a little."

"Change the currency at a bank or something. There'll be extra. And next time, watch yourself with tourists. You never know who's in your back seat."

She got out, slammed the door hard, and ran for the area where the Chinese man had disappeared. She approached a square with a small church or temple to her left. A group of young men were break dancing in the center of the open square to music blaring out of a stereo at their feet. People crowded around to watch and toss coins into an open guitar case.

Past the church, the tables and chairs set out in the blazing early morning sun in front of a line of restaurants were jammed full of tourists eating gyros and other Greek dishes.

To her right, scanning all the faces for the Chinese man, she saw a sign that said Monastiraki Flea Market. In the distance, on a plateau, sat the ancient Acropolis. Momentarily, it made her stop and stare.

Forcing her eyes away, she saw what she had been looking for. The Chinese man was about to enter what looked like an alley that led to tourist shops. She ran down four wide steps, bumped past people, and made it through the square's center to the alleyway's opening before he made it fifty yards.

She slowed her pace to keep a distance. Up ahead, a road intersected the shopping lane. Tourists were everywhere. White Brits looked like lobsters under wide-brimmed hats. She thought she heard Danish being spoken. A couple walked by, speaking French. She got to the road, traversed it, and kept going, the Chinese man still up ahead, not looking back.

Two men walked by, one wearing a Lakers shirt and the other wearing a shirt that said, *They're Either Arguing, or They're Greek.* The taller one said something about loving Plaka, and then they were by her, and she missed the rest of their conversation.

Chinese man turned right up ahead. Sarah ran to catch up. Another narrow street was just ahead. She began to cross it when Vivian screamed at her.

Dive resonated in her head so loud that Vivian's shout caused an instant headache.

Before the echo of that word diminished, Sarah leaped off her right foot, thrust her hands out, and felt the wind of a car as it raced by, missing her by less than an inch.

She hit the marble sidewalk, rolled into the base of a building, and stopped. Pain flared through her shoulder wound. She winced, rolled onto her side, and got to her feet. People had stopped and were gathering around her, mumbling questions in Greek.

"You all right?" one woman asked.

Foreign languages were whispered all around her. She moved past them and looked down the street, but the car was gone.

They had been waiting for her. That car wasn't already coming down the road. It had been parked, engine quietly idling. They expected Sarah to run when she lost sight of the

Chinese man.

If Vivian hadn't shouted, Sarah wouldn't have made it. Clear and simple. She was in the middle of the road when that car was about to make contact. Under the wheels, run over by the front and back tires. That would've really pissed her off.

Barely making it pissed her off, too.

She pivoted to face the way the Chinese man had gone and started pushing through the gathered onlookers.

Up ahead, at a corner in the shopping lane, he turned. She ran, pumping her arms even though it felt like the wound near her shoulder blade had reopened.

At the next corner, she turned left and continued running. The Chinese man was her only connection, her only way to end this. If she lost him now, she had nothing.

A daunting realization swept over her that she was on a wild goose chase. Casper was gone. She was chasing a shadow. This was a setup. It was a waste of time. An ambush.

But if so, why wasn't Vivian stopping her? Questioning if she should be here or not was useless because she wouldn't be if Vivian had told her to stay at the hotel. And wasn't Vivian driving this bus at all times, even when it didn't appear to be the case?

So Sarah ran harder. One full minute later, she caught sight of her target shambling along up ahead, moving faster than when she was trailing him before. He must've thought she got hit by that car. He was probably on his way to getting paid. He thought his part in the ruse was over.

Not by a long shot.

She came up behind him. He hadn't looked back. In front of a large tourist shop, Sarah snatched the book from the

Chinese man's hand and retreated a few feet to examine it.

He grunted a protest and spun around to see who had ripped the book from him. When he saw her, he stepped backward like he would lose his balance, his face a mask of fear.

Sarah rifled through the book. Every page was empty.

This was a joke. There was nothing here for her. Aaron was missing. A Mexican cartel was probably torturing him somewhere in Buttfuck, Mexico, and she was chasing a Chinese man through the tourist shopping streets of Athens. Her anger flared, and what felt like spikes of flame heated her cheeks as she advanced on the retreating Chinese man.

"Who hired you?" she asked.

"Wǒ bù zhīdào," he said in Chinese, his voice nasally and whiney.

He said he doesn't know, Vivian whispered. Then Sarah's sister told her how to respond in Chinese.

Sarah repeated the words in her head as best she could.

The Chinese man's eyes widened when she spoke his language. He responded.

They didn't meet. Phone call.

Vivian asked another question, and Sarah repeated it, unsure of what Vivian was saying. It took all her willpower to not throw a punch, but if what he was saying was true, he was just another pawn in Wong's strategy.

He spoke again.

Meet at the ancient grave on the plateau, Vivian translated.

Then the Chinese man turned and ran as if Lucifer himself chased him through the streets of Athens.

The Acropolis? Where is it from here? Sarah asked.

Vivian directed her, and Sarah started off toward the Acropolis, wondering why Vivian hadn't made it easier. Why translate? Why not read his mind and offer what she learned to Sarah? Unless even Vivian had rules to follow. Maybe there were boundaries and limits. Was it possible Vivian could be in Sarah's head but not anyone else's?

That had to be it. Otherwise, Vivian could just tell her where Wong was and be done with it. Why not tell her where Aaron was and how they could get him out safely?

There had to be limits because if she knew Vivian's talent was all-knowing and she let Aaron be taken and hurt, Sarah would be done with her sister.

Connection or no connection, fucking with family, no matter who it was, cost plenty, and Sarah was all about consequences.

Even Vivian, if warranted, had to be accountable for her actions.

The dead could be hurt. If not, Sarah was confident she would find a way.

Chapter 44

IT TOOK HER OVER thirty minutes to walk back to Monastiraki, get through the center of the square, along a row of restaurants and cafés, and up through what appeared to be a sidewalk sale of some kind where people were selling homemade trinkets.

Finally, weakening under Greece's blazing and relentless summer sun, she approached the ticket booth to the Acropolis, waited behind a dozen tourists that had just been let out of a bus, and eventually bought a ticket.

Once through the main gate, she followed the crowd of tourists up sloping wide steps, stones probably placed there centuries ago, if not over a thousand years ago, and passed an ancient theater on her right. Under any other conditions, she would've loved to stop, listen to a tour guide or study a book in her hand to discover the secrets of a long-ago society, but the secrets of her current one still needed unearthing.

Somewhere ahead of her, with Vivian as her guide, a man waited to pay off the Chinese man for luring Sarah into Athens.

Vivian, why can you tell me when an accident will happen, but you can't read minds?

Sarah waited for an answer as she climbed large marble steps that led between columns that seemed to rise at least thirty feet in the air.

You know, Vivian started, *that we write our earth stories before we come to live them. I examine blueprints. I look into their books, their stories.*

Sarah nodded to herself. *That makes sense. But what about reading their minds?*

Free will. People can change their path at will. Some of that is in their blueprint as their actions change, but only One can understand the free will of earth-bound entities, and I'm not that One.

It all slid into place like pieces of a grand puzzle. It made sense for Sarah. All the car accidents, the gunfire, the running and chasing people. Even her sister couldn't see what people would do until they were doing it, until they *chose* that action. She didn't know about the car until it moved to hit Sarah. She didn't and couldn't know how the Chinese man was connected until Sarah asked him. She saw that Aaron was about to be kidnapped and gave Sarah a way to stop it, but that didn't work in time. In the end, Vivian was always there, but she wasn't God.

I wish ... Vivian's humor echoed through Sarah's head as she thought of the Prime Mover.

Sarah caught herself smiling as she made it through a columned entrance and stood staring at the Acropolis. The large city of Athens lay below, spread out like butter on toast, melting in the Greek sun that sweltered anything in its path at this time of year.

They're watching you ...

Sarah didn't spin around or duck down. She had no idea who was watching her or where they were. With one foot in front of the other, she walked toward the Acropolis like the rest of the tourists.

There are three of them ... keep walking until you've reached the other side of the Acropolis ...

Someone screamed from behind Sarah. She spun around, hands up in a defensive gesture, but it was an overweight tourist who had slipped on a particularly shiny, rounded piece of marble.

She turned back and kept moving forward.

Friendlies are coming ...

That washed over Sarah like a wave of comfort. A helicopter could be heard over the wind that had picked up. Two large American-looking helicopters headed her way. They appeared to be armed.

What the hell? Sarah thought.

Friendlies ...

She reached the other side of the Acropolis and stepped up to a small stone railing. There was at least a seventy-foot drop to the hard, rocky ground below on this side. She watched the helicopters approach, waiting for Vivian's next message.

Tourists nudged past her in the dozens. So many out on this hot day, hats on for protection from the sun, smelling of coconut and Coppertone.

Drop now! Vivian's voice charged through her

consciousness.

Sarah's knees gave way, and she body-checked the stone floor, a grunt escaping her lips as her shoulder blade protested the hit.

She caught a glimpse of clothes and flesh, but then it was gone.

A woman screamed, and someone else cried out. Sarah got up on her elbows, trying to see what had started the raucous. People moved to the edge and looked over.

"I saw the whole thing," a woman said. "He tried to push that girl." The speaker pointed at Sarah.

A surge of adrenaline rushed through her. She got up on her knees and looked over the edge. A man sprawled out on a rock below, a blood splat painting the rock beside his head.

A quick look behind her in case more attackers were coming was fruitless as the tourists crowded her trying to get a look over the edge.

"Okay, spread out," someone yelled.

Sarah got to her feet, ready to move away from the edge of the wall when a man in a Greek police uniform moved in beside her.

"Don't play a hero," he said as he jammed something into her side.

She looked down. A gun.

"Move."

She started walking.

"You're not Chinese. Where's Wong?"

"Shut up."

"Where's Wong?"

He jammed the gun in further. "Mouth closed."

Sarah screamed as loud as she could. She moved away

from the man in uniform and screamed again. He stared at her, stunned, the gun still held out in front of him.

"Mouth open, asshole," Sarah spat at him, knowing the scream for attention was risky. But if he were a hired gun in a Greek police uniform, or an actual Greek cop, chances were low he'd shoot her with this many witnesses. With security tight at the Acropolis, he wouldn't make it out of there if he shot her without probable cause. "I'm so sick and tired of this cat and mouse, cloak and dagger shit." The helicopters raced by overhead, nearly drowning out her voice. "Where's Wong? Or do you want to go over the edge, too?"

People spread out, moving away from them, forming a large circle that continued to widen by the second.

The fake cop looked down at his gun. "I'm the one with the weapon. Are you insane? I could've shot you. I still might."

"I want Wong. That's it. Go shoot someone else. I'm sick of this fucking game." Her anger spilled over. She felt her eyes bulging, spittle escaping her lips. Her patience had become a thin string that just snapped. "I've got to go find Aaron, and you're fucking around with a toy gun." She groaned so loudly it sounded like a warrior cry.

"It's not a toy. See, look." He fired once. The bullet ricocheted off the marble wall behind her, careened off something else, and disappeared. Sarah waited a brief moment to hear someone groan, but no one did.

"Not a toy," he said again.

"You jerk. You asshole." She moved toward him. "You fucking idiot. That ricochet could've hit somebody." She was in front of him now. "Kids are up here."

She punched the wrist that held the gun, grabbed the

barrel with her other hand at the same moment, and twisted the gun's aim skyward. She relieved him of it before it could fire. He stumbled backward in pain, holding his wrist.

"You broke my wrist," he said.

"Fucking amateur." She cocked the weapon and aimed it at him. "Who are you?" Sarah asked as a woman screamed behind her. "Who sent you?"

He backed up to the wall, shaking.

"Just don't shoot. It's loaded."

"As you just demonstrated. I know it's not a toy. Now, who hired you—"

A gun went off somewhere close. Sarah, along with the remaining tourists in the area, ducked out of reflex, but she didn't take her eyes off the fake cop.

A hole opened in his forehead, accompanied by a short burst of red. His eyes widened in surprise and shock. He leaned back with the momentum the bullet had started and slowly tumbled over the small ledge of the wall and disappeared.

More screaming. Someone shouted that the girl with the gun had shot the cop. But Sarah didn't pull the trigger. Whoever pulled the trigger was sick of his hired help screwing up.

Sarah tried to ascertain which way the bullet had come from. She reminded herself that James Wong was a human trafficker. When his girls stepped out of line, he killed defenseless, weak women. He had money and could find ways to hide, but he didn't have mercenaries on standby. Hence the men he hired weren't professional enough to do what was necessary.

"Wong!" Sarah shouted, turning in a slow circle. "Show

yourself."

People scattered away from her. A bullet could end her life at any second, but she had faith that her sister was on the job.

The helicopters were circling. One of them was coming in closer. Squinting in the sun, she looked up. American choppers, for sure.

What were they doing patrolling the skies of Athens? Another NATO arrangement? She doubted it. These men, if they were American, were Casper's men. If that were true, why weren't they with her on the ground, securing the Acropolis, so Wong didn't get away?

Someone broke through the crowd and stepped forward.

A professional-looking Chinese man in an expensive suit.

He met Sarah's gaze and started toward her.

Is this Wong, Vivian?

He kept walking as one of the helicopters hovered not fifty feet above and behind Sarah. The tourists had all but disappeared around the sides of the Acropolis. Only a couple of stragglers stuck around, hiding behind small outcroppings, cell phones up, no doubt filming for YouTube.

Our world has become a strange place.

She waited, the fake cop's gun held down at her side. When the Chinese man was ten feet away, Sarah yelled at him to stop, loud enough to be heard over the rotors above.

The man stopped.

"Name?" she shouted.

"James Wong."

"You're Wong? Yeah, right. Prove it."

"Amsterdam. Five women in chicken wire."

"You read that in the news."

"Amber. Sven. Warehouse. Madam's brothel. Toronto. Torture Club. ITA flight crashed. Believe me now?"

Sarah nodded. Another man approached from behind. A large man in an expensive black suit. Sarah waited until Wong noticed the man. Wong appeared to be unarmed.

"Where's the ledger?" Sarah asked.

Wong didn't answer. One chopper hovered. The other helicopter had disappeared over the ridge.

What the hell is going on?

Vivian didn't respond.

Do these choppers belong to Wong?

The man in the black suit made it to Wong. He whispered in his ear.

"Casper's dead," Wong said to Sarah.

So that's what happened to him this morning. Shit.

"I foiled your plan of ambushing me at the hotel," Wong said. It was easy to hear him as he shouted quite loud. "But it was close. Had I not seen you in the restaurant this morning —"

"I need that ledger," Sarah shouted.

"You'll never find it. It's safe on one of the Greek Islands until I return and pick it up. Too risky to continue to travel with it."

"Which island?"

"I would never tell you," he shouted.

This had gone from insane to absolutely maddening. It infuriated her to no end to realize that this saga may not come to a conclusion. All this shit for nothing. She needed the payoff. Maybe she would shoot him and torture the location out of him. He killed Casper, after all. That had to come with some kind of penalty.

The helicopter moved position but stayed close behind her.

What the hell are they doing?

She took two quick strides toward Wong. As she did, the man in the expensive suit—it had to be hot in that thing—pulled out a silenced handgun. But Sarah was quicker. Her gun was up and firing before the large man could aim in her direction. Three bullets entered the man's chest, with one nicking his neck. Blood spurted out as he fell soundlessly beside Wong, the helicopter blanketing all sounds but gunfire and shouting.

When she aimed at Wong, he opened his Adidas jacket.

Strapped to his chest were cylindrical canisters, all linked to each other with tiny wires that shined red and blue in the blazing sunlight.

That stopped Sarah. She lowered her weapon.

"Now we both die, Sarah." Wong was smiling. "It's over for me. Too much went wrong, and too many people are after me now. I could never continue my business as it was. Authorities in almost a dozen countries want me for murder. But they're not the ones I'm afraid of."

"Who are you afraid of?" Sarah asked, staring at the units wrapped around his chest. There had to be at least twenty of them. That was probably enough to damage the Greek monument behind him. If she survived this moment, she would never be allowed back in Greece *if* they let her leave in the first place.

"I'm afraid of the Enzo Cartel."

Sarah met Wong's eyes, the bomb momentarily forgotten.

"What about the cartel?" she asked. "The one near Tijuana? The money-laundering bastards who have Aaron?"

"See, even you know too much of my business."

"Push the button," Sarah said. "Or put your hands up and get on your knees." She raised the gun, closed one eye, and focused the other on aiming at his throat. "I will shoot you in the throat. I will sever your spine. Hands up. Now!"

As Wong reached for something in his pocket and Sarah's finger applied pressure on the trigger, something behind Wong caught her eye.

Then she aimed the gun skyward and said, "Hey, I'm bluffing."

The other helicopter, which had been out of sight for several minutes, must've landed because a dozen men in tactical gear had crept up behind Wong and were only fifteen feet away. The helicopter behind her had masked any sounds they might have made on their approach.

But Wong now had a small black device in his hand.

"I read about you, Sarah." He held the device higher like he wanted to show it to her.

"Not you, too. Why's everyone I'm supposed to be fighting reading my stories? If you're an enemy, don't read my memoirs." She needed to keep him talking. "That's an unfair advantage."

"I read that you never bluff, Sarah." He grinned a maniacal and twisted smile. "I don't either."

He adjusted something on the black thing in his hand.

Possibly, with only seconds to live, Sarah looked past Wong's shoulder and gestured for the men in combat gear to hurry up.

Wong caught the movement and looked back at her. "I won't fall for that," he said. "You can't make me turn around. Oldest trick in the book. I remember you did that in one of your books to another character. Not me."

The tactical team was close. The leader raised his machine gun and took aim at Wong's hands.

"Wait!" Sarah shouted. She dropped her weapon on the ground. "Any last words, Wong."

He shook his head. "Sadly, no."

As she saw his thumb lower to depress something on the black thing in his hand, the machine gun rattled. Before her eyes, his hands were severed clean off. The black thing tumbled to the ground, useless.

Wong shuddered with the burst of gunfire and turned toward it, even as his wrists—jaggedly cut open, sheets of skin flapping in the wind—shot blood out in a heartbeat sequence. The men approached with speed now, subduing their suspect and tossing him onto his back. As far as Sarah could see, the only bombs he had were strapped to his chest.

Blood poured out of Wong's wounded hands as the men worked on removing the bombs. Sarah advanced. If Wong was going to die here, she needed to know which Greek Island the ledger was hidden on.

She tried to push her way in, but two armed men held her back.

"Get over to the helicopter. Go. We got this."

"No. I need to find out where he hid the black book."

She caught a glimpse of Wong's blanched face, his eyes wide and staring skyward. Then the vest of bombs was off him.

Could he die that fast from losing his hands?

Before they turned her away a second time, she saw the cause of death. It wasn't just his hands that had been shot. A bullet had entered the back of his neck. Blood filled the dirt and marble under Wong's hair. He was gone. She had been cheated out. No black book. All this way and no black book.

The defeat was as if she'd been shot.

"To the chopper, Sarah," one of the men yelled at her.

Resolve gone, fight diminished, Sarah tried to keep her shoulders back as she walked to the chopper. It had landed in an open area on the other side of the Acropolis.

What now? Would Vivian tell her where the ledger was? Would there be a resolution? Or was this all a waste of time?

Casper was dead. How could Wong get the jump on someone like Casper? Or better yet, if Casper was so good, how did he let Wong get to him? That kind of mistake costs lives.

The adrenaline began to fade. Her legs weakened on the way to the chopper. Being up here without the tourists who had virtually covered the area not fifteen minutes ago felt strange.

She got to the chopper's open door and stopped at the sight of a familiar face.

"What the fuck are you doing here?" she asked over the pounding of the rotors overhead.

"I thought you'd be glad to see me," Casper replied.

"Wong said you were killed."

Casper raised his shirt and pointed at bruising about the chest area. "They tried. Succeeded in cracking some ribs and bruising the hell out of my chest. Knowing we were about to go pick up Wong, I had just put on my Kevlar. The idiot who shot me couldn't tell I was wearing it."

They stared at each other for a few moments.

"This is all fucked up," Sarah said. "You know that, don't you?"

He nodded, then winced and raised a hand to his chest.

"No ledger," she said.

"Nafplio," Casper said.

"Nafplio? I know that name."

"It's where Palamidi is. Where Aaron got shot and almost died. Where Parkman followed Oliver Payne a while back."

"You memorized my books, or what?"

"Something like that."

"Why Nafplio?"

"While we were still in Amsterdam, Wong landed in Athens and went straight to Nafplio. He stayed one night, returned to Athens, and was booked in a room at our hotel. We were set up to deal with him near the airport, but he saw us—"

"I get all that. Just tell me about Nafplio."

"I have a witness that says he arrived with a briefcase and left the city empty-handed. The ledger's in Nafplio."

Sarah shook her head. "Unless he handed it off to someone, he told me it was on a Greek Island. Nafplio's not an island."

"All we have is Nafplio as the last known location where Wong was seen with the ledger. Coming or not?"

Sarah hesitated at the helicopter's open door, the rotors' noise already maddening. She looked over her shoulder at the Acropolis and whispered a question to Vivian.

Yes ... Vivian said. *Go with him* ...

Sarah climbed inside, took a seat, and smacked Casper in the arm. He squealed as the pain from his bruised chest flared.

"Don't fucking get shot again, or I'll shoot you," Sarah shouted at him. "Be more professional and stop dying on me.

Fuck, you are one frustrating ghost. Every time I turn around, you're disappearing on me. No more."

The helicopter lifted off, and Athens got smaller below them.

"I'll try not to disappear again. But working with you has been a real pain in the ass."

"If I were you, I would hate to work with me. In fact, I would quit. Someone like me can't be worked with. I'm just happy *I'm* me because I can tolerate myself. If I weren't me, I'd be fucked. And then I'd fuck me up."

Casper frowned. "What was that?"

"Nothing."

The chopper banked left and headed out over the Aegean Sea en route to Nafplio, Greece.

Chapter 45

THE PILOT EXPERTLY LANDED the helicopter in an empty parking lot by Nafplio's harbor. Seeing the ancient prison Palamidi from the air had been bittersweet. The stone prison, built on the side of a mountain, was astounding. But it was the location of Aaron's near-death experience a few years ago when he met up with his sister's murderer. If it weren't for Aaron's three teachers at the dojo, Aaron would be dead right now, and Sarah would never have met him.

Or he could be dead right now because he had met me.

Thoughts of Aaron made her shiver even though the sun baked the earth under her feet. He would be okay. He would make it. Otherwise, Vivian would've had Sarah do something about it earlier.

Right, Sis?

No response.

Sarah followed Casper into a large parking area nestled

by the water, a row of restaurants on the other side. Casper said the helicopter's pilot would shut down and wait for their return. Casper felt this search for the ledger would be easy. No problem. Wong dropped the black book off on his journey to Nafplio, and they were supposed to locate it within hours. Even though she got a confession out of Wong—one she believed was truthful because he was taunting her—that it was on an island.

"Where are we headed?" she asked. "Do you have a destination in mind?"

Casper glanced sidelong at her. "Yes, I do. We're going to start at his hotel. Then work our way to the wharf where my informant states he rented a boat."

"Fine. I'll follow. But take notes. A boat means he went to an island. This leads me to believe the ledger's on an island, just as Wong said."

Nafplio was a gorgeous city. It made her yearn for a time when she could experience it as a tourist … with Aaron.

Thoughts of Aaron intruded. Wasting time like this drove her nuts. Every minute they wandered around was another minute further from freeing her man.

They walked by an Italian restaurant called Scuola. Sarah knew that meant *school* in Italian. The restaurant's décor, even the tables outside on the patio, were all very Italian looking. They passed The Trendy Grill, where gyros were advertised for just over two euros.

A vacation was definitely needed. Aaron was needed.

"Wong knew he wouldn't leave the Acropolis alive," Sarah said.

Casper looked over his shoulder at her. "Your point?"

"He told me the ledger was on one of the Greek Islands

and that I would never find it."

"He must've lied. He left it here somewhere."

"How can you be so sure?"

Casper slowed his pace and stopped outside a post office. "I told you we monitored his travel to Nafplio and back."

Sarah nodded. "He came here with it and left without it. I know. That's what you said. But this isn't an island."

"I didn't tell you that the limo driver he hired to bring him here is an old, retired friend. He's my informant."

"Wong hired a limo?"

"Not one of the stretch kind. He had a BMW SUV and a driver. You can get that sort of thing in any major city."

"Right. Okay. So what did this old friend say?"

Casper started away. "Keep walking. I don't want to waste time."

Sarah caught up to him after crossing a street. They started down a shopping lane, like a walking street, that appeared to be leading them into old town. Again, it reminded her of Italy with the small shops, elegant little balconies one floor above, with everything draped in bougainvillea. The view of this older part of Nafplio almost brought tears to her eyes. Tourists wandered everywhere, sipping beverages, licking gelato, and laughing, their cares forgotten. It was so foreign to what Sarah was used to in her life that she felt like an outsider, almost like she didn't belong there like she stood out for all the wrong reasons.

"My friend told us the hotel Wong stayed in while in Nafplio. That's how we knew Wong would end up at the Sofitel outside the Athens airport."

"What about the ledger?"

They entered Nafplio's main square. Children kicked a

ball around while parents looked on with admiring eyes. Restaurants and cafés were jammed, and almost every seat was taken as the summer sun promised life and hope for this economically torn country.

"The driver confirmed Wong had a book with him, something he browsed, flipping pages in the back seat, on the ride to Nafplio. He didn't get a good look at it but thought it was a binder of some kind. When he drove Wong back to Athens, he had nothing on his person. Just Wong, no luggage."

They exited the main square on the other side and started up a narrow cobblestone street. It wasn't where they were going that bothered Sarah anymore or the fact that she worried this was a waste of time. What bothered her now was that someone was following them.

"Do you have someone shadowing us?"

"No. Just you and me and the pilot. Wong's dead. It's over. Don't get paranoid, Sarah. The only danger now is in Mexico, and we're heading there next."

"Not in that helicopter, I hope," she said as a joke.

He blew air out through his lips. "Of course not. The Athens airport. Transfer in Rome, then land in Los Angeles."

"Why Los Angeles?"

"We're driving over the border under a cloak of secrecy. It's being set up and arranged right now while we are here in Nafplio."

They turned a corner, and Sarah stopped. Casper carried on two more steps until he noticed. She held up a hand for quiet. He waited. She counted to five and then jumped back around the corner.

The street was empty.

"Anyone?" Casper asked, doubt in his voice.

Sarah shook her head. The feeling of being watched was almost like an innate skill, one she just felt and knew to be true. But the evidence was to the contrary, which couldn't be disputed. If she was right, and someone was trailing them, then that someone was an expert.

She turned and jogged to catch up to Casper, who had already started walking again.

They came up on a stunning hotel on their left, the walls constructed of fieldstone. It was built up on a hill overlooking the Aegean Sea. To her right, along the pier, restaurants lined the walkway. Almost every seat was taken. She concluded that Nafplio had to be one of the most popular cities for tourists.

"This is where Wong stayed the night," Casper said. He stopped and looked around the area. "I'll go in and talk to the clerk at the counter. Hopefully, it's the same clerk that checked Wong in. Give me a minute."

Sarah headed to the railing and stared out over the sea. A light breeze had picked up at this level, cooling her skin. Out on the water, someone had built a castle. The plot of land it sat on was the exact size of the castle's base. Whoever constructed the stone building with turrets used every square inch.

She watched tourists, stared at the waves rolling in softly, and wondered what would happen to her, to Aaron. How could she deal with a cartel and walk away with their lives intact? Mexican cartels were known for their brutality. Thinking about the coming fight stirred acid in her stomach. Would she be up for it when the time came?

The only saving grace was she had the support of the

American government in the form of Casper and his powerful influence.

She would do anything to get Aaron back. Not following through wasn't an option. Burning the cartel to the ground and anyone stupid enough to get in her way was all she had left if she lost Aaron. She had never really loved anyone like Aaron before. Without realizing it, Aaron had found a home in her heart more than she knew. When he left California while Sarah was dealing with that maniac Cole Lincoln, it had hurt her. Heading to Toronto to meet up with him and discuss things had been all she could think about. But Vivian had needed her to do a little job that involved shooting and killing a girl in front of the Toronto police.

So much for meeting Aaron, having dinner, and chatting a little.

All that led to this. And here she was in Greece, still looking for a black book. This was supposed to end here. Get the book, fly back, and then see where things went from there with Aaron. But now he had been kidnapped because of her actions.

The plot thickens ...

"Sarah?" Casper said from behind her.

She jumped. "What?" she said without turning around. She placed both hands on the railing and squeezed.

"The clerk was the same one who checked Wong in but had nothing for me. He barely remembers Wong and doesn't speak very good English."

"So, where's the ledger?" Sarah asked, taunting him, knowing he was no closer to solving the mystery of its location. By now, the black book could be anywhere in the world. Unless they solved this mystery today, it would remain unsolved as far as she was concerned. With or without Casper, Sarah had a cartel near Tijuana she had to make a house call on.

"I have no idea, Sarah."

She turned to look at him. His voice was low like he regretted having to admit defeat. Casper squinted into the sun, shaded his eyes with his hand, and then looked back at the hotel.

"What now?" she asked. "Any ideas?"

"The pier. Try to locate the boat he rented. Maybe we can discover where he went."

Something clicked into place. "Boat?" she whispered. "Rented?" Casper had mentioned that before entering the hotel to talk to the clerk. She turned back and stared out over the sea. The castle appeared to float on the water. It sat an easy five hundred yards from Nafplio's shore.

"Come on," Sarah urged. "I think I found the Greek Island Wong said he put the ledger on."

"What?" Casper called behind her.

Sarah ran along the wall until she found stone steps leading down to the pier. She bounded down two at a time, Casper close on her tail.

"Sarah?" he called. "Wait."

But she kept running, dodging people, passing a line of restaurants, until she made it to the first boat moored to the concrete pier that had someone on it.

"Excuse me," she said, trying to catch her breath. "Can you take me to that little castle out there?" She pointed.

The man had been lounging on a loveseat-sized cushion on the back of a small yacht. He turned and looked at the castle, then back at Sarah.

"You mean Bourtzi," he said in Greek. Vivian was so fast at translation that Sarah caught it within seconds of the man finishing his sentence.

"Naí," she said, repeating Vivian's whisper of how to say *yes* in Greek.

Casper had caught up and stood wide-eyed beside her as she spoke Greek to the man.

"There's a water taxi at the end," he said in Greek and pointed. "Four euros, and they'll take you over. They're taking tourists all day."

"Efcharistó polý," Sarah replied.

She started toward the water taxi at the end of the concrete pier, dodging slow-moving tourists the entire way.

Casper caught up with her. "Slow down."

"Can't."

"How did you do that?"

"Do what?"

"You speak fluent Greek?"

"No."

"Then what language was that?"

"Greek."

"What?"

Sarah kept walking. Casper kept up.

"That was Vivian?" he asked.

"Yes."

"She translates for you and tells you what to say?" he asked, his voice rising to falsetto.

"That's about it. Chinese too." She looked at him. "I'm surprised as shit as well."

"You don't look surprised."

"Didn't know I could do it until today."

"What? I mean, *what*?" Now his voice was squeaky. "You've got to be kidding. That kind of talent would be extremely useful in—"

"Casper," she shouted. People around them turned to see what was going on as they passed. "I'm not a guinea pig. No governments. No tests. If Vivian goes silent, I'm not useful to anyone but Aaron. We work together but do not mistake who I am and what I represent. I'm only there for Aaron, and if this cartel dies in the process, so be it." They were almost at the water taxi. From what Sarah could see, it appeared there were two water taxis. "Our agendas are different. We just happen to be on the same train speeding down the same track that might be a dead end."

"There's no dead end. Aaron's alive. They need proof of life to get to you."

The truth in that statement sent a wave of relief and a shiver down her back.

People were getting on the boat. Sarah counted a family of four and two teenagers talking to an older woman, probably their mother. Seven people. Sarah and Casper made nine. The boat's operator stepped off the boat and asked for eight euros for the two of them.

Sarah got on the boat first and sat beside the father of the small family. Casper sat on the other side, facing her. Probably a routine response for him. A better way to watch her back and she could watch his.

After a two-minute wait, with no other tourists approaching the boat, the operator unhooked the ropes and started away from the pier.

"Beautiful day, eh?" the man beside her said in English.

Sarah turned to look at him, then jerked back, moving a

few inches away. "I've seen you before." She thought about where, then it hit her. "In Italy. I met you on a train."

The man nodded, a wide, teeth-revealing grin on his face. "That's right. You remember well. I live here now, in Nafplio. I'm traveling with my daughters, Bethany and Odette." He pointed at each girl as he said their names. They nodded at Sarah, wide smiles on their faces.

Why is this family so bloody happy?

"Jonas something, right?" Sarah said, remembering that he'd given her a business card when they last met.

He nodded. "Good memory."

Sarah caught a glimpse of Casper. The question of who these people were was written all over his face. Sarah ignored Casper.

"Coincidence?" Sarah asked. "Or are you following me?"

"I'm following you," Jonas said in a deep voice, then burst out laughing. "Of course not. Do you think I have time to follow people around the globe? I'm busy traveling and killing people."

Sarah started again. She leaned in closer. "Killing people? What are you talking about?"

"I'm a writer. I try to find inventive ways to murder people and research locations for scenes worldwide. You know, dead body disposal and things like that."

The island was approaching, and the operator was already revving the engine lower.

"Something strange is going on here," Sarah mumbled. "I don't like this."

"What's not to like? It's a beautiful day. You're in tropical Greece. Have an ice cream. Drink a cold beverage.

Read a book. Nap. Do what humans of leisure do. Relax—Sarah, you have to relax. You'll live longer."

Muscles in her face tightened. "Is that a threat?"

Jonas leaned away from her, his expression one of fake shock. Then he shoved his face close and said, "A threat? That's hilarious. Who writes your material? A threat. Sarah, you're the last person in the world I'd threaten."

The boat bumped the dock. They began tying the ropes up when the operator announced that the boat would take them back in thirty minutes.

Jonas's family got up and exited the boat. Sarah followed with Casper close behind.

"Who was that?" Casper whispered.

"Someone I bumped into in Italy. Pure coincidence."

"Really? Coincidence or synchronicity?"

"What?" She looked sideways at him as if he was crazy.

"Nothing. Just something I was reading lately that Carl Jung said."

Jonas's family had headed toward the center of the castle. "Come on, Casper. Let's find that book and get to Athens. The chopper is waiting."

Something about meeting Jonas and his family bothered her. Maybe it was something Darwin Kostas had said when she told him about Jonas.

Jonas Saul.

Darwin had said something about suspecting that everything he had gone through was Jonas's fault somehow. But that didn't make sense.

Was he following her? Why didn't Jonas have the girls with him in Italy? And now, suddenly, he shows up with two daughters, the youngest at least fifteen or sixteen. What was going on?

She quickened her pace and rounded the corner where the Saul family had gone, but no one was there.

"Casper, find that family for me. I want to talk to the father again."

Casper moved away and ascended a set of stone stairs to her right.

Alone, she turned in a full circle, waiting for Vivian's response. Nothing came.

To her left was what looked like an old restaurant. Maybe the economic crisis aided its demise. Or maybe it closed down a long time ago.

She walked over to its door and tried the handle. Locked. She tried to peek through the windows that were covered in newspaper, but that proved difficult. She dropped to the bottom part of the window. Sunlight filtered through on the opposite side of the room behind the glass. There was enough light to see the dirty floor covered with papers strewn about. But what caught her eye was the footprints that had waded through the dust, leaving tracks toward the back. Those prints were recent. Nothing else appeared disturbed.

She tried the door again, firmer this time. Using her shoulder, she tried to bump it open. Nothing.

The glass would have to be broken. There was no other way. A quick entrance and exit and then off the island with the ledger, provided it was in there.

Someone was coming down the stairs behind her. She turned around to see Casper.

"I couldn't find them. I even asked those two teens with their mother, but no one has seen the family you were talking to on the boat."

"It doesn't matter now. I think the ledger's in here."

"What makes you think that?"

"Footprints in the dust are recent. Look." She pointed at the small hole in the newsprint, and Casper bent down to look.

"You're right." He tried the door, putting his shoulder into it.

"The glass," Sarah said. "Break the glass."

Casper pulled his gun, flipped it around, and hit the glass with the butt end. It broke and made a huge racket as it clattered to the floor. Sarah hopped over the sill, careful to not get cut, and disappeared inside.

"I'll wait out here," Casper said behind her.

Old furniture was piled up along one wall. Tables lay on their sides, and chairs were piled one on the other. Two grime-covered carpets were rolled up and shoved into a corner. Sarah followed the footsteps toward the back of the restaurant, wondering how Wong got in there if those were his footprints. If he didn't break the glass, he must've gotten the key from the owner or picked the lock.

The prints led her into what was once the kitchen of the small restaurant. Most of the cupboards were open and empty, with two broken off. A large walk-in freezer sat to the side, the door open wide. The only door that remained closed was the oven.

Gingerly, Sarah touched the oven's door handle and figured she would count to three and yank it open. This had to be the place. Could the oven's door be rigged to blow? Wong was into explosives, after all.

"Sarah!" Casper shouted.

She jumped again and let go of the oven door. "What!"

she yelled back.

"Come quickly."

Moving away from the oven, she left the kitchen and retraced her steps to the broken glass window.

"Come on out," he said. "You're going to love this."

Sarah eased out of the restaurant and turned to face him. Casper had a large black book in his hands.

"Is that what I think it is?" Sarah asked.

"It is."

"Since my nerves are frayed, and my patience has dried up—think Sahara Desert dry—would you like to tell me where you got that?"

"The guy you talked to on the boat over here. He gave it to me."

"Jonas?"

Casper nodded like he had just told her a dirty joke, his grin devilish. "Apparently, they had walked outside the castle wall and discovered a small hole in the stones, sheltered from the sea and wind. When Jonas took a picture with his flash to capture whatever was inside the hole, he saw this sitting in there. He grabbed it and was heading toward the boat when he passed me standing there. I asked him where he'd found it, and after a short conversation, I relieved him of James Wong's black book. We're golden. We can go and prosecute nearly a hundred people because of this gem."

"This is unbelievable. Too easy." Sarah started back toward the boat. "I want to talk to Jonas. No, I *need* to talk to him."

Casper caught up with her. "You can't. Another boat came in and took his family off the island."

She stopped walking and faced Casper. "So, he's gone?"

Casper nodded.

They boarded the boat without another word. She shoved thoughts of Jonas away and focused on Aaron. Miraculously they had the ledger. It was over. She could go and get Aaron.

The boat started back for shore. Sarah remained silent on the way back. Once off the boat and back on the pier, she recalled that she hadn't eaten since breakfast.

"We need to grab something before we get on the chopper. I'm famished."

"Okay, we'll grab a gyro and walk with it. A plane is already waiting at the Athens airport. You can sleep on the way to L.A. It's a little over sixteen hours of total flight time."

"Great," she said sarcastically.

They found a small restaurant that served gyros, and Casper reluctantly agreed to sit and eat instead of walking back to the chopper.

"It'll only take us five minutes to have a meal," Sarah said. "Sit down and eat and shut up. We've got the ledger. It's over."

"Yeah, thanks to your friend."

"Jonas is not a friend. In fact, I think he's responsible for something. I just don't know what, though."

"You don't make much sense sometimes."

"Good."

They ate, Sarah devouring hers before Casper finished.

"I have to use the boy's room before we go to the chopper," Casper said. "Wait here."

Sarah leaned back in her chair and looked around. She watched the people come and go. The carefree vacationers were having a good time. They felt safe and comfortable.

They laughed and appeared to be enjoying life. Would she ever have this? Could it be possible with who she had become?

"Excuse me," a man said beside her.

She turned to look up at him, but the sun blocked her vision. She brought a hand up to ward off the sun. With one eye open, she caught a glimpse of his face. A dark-skinned, Spanish-looking man held a small white box in his hand.

"This is a gift from a common friend," he said in a Spanish accent.

A gift? That made her wary.

"What friend?" she asked.

"When you open it, you'll understand."

The man set the box down on her table and walked away. *That was weird.*

She undid the green string and slowly opened the top. Inside, there was a small envelope. She picked it up and looked back at the figure of the man retreating toward the parking lot. Then she opened the envelope.

It was an invitation card. It told her to join them at their horse ranch for a race one week from then to see who lives or dies. Miss the race at her own peril.

That was odd. What ranch? Where?

She saw the man still walking away. He hadn't looked back once.

She flipped the card over and saw Tijuana, Mexico, written in a dark red substance like melted wax. It reminded her of those old feather pens dipped in ink.

Could it be blood?

Tijuana, Mexico? The Enzo Cartel? Spanish accent? She looked sideways. The man was far away, but she could still see him meandering through the parking lot. He wasn't Spanish. He had to be Mexican.

Inside the box, below where the card had sat, was another smaller box. She flipped the top off it just as Casper stepped up beside her.

Then she screamed. She cried out and almost lost her balance. Her eyes welled up in tears, and she struggled to stay on her feet.

Inside the smaller box was an index finger. One she knew all too well. They had cut off Aaron's finger and found her in Greece to deliver a message. There was only one response to this horror. The cartel would die for this. All of them. Every last one.

Casper was shouting something beside her. She spun him around, yanked his weapon out of its holster, and ran toward the parking lot, her eyes blurring with tears.

Casper shouted behind her again, but she knew he could never keep up with cracked ribs and a severely bruised chest.

Sarah ran with purpose. She ran, fueled with anger. The rush of wind dried her eyes. Every last cartel member would pay for this. Aaron's hands were his career, his karate. All this because she stopped their laundering connection. It was her fault. She had to make things right. And she would, starting with this Mexican.

"Sarah!" Casper yelled behind her. "Don't do it!"

She ran harder. The Mexican had disappeared from sight. He had to have gotten into a vehicle. But which one?

She was closer now. Close enough to see the cars leaving the large lot. An Audi pulled out. A female driver. A Fiat came next. Then she was at the entrance to the parking lot, running along the line of half a dozen vehicles waiting to move out into traffic.

He wasn't in any of the cars.

"Dammit!" she shouted.

She looked around, scanning cars close to her. Nothing. Casper was catching up, lumbering along.

Then she saw the Mexican.

He had traversed the parking lot but not to get in a car. He was still walking away, on the far end of the lot.

She started running again. Casper shouted behind her to stop.

In less than a minute, she was twenty feet behind the Mexican before he turned around, a gun in his hand.

Between breaths, she said, "Tell me who sent you."

"Go to Tijuana," the man said. "They will know you're there. Someone will come to pick you up."

"How do I know Aaron's alive?"

"You have my word. That was only one piece of him. The other piece is waiting for you in Tijuana. Trust me."

"I don't trust anyone."

The Mexican pulled a cell phone from his pocket. "They told me you would come after me. Here," he tossed the phone. She caught it. "There's a video of Aaron on that. Taken an hour ago. They texted it to me."

Sarah turned the video on from iMessage. It was Aaron saying he was okay. They had fed him and offered water. He raised his bandaged hand to the camera, then forced a smile. Before the video ended, he did a subtle shake of his head, and his eyes clouded over. Then it stopped.

He was warning her to stay away. In that brief second, Aaron told her to leave him there, to leave him to die. She didn't just feel it. She knew it.

But she would never leave him there.

Casper caught up and stayed behind Sarah, panting and wheezing.

"I've done what I was supposed to do," the Mexican said. "I've delivered the message. Now I must return safely, so Aaron stays safe. If I don't return safely, you will receive one hundred more packages like that one, piece by piece."

"Send a message back to them in Mexico," Sarah said.

The Mexican lowered his weapon, then slipped it in his pants at the back.

"What is it?" he asked.

"This."

Sarah shot him in the forehead without hesitation. He stumbled backward, tried to catch himself, then fell. Sarah walked up to his fallen body. His eyes roved around, trying to see her. She shot him three more times in the chest.

"Nobody takes my family and dismembers them without consequences." She kicked the man's dead body. "I'll burn the cartel to the ground before I'm through. Pablo Escobar ain't got shit on me. Little Mexicans will hear horror stories about the white American girl who came to Mexico and destroyed the drug business single-handedly. You hear me," she shouted. "No one fucks with my family." She was nearing hysteria and felt good about the loss of control. The wonton abandonment released the pressure racing between her temples.

Casper's hands gently touched her arms. He leaned in close as her breath seethed in and out between her teeth.

"We have to go," Casper whispered. "People are coming."

He pushed a little, but she resisted.

"We need to leave now, Sarah." His voice was firmer. "Give me my gun back."

The spell broke. She blinked. A moment later, she handed Casper his weapon.

"Come on. The chopper's just over there."

Casper got on his cell phone and texted something. Sarah started walking in a daze.

The chopper's rotors began turning.

"We have to move faster if we're going to make it out of Greece. The police are already coming. They heard the shots."

Sarah's pace picked up. Getting out of Greece meant going to Mexico.

She started running. Mexico. Where she could kill more Mexicans.

Enzo Cartel Mexicans.

They made it to the helicopter as three small Greek police cruisers raced toward them.

Less than ten seconds later, the pilot lifted the machine off the ground and out over the sea.

Sarah closed her eyes. She wanted to cry. She wanted to scream. Would it ever end? Would she ever catch a break?

"You know, he was probably right," Casper said.

"Fuck you."

"Killing him sends a wrong message."

"They want me. Aaron won't die until I get there. Too risky for them. If Aaron's dead, I don't have to come. Aaron will be fine."

"Still, wrong message to send."

"Fuck you still stands."

"Clearly, you're not interested in talking to me. And you

seem quite angry."

Sarah kept her eyes closed. The gyro wasn't sitting well in her stomach anymore. Maybe she shouldn't have eaten.

Mexico …

The tears couldn't be held back. The helicopter shook with the winds coming off the Aegean as they raced back to Athens and, ultimately, Mexico, where a fight was brewing for Sarah. A fight she was ready for.

The Enzo Cartel had taken family. Her family. This fight was personal.

She tightened her fists as she wept.

The cartel had no idea who was coming for them.

None whatsoever.

She kept her eyes closed and thought of murder.

Dead bodies enveloped her thoughts when she envisioned *The Cartel.*

The Cartel …

Afterword

Dear Reader,

With *The Abandoned*, I wanted to explore Sarah's life more deeply. I wanted to reach inside and see what she felt about Aaron. We saw more of Aaron's feelings in *The Unlucky*, and now it was time for Sarah to open up. I decided to do that by having him in peril *because* of her.

I asked myself, what would happen if Sarah ran to help others in need when the people who needed her the most were her own people, her family? How would she feel if she discovered that Aaron's kidnapping and subsequent torture were laid at her doorstep?

Part of my madness here is that I want to display another side of Sarah. A maniacal, insane, and brutal Sarah is coming to *The Cartel*, book fifteen, one that will stop at nothing to free Aaron. The ride in the next book will be one of the hardest runs for Sarah. I'm worried at times, she might not be able to endure it and still maintain a level of kindness, her heart intact.

We'll have to see …

As with most—not all—Sarah Roberts novels, there's a beginning and an end. The bad guys get taken care of, and all ends well. But in my head, Sarah's life continues beyond the limits of the page. I even have people ask me, "What would Sarah do in this instance?" and, "How would Sarah feel about this?"

I felt it important in this novel to have a subplot—Aaron's story—to begin in this novel and come to completion in the next as it would happen in reality. Several authors do this—Jo Nesbø, Mo Hayder—and I've often wanted to but hesitated until now.

As Sarah's life isn't bound to the pages of a book's formula, things can happen behind the scenes that set in motion the next book or even the next few books. Yet at the same time, *The Abandoned*'s bad guy, James Wong, and the overall story arc doesn't continue on to other books, like when Sarah was hunting Armond Stuart in *The Warning* and didn't catch up with him until the end of *The Crypt*.

So there you have it. Aaron is in trouble, and Sarah's on her way. *The Cartel* will be explosive and extremely dangerous and should be out by September 2015.

***

I've been traveling through Europe again this year. We're currently in Greece, will be in Denmark for June, and back in Greece for the summer. Because of this, I like to add locations I enjoy visiting during my tours. Having Sarah come to Amsterdam and walk the canals as I did was fantastic for me as a writer. I loved Amsterdam as well!

To have her land at the Athens airport and stay a night in the Sofitel, where I stayed several times, works for the story and for me. It's like revisiting places I've been to and bringing deeper meaning to the phrase, *write what you know.* I am *literally* writing what I know.

The town in Greece I currently live near is called Nafplio. It was Greece's first capital before Athens took the title. If you've read my other novels, you would have heard of Nafplio from *The Specter* and *Killing Sarah*. I love this town and have returned often because of the wonderful people and food (I came back for another year during the pandemic from 2019-2020, and now I live in Athens, Greece). As mentioned in the novel, Scuola is one of my favorite Italian restaurants in Nafplio. I had Sarah walk through the old town—designed by the Italians—and into the square. I've never stayed in the hotel where Wong stayed— it's one of the most expensive hotels in Nafplio—but I figured Wong would've chosen that one, so that's why it's in the story. Besides, it's near the water, and I needed Sarah to see the island Castle of Bourtzi.

I took the water taxi over to Bourtzi, toured the castle, and routinely found holes in the wall similar to the one where "Jonas Saul" located the ledger.

This brings me to my next point: I have added myself to the novel this time, as well as my daughters. I've done this once before in *The Rogue*, but I felt I needed to do it this time for several reasons.

The first reason is the same one I offered in *The Rogue*:

I've always loved when other authors did this, such as Alfred Hitchcock and Clive Cussler. When writing *The Rogue*, I was in Italy touring the countryside by train, so it made sense to have Sarah bump into me on the train. While writing *The Abandoned*, I'm touring Greece by boat and living in Nafplio, so again, it was natural to assume my character—Sarah Roberts—would bump into me.

Lastly, I added my daughters as a tribute. They often shoot out questions and ideas for Sarah. What if Sarah did this? What would Sarah think of that? When Odette said, "Sarah hadn't been in a plane crash situation yet, and if she was, how would she go about saving people?" I added that to the beginning of this novel. So, a big thank you goes out to Odette, my daughter, for adding a plot point to this novel.

Another thank you goes out to Bethany, my oldest daughter, for the ideas she has added to the upcoming Sarah Roberts Series. We sat down and discussed a scene for the forthcoming pregnant Sarah story. And a dynamic scene for Sarah's baby once she's born. But I'm getting away with myself here as that's not until *Sarah's Return*, book twenty-one, further down the line.

I enjoyed my stay in Nafplio. Whether you want to tour the ancient theater Epidaurus, built around the sixth century B.C., or visit Agamemnon's Tomb, built around 1500 B.C., or even tour Argos, a city that has been continuously inhabited for the past 7,000 years—the longest in European history—the area is rife with history and museums.

And finally, I need to send out a special thank you to Conner Quinton and his mother, Sara Quinton. I added them to the final scenes of the plane crash. Sara is a reader of the Sarah Roberts Series and allowed me to use her and her son's names. Conner is fourteen and lost his father, a soldier, to the war overseas, and Sara lost her husband. Their story moved me to tears, and I wanted to add them to *The Abandoned* in a way where they helped save lives in the story, as they did on the plane. Similar to the man in their life who saved lives and lives on in their memories. He's the true hero here, and I salute him.

May he Rest In Peace.

Also, thanks to Holly Tuell, who allowed me to use her husband's name, Buck as my disappearing black ops agent, Buck Schaffer, also known as Casper. He's in *The Cartel* as well. So to Buck … thanks for the use of your name and thanks, most of all, for reading the Sarah Roberts Series.

Until next time, and you're lost in the pages of *The Cartel*, please forgive me in advance for what happened to Sarah and Aaron. All I can tell you is that their love never dies. I won't reveal more except to say that the next ride is absolutely crazy. It frightens me, too!

Then, onto book sixteen, *Losing Sarah*. There's so much more to come.

Stay safe. Stay healthy. And get caught reading.

I love you all!

Jonas Saul

About Jonas Saul

Jonas Saul is the bestselling author of the Sarah Roberts Series—more than two million sold!—and has written and published over sixty thrillers. After acquiring an agent, he signed several deals in Los Angeles, with MadRiver Pictures optioning his Sarah Roberts Series— over forty books!—(currently in development).

Jonas has often outranked Stephen King and Dean

Koontz on Amazon over the past decade. He's regularly invited to be a guest speaker, teacher, or workshop presenter at international writing conferences and film festivals worldwide. He hosts an annual writer's retreat in Greece, where he currently lives. He focuses his teaching on how to get tension and emotion in every scene, on every page, how he made it as a creator/writer, the path to success in this business, and the pitfalls to avoid. He also hosts a reading retreat in Greece with guest authors, yoga retreats, and hiking retreats. Visit the Imagine Greece Retreats website at www.imaginegreeceretreats.com, or email him directly to discuss an opportunity to join one of the retreats at jonas@imaginegreeceretreats.com.

Jonas is also a professional freelance editor. He works for several publishers and does private editing for clients, with many testimonials on his website at www.imaginepress.org, which details each author's response to Jonas's editing skills. Email Jonas directly for an editing quote at editor@imaginepress.org.

To book Jonas for a speaking engagement at a writer's conference/festival, to have him on your jury at a film festival, or even to say hello, email Jonas directly at jonassaul@icloud.com.

For updates on releases, hit the "Follow" button on Amazon or Bookbub, and join Jonas on Facebook, where he's most active.

Contact Jonas Saul

Linktree: Find me here

Email: jonassaul@icloud.com

www.ingramcontent.com/pod-product-compliance
Lightning Source LLC
Chambersburg PA
CBHW022009310726
48972CB00006B/1583